Seeds In The Wind

Doris Fleming

Seeds In The Wind

Doris Fleming

Seeds In The Wind

© Doris Fleming 2012
Cover design by Kim Gardell

Published by
Lighthouse Christian Publishing
SAN 257-4330
5531 Dufferin Drive
Savage, Minnesota, 55378
United States of America

www.lighthousechristianpublishing.com

CHAPTER ONE
Alberta, Canada 1924

The train bellowed its approach into the small town of Didsbury, Alberta, Canada.

Finally, Lizzie thought.

Why it had to take so long to travel fifty miles, she had no idea. Sixteen year old LIZZIE VAN ANKUM pulled her cold hands from beneath her lap and gripped the empty train seat ahead of her. She wished she had listened to Aunt Emma and worn her winter coat and mittens, instead of her spring things.

"Just because it's March doesn't mean spring is here," Aunt Emma had warned.

Lizzie pulled off her flimsy right glove, rubbed a spot clear on the frosty window and peered out, but she could see nothing. Nothing, that is, but billowing steam and blustering snow whirling wildly about the train.

She squinted through the thawed spot on the glass, trying to see if Dr. Martin was waiting as promised. The telegram she had received from him yesterday was short. Too short, she felt, and much too vague. "Mother beckons," the message read. It stated simply that Dr. Martin would pick her up at the Didsbury station at ten o'clock the next morning.

"BE THERE," the message demanded.

Aunt Emma said it wasn't a good sign, but Lizzie preferred to take the unexpected telegram a different way. Perhaps Mother had prepared a surprise for her, a celebration recognizing Lizzie's acceptance into Calgary's School of Nursing. Hadn't everyone said she was the youngest Canadian woman ever to enter such training?

But in her heart Lizzie knew Dr. Martin wouldn't order her home for a celebration.

The whistle blew again, cutting into Lizzie's thoughts. It blasted out one long deafening call, followed by a shrill staccato burst then another two long bellows. Steel screeched on steel as the great iron machine came at last to a grating halt beside a narrow railroad platform. Clutching her satchel under her arm Lizzie made her way down the narrow aisle toward the exit. Aunt Emma had urged her young niece to pack a larger bag, but again, Lizzie had disagreed.

"I won't need much, Auntie. I have to be back by Monday morning for class, remember!"

"But what if..." Aunt Emma began.

"Whatever Dr. Martin needs, I'll do," Lizzie interrupted. "But then I've got to get back here. Whatever it is, it won't take more than three days."

The train whistle cried out yet again, steam hissing and spitting in every direction. From the train door Lizzie scanned the station yard for Dr. Martin's Model T, but blowing snow kept her from seeing anything beyond a few feet from the great bellowing beast. As she stepped down the wet metal steps, a torrent of bitter wind struck her in the face. It caught hold of her long golden hair, lifting and tossing it like a pitchfork spreading hay. She hurried toward the station house, squinting against the driving snow and drawing her meager collar together at her throat.

Dr. Martin must be waiting inside, Lizzie thought, warming himself at the large potbellied stove. It would feel good to do the same. She swiped a hand around her strewn hair, gathering as much of it as she could catch and tucking it inside her collar. She should have listened to Aunt Emma and pinned it down.

A sharp bird-whistle sliced across the morning storm, drawing Lizzie's attention to the right. There, off to the side of the rail-road station, Dr. Martin sat as stiff as a tree on the bench of his winter sleigh. The reins were gripped tightly in one hand while the other hand beckoned urgently. The horses' heads were bent low against the piercing wind and snow. Lizzie ran to the open sleigh.

She stretched out her hand in greeting, but the doctor waved it off.

"Hurry up, Lizzie, get in!"

His face was taut and his cheeks badly chapped. The usual sparkle in his bright Irish eyes wasn't even a flicker. Lizzie knew that look. Trouble!

She tossed her bag onto the floorboards and leaped onto the bench beside him. She wished he had come to fetch her in his new Model T instead of with the team. For all the boasting he had done about the thing, she had yet to see him drive it. The prospect of the eight mile ride to the farm would have been much more bearable had he brought his shiny automobile today.

"Git-up!" he ordered, snapping the reins before she was fully settled into place. The large bays lurched ahead, jerking the sleigh free of its spot in the snow and causing Lizzie's head to snap back. She pulled her collar tight around her neck and fastened the top button. If only she had listened to Aunt Emma. But there was no sign of a blizzard when she got onto the train in Calgary. She could see now that winter was still alive and well even though the calendar said it was spring.

"What's the matter?" she asked against the howling wind.

Doctor Martin didn't answer. He leaned forward, spanking the reins against the team's hind quarters and urging them through the deepening snow.

"Why did you call me home?" she called, louder this time.

Still he gave no answer. The wind, it seemed, gathered up her cries and carried them to the skies before they reached his ears.

An unexpected gust swirled snowy crystals into Lizzie's eyes, forcing her head down. She covered her face with the insufficient Sunday gloves and stayed low until it passed. Quickly she dug the yellow cotton scarf from under her coat collar and wrapped it over her head and ears, tying it tightly under her chin.

Dr. Martin looked straight ahead, clucking at the horses and working the reins. Lizzie shifted slightly to look directly at him. Perhaps a stern stare would coax some information out of him. But no, it produced no response.

What was going on? Why wouldn't he tell her what was happening? Why all the hurry and worry? She glared at him, supposing she could be as stubborn as he.

4

After all, didn't she have a right to know why he had called her home so urgently? He seemed not to notice her efforts and continued hawing at the horses.

A sudden tightness clutched Lizzie's chest as she watched his sober face, Aunt Emma's words ringing in her head.

"I don't like it, Lizzie. Something awful has happened."

Lizzie turned to watch the road. It was better than watching him. Watching him was unsettling. The look on his face was beyond worry; he looked grim.

The wind bit into her face, the large horses doing little to deflect its fury.

As they approached Main Street, Dr. Martin looked both ways and without the slightest hesitation hastened the animals across the intersection. With vigor that seemed more fitting of a much younger man he smacked the reins and directed the horses out of town and onto the straight stretch leading east to Lizzie's home and family. Lizzie rode quietly, jouncing along and gripping the steady bar.

She looked again at Dr. Martin, wishing he would say something. That's when she noticed that the flaps of his winter hat were down over his ears and the wool scarf wrapped so tightly around his head and throat that he probably hadn't heard a single word she had said. She leaned her petite frame closer to the doctor and tugged on his heavy sleeve.

"Doctor!" she called out. "What's wrong?"

"We'll talk once I get you home," he said firmly. He pointed toward the floor and said, "Cover up or you'll freeze to death before we get there."

Lizzie pulled a dark wool blanket from the pile at

her feet, laid it over her lap and tucked it in around her legs. Grabbing yet another, this one a heavy patchwork quilt, she flung it around her head and shoulders, clasping it tightly at her throat.

She peeked across at the doctor, hoping she could find something reassuring in his face. But she couldn't.

Aunt Emma must be right.

CHAPTER TWO

A sharp northeasterly wind blasted its fury against the aging farmhouse sending a shiver clear through Lizzie's petite frame. Swirling snow spit icy pebbles against the bedroom's only window, pushing cold air in around the edges and adding to the chill in the room.

Sarah Van Ankum, Lizzie's mother, lay in the bed, beneath a pieced-together quilt, looking very weak and ill. Zachariah, Lizzie's father, sat on the foot of the bed, his head in his hands.

"I'll explain it as best I can, medically," Dr. Martin said. With some vigor he cleared his throat, but he still sounded froggy. "So you have an idea what she's up against." He started in with the diagnosis, choosing his words carefully, speaking them softly—Sarah's diseased liver, its deteriorated condition—cancer.

"No!" Lizzie gasped, immediately covering her mouth with her hands. She glared at the family's long-time doctor and friend, shaking her head at him and longing for Father to shush him up.

Each word the doctor voiced, each explanation he expressed, stabbed a fresh hole in Lizzie's heart. Soon she could no longer stomach watching the doctor's face. Instead, she turned to the window, choosing to watch the fury of the storm outside. She suddenly felt so cold and hollow inside that she imagined herself standing on the sunless side of the universe, far from everything warm and right and wonderful. The awful news had moved in and stationed itself like an ominous cloud between herself and Mother.

Between the tears welling up in her eyes and the blowing snow it was difficult to make out the large maple tree standing alone near the barn. She loved that tree. Since she was a girl she had claimed it as her very own, even though she knew it wasn't. She could barely see the cluster of cows huddled together under its wide network of naked branches, but she knew they were there. Every last one, waiting for the barn door to slide open and welcome them inside.

Grasping hold of the worn cotton curtain in her parent's bedroom, Lizzie clenched with all her might, keeping her face close to the window. She didn't dare look at the doctor, or Mother, or Father. It was all she could do to restrain the tumult tearing at her innards.

Mother won't die! She can't! Not now!

The doctor attempted to elaborate on the particulars, going on and on about things Lizzie didn't want to hear. Daggers, every word—each one slashing her dreams afresh, each one threatening to make mincemeat of her well-laid plans. She focused outside the window and watched as snowflakes continued to fall, larger now than when she first arrived home.

Medical terms and explanations flowed from the

expert, her mentor and model these last two years. And for the first time in her life Lizzie wanted to throttle him. Tears filled her eyes, but she blinked them back.

How on earth can this be? And in just two weeks?

Another bitter howl burst against the windowpane, pushing cold air through the crack along the bottom edge. Annoyed, Lizzie reached for a towel from the pile on top of Mother's dresser. She snapped it loose then rolled it up lengthwise, laying it along the window sill. With determined fingers she tucked it snugly into the corners, covering the crack that ran the width of the window sill before taking her place once again to the right of the window. She wrapped her sweater tightly around her slender waist and watched as pieces of loose straw flew recklessly about, driven by the demented squall.

"Sarah asked me. . ." Dr. Martin continued, clearing his ragged throat. "Well—she wants me to give you both the plain truth."

The plain truth? Lizzie screamed inwardly, the breath of her nostrils fogging up a spot on the window. *Mother is going to get well, that's the plain truth! And as soon as she does...* Lizzie fought the urge to take a punch at the measly excuse of a window.

She glanced across the room at her father. He was no longer sitting on the bed, but was instead perched on the edge of the painted kitchen chair positioned near his own chest of drawers. The color was gone from his face, but his eyes were pressing the doctor for more.

Dr. Martin dabbed the back of his neck with a wrinkled blue and white handkerchief then reached for the bedpost. It seemed that he, too, was in need of an anchor. Lizzie moved to her mother's side, kneeling beside the bed and jacketing Mother's pasty yellow hands in her own. What she really wanted to do was plug Mother's ears so that she wouldn't have to listen to any more of these lies.

"Sarah is dying," Dr. Martin managed, his words coming out in a half whisper.

Instantly Zachariah collapsed to his knees on the floor. Lizzie jolted, bumping the three-legged stool beside the bed and knocking the bedpan to the bare floor.

"No!" she cried out, oblivious to the clanging.

Dr. Martin stilled the ringing pan and slid it under the bed. He moved closer and rested a hand on Lizzie's shoulder. "I'm sorry Lizzie, but there's no cure."

She twisted away from his touch and leaned against her mother. The whole thing was unthinkable. Mother was too young to die! People don't die when they're forty-two.

"Dear Lizzie," Mother said weakly against Lizzie's cheek.

Straightening, Lizzie aimed her words at the doctor. "How could she get this sick in two weeks? She was fine when I left. There's got to be something—"

Dr. Martin shook his head.

"Just tell us," Lizzie insisted. "We'll do it! Is it special food she needs? Medicine? Sunshine? What?"

Dr. Martin reached for Lizzie, prying her clammy hands from her mother's and pulling her upward.

"Come with me, Lizzie. Come to the kitchen."

She resisted his tug, but Mother gave Lizzie that look that needs no verbal instruction and gently pressed Lizzie in his direction.

Dr. Martin took her by the elbow and drew her resistant body from the room, holding aside the wool blanket that hung as a door, and stuffing a fresh handkerchief into her hand. He guided Lizzie through the big room and pulled out a chair for her at the kitchen table.

"I'll make some coffee," he said.

"No!" she cried, almost squealing. "No! I don't need coffee! I— I—" She threw the handkerchief onto the table and ran for the door. "I need air!"

Once in the shanty, a porch-like room connected to the kitchen end of the house, Lizzie yanked a large coat from a spike on the wall. She pulled it on then punched her hands into a pair of blue knitted mittens that lay atop a cream can. Tears gathered as she stomped into a pair of her father's barn boots. She slammed the door shut and ran toward the barnyard. Because of the oversized garments she decided not to climb up to the loft, her favorite place to go when things were not going well. Instead, she passed through the barn. Emerging from the other side she kicked a chunk of frozen snow and booted it along the cow lane for several yards. Each jab and roll shaved its jagged edges and by the time she reached the pond, it resembled a dirty worn out baseball. One final angry strike sent it sliding across the pond's frozen surface. If only she could do the same with Dr. Martin's words and predictions. She'd wad them up and kick them to kingdom come—never to be heard again.

She scowled at the troubled sky, her sapphire eyes appearing almost gray. The wind bit into her cheeks, stinging them. She leaned forward, hands on her knees, trying hard to sort out her raging thoughts. She drew in a chest full of air and blew it out slowly, three times, but it didn't help.

Mother can't die! She can't!

Lizzie straightened to her full height. Her hands

tightened into fists inside her mittens as the cold wind continued to blast against her body.

How will Father manage without her?

Lizzie couldn't imagine it.

And her younger siblings Jake, Rosie, and Anna— how could they survive without a mother? Children aged twelve, eight, and five could hardly be expected to raise themselves. Father wouldn't be able to do it, not with all the outside demands. Not to mention the expanding cream routes.

"And who will keep food on the table?" she suddenly yelled at the sky. "And wash the clothes, and scrub the floors?"

And what about Willie and J.C., her older brothers? They could make it on their own if need be, she was sure of that. But still, while they remained under this roof, they, too, relied on their mother in many ways.

Lizzie stomped the heel of her boot into the ice at the edge of the pond. It was crusty and gave way easily, crackling like shards of glass.

Why did it have to go and storm again, she cried inwardly, angry that winter was still so apparent. *This is March, for pity sake! It's supposed to be spring.*

Grains of blowing snow bit at her face, forcing her to turn her back against the wind. The sky was hinting sweet blue promise in the far southwestern corner, but the nasty mixed-up wind kept slapping at Lizzie's hair and wouldn't let her see it.

"Why?" she screamed, her long golden hair flying loose in the wind. Slender fingers picked at a loose thread in the tip of her right mitten. Agitated, she pulled the mitten off, turned it inside out and bit off the dangling strand, spitting it to the ground.

Last week's Chinook temperatures had brushed the dormant prairie swells with softening strokes and had caressed the pond, wooing its edges back to liquid. Four straight days of sunny skies and warming winds had quickened fallow ground. Soon spring would have its way. The fields would trade in their white cloaks for jackets of green, and the cattle would be out grooming the grasses and trying the fences. Leaves would bud on the great maple beside the barn, and the crocuses in the meadow would burst forth in pretty patches of purple and white.

But not yet! Wintry winds still exercised judicial control over all the outdoors, and seemed even now to jeer at Lizzie. A dark foreboding cloud pushed its way into Lizzie's soul, and her cheeks felt the heat of angry tears.

If Mother dies, I don't have a chance.

She stooped down and picked up a large wedge of ice. With both hands she heaved it as hard as she could out onto the ice-covered pond then sank to the snowy ground, her face in her mittens.

O, God! Why is she dying? If she dies, I'm trapped. I'll never get off this farm.

***

In the kitchen Dr. Martin scooped up a dipperful of warm water from the cook stove's reservoir, poured it into the dishpan, and vigorously washed his hands. He combed wet fingers through his perspiring head of white hair then reached for the brown towel hanging on a nail behind the stove.

"We're all in need of air," he confessed, sucking

in a chestful for himself. He didn't fault Lizzie for needing a little space to sort it all out. He had expected as much. He just hoped she wouldn't insist on trying to reason the illness away. He didn't like the thought of having to get stern with her. Not at a time like this.

A slice of frosty air sneaking through a crack in the kitchen window made him ache for more air. He crossed the floor, stepped through the fair-sized room the Van Ankum's called their "shanty" and opened the outside door, filling his lungs to capacity. He bent down, scooped up a handful of snow and walked back inside, pressing the frozen shavings against his cheeks and forehead. The melting remains were tossed into the dishpan on the stove.

It had been a long afternoon, and now the stove was no longer hot enough to bring water to a boil. Sighing, he took up the poker, spread the dwindling bed of yellow and orange embers and selected several small sticks and four larger pieces from the wood box.

If only practicing medicine could be so easy, he thought. A poke here, a poke there, add a fresh prescription, and everything is fine again. He glanced out the window hoping Lizzie had stayed close, then pulled the coffee pot to the front. The past few days he had become a regular fixture in this house and maneuvered easily from cupboard to drawer, choosing cups, cream and sugar, and spoons.

***

"Here you go," Dr. Martin said, placing a hot cup of coffee on the table in front of Lizzie. He was thankful she had returned without having to be called. "Drink some. It'll warm you up."

Lizzie said nothing. Her head was buried in her arms, and the handkerchief she had tossed onto the table earlier was now clenched in her fist.

He pulled out a chair for himself and sat with his elbows on the table, his face in his hands. He had, for the better part of the afternoon, tried his level best to explain what was going on with Sarah's health and what they could expect over the remaining weeks. He'd been as honest and forthright as he knew how, and now he was exhausted through and through. He longed for a spray of salty ocean mist in his face, something he hadn't thought about in a very long time.

And now he had to deal with Lizzie. What could he say that hadn't already been said? How could he make the truth easier to bear? She, with all her dreams and plans for nursing school, had been his prize medical trainee this past while. She was a natural, eager to learn, and willing to do the hard work of nursing. So what if much of what she knew had been learned in the barn, tending the farm animals? Because of her age, he hadn't been willing to let her practice on people, not just yet.

He couldn't tell them exactly why the cancer was taking over Sarah's liver and other internal organs. All he knew was that he was completely sure in his diagnosis. She was dying, and she didn't have long. A couple weeks, possibly. At best, a month. He had seen these same symptoms many times in his early training, usually due to heavy drinking. And although alcohol was not the cause in this case, explaining even that seemed difficult today.

He had been fortunate since moving to this western district some years back. Only once had liver cancer made its way into his constituency. But now, here it was again, roaring like a famished lion, seeking someone to devour. Here, right in the middle of this happy household, and friends to boot. And all he could do was watch. He had nothing to offer. No remedy. No prescription. No hope.

"Lizzie," he said, startling her. "There's nothing left but to make her comfortable from now on. Nothing you suggested earlier will make her well."

Both of Lizzie's hands shot up against his words, palms out, the handkerchief dangling. She shook her head stubbornly, unwilling to hear his explanations.

"You're wrong!" she cried, trying to keep her voice down. "If you think Mother will give up that easily, you're wrong."

She laid her forehead directly onto the dark oak table and curled her arms around her head. "Mother's strong, you know that," she mumbled, face down.

What's he thinking? Mother's always been strong. Only once before was she ever slowed down by illness. Why won't he stop with this talk? He doesn't know everything, and besides . . .

"Lizzie, you must face facts!" he said, all raspiness suddenly gone from his voice.

"Face facts?" Lizzie picked up her head and stiffened her neck. "Facts are: Mother is going to get better. And as soon as she does, I'm on that train and heading back to school."

"Now you listen t' me, young lady!" There was edge in his voice. When his dander was up the Irish accent came through more than it usually did. "Everything's changed, Lassie. Do you hear what I'm a sayin'? It's all different now. I know how you've been livin' for your new opportunity, and how you been

longin' to follow your dream 'n all. I know how you and
your mother have been a plannin' your hearts out. For
Pete's sake, child, I had a part in that plan, remember! But
it's not about you anymore, Lizzie. Are you hearing me?
Your dreams will have to wait. That's all there is to it."

He swung from his chair and went for the towel.
He took his time swabbing his neck and forehead before
returning to the table.

"I'm going to give you some instructions," he said
in a quiet, gentler tone, "but not right now. I'll be back
first thing tomorrow morning with everything written
down, and we'll go over it together. You are the key and
the hub right now, Lizzie. Nursing school has come to
you. Everything hinges on you from now on."

Her hands were fumbling with the handkerchief
and her eyes were squeezed shut. With a burdened sigh
the doctor patted her hands and made another attempt to
get through.

"Lizzie, your mother needs your strength
desperately right now. She is very weak. She needs your
constant care, and I know she is counting on you to keep
things as close to normal as possible for the children."

"O God." Lizzie cried. Suddenly she grabbed the
old man's warm hands, clenched them in her own, and
rested her head atop the pile of hands. Tears tumbled
freely over the entangled fingers, much like maple syrup
cascading over a stack of flapjacks.

***

Sitting alone at the table Lizzie fought frantically
with Dr. Martin's hankie, twisting it this way and that and
wringing it until it tore. She heard the soft jingle of the

harness bells as the doctor steered the large bays around in the yard and turned them toward town.

What was it he had said? Liver failure? Internal cancer? Was that it? She couldn't remember exactly. A barrage of unanswered questions jumbled around in her head eradicating every attempt at logic. Nothing made sense. She didn't want to think about it anymore and pushed away from the table. She started toward Mother's room, and then stopped.

No, Father needs time with her.

She sat down again, only to get up immediately and cross the kitchen to the stove. She rummaged about in the kitchen, opening and closing cupboards with no particular purpose in mind, just trying to bring her boiling thoughts to a simmer. If ever she had an opportunity to learn nursing, this was it. But no, not on Mother! She couldn't nurse Mother! Not the way she needed to be nursed. Dr. Martin must know that. How could he expect it of her? If things were as he diagnosed, Mother would need a real nurse; she would need someone who knew how to relieve her pain and monitor her body functionings and do all sorts of things Lizzie didn't know anything about as yet. Besides, Mother wasn't going to die. She'd be well again soon, hopefully in time for Father's birthday. Why wouldn't Dr. Martin reason with them and give them some hope?

"Isn't that a doctor's job?" she moaned aloud. "They're supposed to keep people alive."

Lizzie went to the window facing north, knelt on the large kitchen chair that always sat in that spot, and rested her elbows on the window sill. She could see the cows gathering at the barn door, anxious, no doubt, to get in out of the wind.

A nasty gale swirled loose snow across the yard making her shiver as she watched. It wasn't snowing anymore, but the wind lifted and played with what it found on the ground making it waltz hither and yon, shooing clouds of white powder every which way until they finally smashed against the buildings or were stopped by the Caraganna hedges. What didn't get caught up in the yard was carried off across the fields until she could see it no longer. Everything was in chaos; even nature itself reflected the uproar.

Lizzie turned sideways in the chair, pulling her feet up onto the seat, and hugging her knees. Tears blazed slender trails down her cheeks as she stared out the window, her mind attempting to replay the doctor's words in the order they were spoken.

Suddenly, a loud thud and noisy clang rang out from Mother's room. Lizzie bolted, nearly tipping the chair, and ran to the bedroom. She burst through the curtain to find Father on his hands and knees, looking bewildered.

"Het is goed," he said in a low voice, surprising Lizzie with his Dutch. His arms were scooping up the toppled items. Mother had raised herself onto her elbows and was gasping and blinking wildly, surveying the room with troubled eyes.

"I'm sorry, Mother," Zachariah said, looking first to his wife then back to the mess on the floor. "I ... I don't know how I knocked your basin down." All his words were in Dutch.

"Father, let me do that," Lizzie said, quickly pulling another towel from the dresser and kneeling beside her father. "I'll clean this up; you go get some coffee. There's a hot pot on the stove."

Mr. Van Ankum reached for the leg of the toppled chair. Using it as a prop, he pushed to his feet. Sarah eased back onto the pillow, sighing. Zachariah glanced back and forth between his wife and daughter like a confused child, reluctant to leave the room, still looking dazed.

"Father, please go have some coffee," Lizzie insisted, pulling on his hand and leading him to the bedroom door. "I'll be there is a minute to slice some bread. A bit of bread and jam will do us all some good."

Zachariah started through the door, then came back to the foot of the bed and squeezed Sarah's blanketed toes before leaving the room.

"Father will like the coffee," Lizzie said to Mother as she mopped up the floor. "Dr. Martin made it."

Mother let out a relieved breath and closed her eyes.

Lizzie sopped up the spilled water and wrung out the towels into the metal bedpan Dr. Martin had brought out earlier in the week. How had both the bedpan and Mother's precious porcelain basin gotten involved in the incident? Mother always kept her special basin on top of her dresser. The only time it was ever down was when Mother had it resting in her lap, caressing it, or explaining to one or the other of her children their Dutch ancestry. Lizzie examined it now and found only a small chip along the basin's edge. She placed it back in its usual spot, pulled the chair into place beside the bed, and was gathering up the pan and towels when Mother spoke.

"What's to become of us all, Lizzie?" Sarah whispered, reaching out to Lizzie. "Things are crashing in on us, and I'm the cause of i'tall." Tears were sliding from the creases of Mother's eyes and into her hair.

Lizzie's throat went dry. She squeezed her mother's hand and looked into her eyes, trying to conjure up some words of comfort. That's when Lizzie noticed it. The dark circles around Mother's eyes. She hadn't seen that before. And they were sunken. Her skin, too, looked odd. A dull yellow. And the whites of her eyes were yellow as well.

Dr. Martin's words came flooding back, and Lizzie saw her mother as she really was. Dying.

A ball wadded up in Lizzie's stomach and she leaned close to Mother.

"Shh, Mother. You rest." She stroked her mother's wavy hair away from her forehead. "It'll be getting dark soon. Just rest. We'll talk about it tomorrow."

"Where are the children?" Mother asked.

Good question, Lizzie thought. They should be home from school by now. But she wasn't about to say that out loud. With the storm as bad as it was, Miss Patchin probably held them over. She'd ask Father.

"Shh, Mother, rest now. Everyone's fine. Everything's going to be all right. Dr. Martin will be back in the morning." Lizzie smiled and wiped Mother's forehead with a dampened cloth.

The tears continued to cascade from Mother's eyes, wetting her dark brown hair.

"Don't worry." Lizzie spoke softly, tenderly touching Mother's cheek with her lips. "Everything will be fine. You'll see."

Then straightening and heading toward the door, she added, "I'll put on some potato soup. How does that sound?"

Mother smiled faintly and turned to face the wall.

CHAPTER THREE

Rosie and Anna screamed hysterically, begging Lizzie to come and get them down. Lizzie could make them out in the darkness, just barely. She squinted, trying to sharpen her focus. They sat perched on top of a high, wobbling set of steps, their arms and legs flailing as they balanced on their bottoms. Shadows covered their faces. Their frantic cries drew Lizzie upward. Up she went. Up the wicked staircase.

With legs as heavy as an elephant's and her arms as spindly as willow branches, she pressed on. Up, up Lizzie climbed. She tried to call assurances to her young sisters, but no sound proceeded from her lips; her cries of comfort piled up in her voice box and got stuck there. She was close enough now to see their faces and read the fear in their eyes. But the moment she made eye contact with them, the staircase turned into a tall splintering ladder standing straight up in mid air. Lizzie grasped tightly, leaning hard into the thing to keep from falling over backwards. She edged her way upward, clutching the slivery rungs. At last she reached them; she was near enough to touch their outstretched fingers. But before she could take hold of their wrists, the ladder buckled and sent them all tumbling headlong, plummeting into the deep black hole far below. Gasping, Lizzie bolted up in bed.

She swayed slightly as a wave of dizziness passed through her head, then flopped back onto her pillow. She could feel her heartbeat thumping in her ears. The darkness surrounding her brought little consolation, but the sound of the girls' breathing in their bed nearby brought considerable relief. Lizzie took up a corner of her top sheet and wiped her dampened hairline then kicked away the rumpled bedding.

With hands still shaking she arranged the blankets back into place, layer upon layer, and settled once again onto her pillow. But instantly, the moment she closed her eyes, the stairway reappeared just as vivid as before. Quickly, she sat up, determined not to be swallowed up again by the dreadful dream.

Shaking fingers combed the tousled hair away from her neck and held the full load on top of her head. Drawing in a very deep breath she started counting to one hundred. She began kneading her hair into a French roll. Once it was rolled up tightly, she let it go and the tresses fell against her back. Again she twisted the shiny strands into another roll, only to let them drop once again around her shoulders. She repeated these motions until she reached the full count of one hundred. Now she was fully awake.

That was the plan. She had learned this counting trick when she was twelve, and it had never failed in chasing away nightmares. Hopefully, tonight would be no different. Now, fully alert, Lizzie snuggled down into the blankets, her anxious thoughts turning once again to Mother.

Dr. Martin's announcement pealed anew in her head, Mother's prognosis resounding in her brain like a deafening gong. Lizzie rolled over and buried her face in the pillow.

"I don't want to be the hub," she moaned. "I can't do it. Mother, please, you know I can't do it."

Anna stirred in the bed she shared with Rosie and sat up. Lizzie quickly turned to the wall, clenching the pillow slip between her teeth. Anna looked around sleepily then settled back down, snuggling close to Rosie.

Without Mother Lizzie's dream of becoming a nurse was dead—stone dead! With no more hope of fruition than a handful of seeds stored in a rusty old can.

"What good are seeds if they don't find the soil?" she whispered through gritted teeth. "I need that schooling."

Lizzie couldn't remember how old she was when she started dreaming about becoming a nurse. But she knew for sure it was Mother who had cultivated the idea. It had probably been Mother who had planted the desire in Lizzie's heart in the first place.

However it got there, as far as Lizzie was concerned, Mother deserved the credit for keeping the dream alive. It was Mother who made sure Lizzie was in the middle of every medical emergency and opportunity that arose on the farm. She had been especially attentive to Lizzie's dream the past couple years. Once Mother started going to church and reading the Bible, she had become a firm believer in "seed planting." And she never neglected any of the seeds she planted. She said it was her "calling" to plant seeds in her children's hearts. Along with sowing the seed, she also embraced the task of keeping those seeds well watered. And the weed picking? That, too, Mother took very seriously. If ever she saw a weed growing up in the garden of her child's life, she mercilessly plucked it out, roots and all.

Mother had carefully tended Lizzie's dream and had, on occasion, thrown in a seed or two about Lizzie becoming a doctor. Lizzie felt those were dead seeds and told Mother so, being that she was a girl and all. And a farm girl to boot.

"Who ever heard of a farm girl becoming a doctor?"

"We'll see," Mother had said.

Lizzie wrestled anew with the blankets. Why did they have to be so hot and heavy? Agitated, she kicked the corners free, threw back the top quilt, and lay staring into the darkness. Today Dr. Martin had tossed her seeds out the window, pitching out her future in the process.

J.C. and Willie wouldn't need her to stay for their sakes, she felt sure. They were grown boys now, both over twenty, and besides, they each had a girl who would soon take them away and feed them. But the younger ones: Jake, and Rosie, and Anna—how would they manage? Lizzie turned again into her pillow and wept.

At last her worries were swallowed up in slumber, but again, just as she touched the girls' fingertips, she plunged backwards, falling head-over-heels into the deep dark hole.

CHAPTER FOUR

At the rooster's first boisterous cawing Lizzie pushed back the disheveled blankets and rose from the bed, weary and numb. Her thoughts were a blur and her eyes barely seeing as she pulled on a long-sleeved flannel shirt and a pair of Willie's hand-me-down overalls and made her way to the cold kitchen. Half asleep, she swung her hair forward over her shoulder and tied a loose braid, secured the end to the top of her head with a hair pin, and made her way down the dark stairway. She'd brush it out later.

Using the poker Lizzie scraped the ashes into the lower holding tray of the cook stove then carried them outside and tossed them onto the garden spot. Typically Father was up by now, but she saw no sign of him. She got the fire going then went outside to start her barnyard chores.

Spring was whispering "good morning" but Lizzie couldn't hear it. The morning sky smiled a bright happy greeting upon her, but she saw only the ground. Yesterday's stormy tempest had twirled itself out leaving little more to show for itself than some moderately adjusted snow drifts. But Lizzie noticed none of it. She gathered the eggs, oblivious of the four extras. The pigs grunted and shoved against the walls of their enclosure insisting on liberty, then squealed their delight when she finally lifted the gate to the larger pen.

During breakfast Jake was talkative, as usual, and offered to pull the girls to school on the sled.

"Might not have many sledding opportunities left this year," twenty year old Willie advised his youngest sisters, pushing away from the breakfast table. "Better take him up on it."

"Oh, we intend to, don't we, Anna?" said eight year old Rosie.

Anna's head bobbed up and down and she bounced excitedly in her seat as she stuffed a corner of milk soaked toast into her mouth on top of the piece she hadn't yet fully swallowed. She reached for her tumbler of milk and answered, "Uh ha!"

Five year old Anna was gushing with giggles and chatter. It started the minute she saw the bright blue sky. She recognized spring's happy message and it set her to burbling like a mountain spring.

Anna had turned five on New Year's Day and though she was still too young to truly be labeled a first grader, she had been included in the student count. Including her on the student roster enabled the community to meet the quota for getting another teacher into the growing district. Anna was thrilled about being the youngest student in the whole school. She seldom received individual attention from the teacher, young Miss Patchin from Prince Edward Island, but Anna didn't mind. She was just glad to be a "pupil." Mother's "maybe you'll be a teacher someday" seeds were finding good ground in Anna.

She was not expected to read aloud or do sums or multiplication or any such thing, but she had her own spot at a table for two, and kept herself busy painting fancy seashells on serviettes and marking up her scribblers, imitating as best she could what she saw in the older student's writing tablets.

Lizzie was thankful that Anna would be out of the house today. Those little ears often picked up mighty big things, and Lizzie didn't want them near enough to hear what Dr. Martin might say.

During the cold winter months Mother had not often let Anna attend school, but by early March the weather had warmed up enough to take the worry out of sending her, so for the past few weeks she had not missed a single day. She was thrilled about yesterday's storm. All the students got to spend the last two hours of the school day in Miss Patchin's small home next to the school building, eating chicken salad sandwiches and singing around the piano.

"I never had chicken salad sammiches before, y' know," Anna reminded Lizzie as the buttons of her coat were being double checked and the ties of her wool bonnet secured. Lizzie smiled and kissed the child's cheeks then settled her in front of Rosie on the sled.

Jake, although short for his age, was strong—much stronger than other twelve year olds Lizzie knew. He yanked on the rope and the girls squealed their delight as he whisked them away. Lizzie was watching him pull them across the field when Dr. Martin steered his team into the yard.

Father was still holed-up in the bedroom with Mother, curled up beside her on the bed when Lizzie last checked. As far as she knew he hadn't had anything to eat, or drink, since his cup of coffee last evening. She had encouraged him to eat some soup, but he denied being hungry, and promptly insisted that he be the one to spoon a little to Mother. Then, once Mother waved the bowl aside, he put it on the window sill and crawled into bed beside her. He had snuggled close and fallen asleep holding her tightly in his arms.

J.C. and Willie had left the house earlier than usual this morning, milking the cows Father usually milked then taking a few minutes for a quick bowl of porridge before assuming full responsibility for the cream routes. Lizzie had told them Father was not feeling well and they should go on ahead without him. They had never done the cream routes without their father, and this was the day of the week that took them to the city, but she knew they could handle it. They'd been working the various routes with Father for two years. They could manage.

Lizzie watched as Dr. Martin urged the team of horses into the yard and up to the house. Here he was again with the sleigh and team instead of his new automobile.

He brought them to a halt and secured the reins. Lizzie stepped toward the horses and took hold of the halter to lead them to the barn. And there, to Lizzie's astonishment, sat Nadine—there in the belly of the sleigh. Lizzie's knees suddenly went spongy. She leaned against the nearest horse, burying her face in its mane.

Why is she here? Lizzie cried inwardly. *Surely Mother's not that close to death.*

Dr. Martin and his nurse climbed out of the sleigh and carried their black bags to the house. Lizzie gathered strength by squaring her shoulders, then gritting her teeth she gave the leather strap a sharp yank and led the team to the barn.

Nadine rarely accompanied Dr. Martin on country house calls anymore. When she did, it was for one reason only—to usher the patient through death's door. Everyone knew it. Some said it was her life's mission; everything else she did was secondary. Even the school children knew of her and called her the "death angel."

At the barn Lizzie grudgingly removed the harnesses and trappings that made the two a team and shooed the horses into separate stalls. She broke up a bundle of hay and forked it to the grateful animals before grabbing up two handfuls of oats from the sack in the corner. She offered them each a handful and their soft full lips tickled her palms for every last flake.

By the time Lizzie returned to the kitchen, Dr. Martin and Nadine were both backed up to the stove, sipping hot coffee. Their bags rested against the legs of kitchen chairs.

"Good coffee, Lizzie," Dr. Martin praised. "The boys haven't left yet, have they?"

Lizzie nodded, indicating that they had. She pulled the scarf from her neck and tossed her gloves on top of the stove's warming closet.

"I was hoping to get here before they headed out." Dr. Martin said. "Thought they might have a few questions of their own."

"I didn't tell them," Lizzie admitted then pulled out the chair at her spot at the table and collapsed onto it.

Dr. Martin glanced at Nadine, and she at him.

"But your father? He's talked to them, hasn't he?"

Lizzie shook her head.

"Have you and your father talked a'tall since I was here yesterday?"

She shook her head again. Why should we? she thought. What's to talk about? Mother will prove you wrong, and both Father and I know it.

Lizzie pushed up wearily from the table and went to her parent's bedroom. After some time she returned with her father. She led him to the table, her right arm supporting him around the back.

Zachariah seemed not to see anyone in the room and sat in the chair Lizzie pulled out for him. His eyes were red and the thin strands of hair that were typically combed from left to right over his bald top lay limply along the side of his face and ear. Dr. Martin sat down across from Zachariah and cleared his throat. Lizzie could see he was readying a discourse.

"Zachariah...and you too, Lizzie." He paused to clear his throat, yet again. "First I want to say how sorry I am about Sarah."

Zachariah's glazed eyes fixated on his hands. Nadine offered him a cup of coffee, but he did not acknowledge her gesture. Lizzie watched Nadine take the coffee pot back to the stove.

"I'll tell you again," the doctor continued, "as best I can, what I believe the situation to be, and what we can do to help her, but—"

He choked slightly and reached for his cup. He sucked in a mouthful of his creamy sweetened coffee. Nadine sat down and pulled a pencil and writing tablet out of the flat pouch at her feet.

Zachariah snorted, pulling all eyes his direction.

"I need to know," he asked in English, his eyes not moving from his hands. "Is she dying? Or is she deathly ill?"

"You're right, Zachariah. There is a difference," Dr. Martin answered. "I'm sorry to say it, but Sarah is dying. Her time on earth is likely very short."

The men's eyes met briefly then Zachariah, shaking with fatigue, got up from his chair, went to the other side of the table and placed his hands on Lizzie's shoulders.

"Lizzie here is everything her mother will need," he said. "Show her what to do. I want Sarah comfortable, you understand?" Lizzie's head dropped, fresh tears spilling to her cheeks.

"I understand, Zachariah," Dr. Martin said. "We'll do the best we can, but—"

Zachariah turned from the table and exited the kitchen as if there was nothing left to be said, dragging his trembling legs toward the bedroom.

"Father?" Lizzie called after him.

He looked at her, telling her in Dutch. "It's up to you, Lizzie. I can't bear to hear it."

Dr. Martin didn't know what Zachariah had just said to Lizzie, but there was one thing he did know. Yesterday he had made Sarah a promise, and he intended to see it through, today.

"Zachariah, we're coming with you." The doctor's voice was a bit stout. "All of us. Sarah has something she'd like to say, and I promised to let her say it first thing this morning."

They each fell in line behind Zachariah and followed him to the bedroom.

"Push back the curtain, Lizzie," Nadine said, taking charge inside the bedroom. "Let that sunshine in."

Lizzie did as she was told. Mother flinched at the

brightness hitting her face, but then relaxed and seemed glad it came in. Mother's face looked extremely yellow, Lizzie thought, almost greenish.

"Good morning, Sarah," Dr. Martin greeted, gently squeezing her hand. "How are you this morning?"

"Same, I guess," Sarah answered, smiling weakly.

"I've brought Nadine with me today, as I promised."

Sarah nodded at Nadine and Nadine patted Sarah's hand.

"Nadine's brought along some supplies, lotions and the like, and will show Lizzie what she needs to know." Then he turned to his nurse. "Nadine, go ahead and set things up, and rearrange the room however you see fit."

Lizzie watched as Nadine pulled various items from her bag and set them in a row next to Mother's basin on the chiffonier. Nadine drew from her bag a dark brown bottle of Calamine Lotion, a container of soda powder, a syringe, Ether Squibb, and a small bundle of something Lizzie didn't recognize, tightly wrapped.

Mother issued forth a peculiar whimper. She was reaching one hand out toward Lizzie, and with the other, beckoning Zachariah. They moved closer.

"Please, I want to speak with you both. I need each of you to make me a promise." Sarah licked her dry lips. Her tongue looked parched, and her eyes rolled upwards and away just briefly before focusing back on Lizzie. Nadine offered to get a dipper of water.

"First you, Lizzie," Sarah said, gently pumping Lizzie's hand. "I have a request to make of you. Two, really. Can I count on you?"

"You know you can, Mother," Lizzie answered,

anxious to help her mother.

"Well, then—" She licked her lips again and tried to swallow. Lizzie took the dipper from Nadine and lifted it to Mother's lips. Mother took a sip then lay back again. The water seemed to revive her somewhat.

"Lizzie, I want you to be in charge once the Lord takes me home."

"Mother!" Lizzie gasped, unable to believe what she just heard. She crawled onto the bed beside Mother. "Don't talk like that!"

"Lizzie, now listen to me. I know it's an incredible thing I'm asking a girl your age to take on, but God will help you. You can count on that. I've been battling over it all night, wondering whether to talk to you now, or wait. I've decided I can't wait. I need to ask you now while I can still think straight. Will you promise me, Lizzie? Will you promise to take care of Father and the children in my place?"

Lizzie felt like she'd been hit in the stomach. Hard! With a baseball bat…and kicked to the ground. How could she make such a promise? Mother knew nursing classes were scheduled to start Monday morning. It was too soon to talk like this. No one knew how things would turn out. And anyway, consenting would mean it was all true; she'd be verifying the doctor's verdict. No! Mother was rushing things.

She couldn't say "yes." She just couldn't. She didn't know how to do the things Mother had done for the family. She wasn't ready. Not yet. Lizzie closed her eyes tight, hoping to hold back the fresh threat of tears, but they escaped all the same. She bent her head into her mother's shoulder and started crying aloud. She couldn't make such a promise. She just couldn't.

But then, how could she say "no" to Mother? She never had in all her life. It wouldn't be right.

"Mother, please," she begged. "Don't talk like this. You can't leave us alone!"

Mrs. Van Ankum tutted softly and took Lizzie's face in her hands.

"Lizzie, you know better than that. I'm not leaving you alone. You are never alone. The Lord thy God is with thee, and will be with thee through i'tall." She pulled Lizzie close and smoothed her hair in long even strokes. "God is calling me home, Sis, and now that he is, I am asking you to raise your brother and sisters in my place. Can I count on you?"

The room felt suddenly tight, and hot. There seemed not enough air to go around. Lizzie clung to her mother, noticing that Mother's skin felt as dry as paper. She turned her head the other way.

Making such a promise would mean she wouldn't get to nursing school. And if she didn't go now, who's to say she would ever get there. It meant laying down her hard-earned dream. Giving up on what mattered most and taking up Mother's life instead. It was too much! Too much!

But what choice did she have? There was no one else.

At last she moved her lips close to Mother's ear and whispered, "Yes, Mother."

Mother held her as tight as her ebbing strength allowed.

"There's something else, Lizzie," Mother whispered against Lizzie's hair. "I want *you* to be my nurse."

Lizzie jerked back.

"Mother! You know I can't do that! I don't know a single thing about it."

"Yes, you do! I know you do. You haven't been practicing on everything under the sun these past two summers for nothing. Nursing is what you want to do, and I'm asking you to start with me."

"But Mother! I can't!"

"Shh, will you?" Mother persisted. "Please don't let someone else nurse me. You can do it, I know you can. Dr. Martin and Nadine will show you what to do. Please, Sis, promise me you will."

Mother pulled Lizzie again into her feeble embrace and Lizzie wondered if perhaps Mother's reasoning power was not quite what it used to be.

"I'll try," Lizzie whispered at last. She knew it was beyond her capability to fulfill such a promise, but how could she say no.

"Father," Sarah called softly, reaching out to her husband. Lizzie slipped away and moved to the foot of the bed as Father knelt on the floor beside his wife.

Sarah brushed the palm of his hand with her lips. "I have something to ask of you, too, Dear. It has to do with Lizzie."

Lizzie slid off the bed and started to the door.

"No, Lizzie. I want you to hear this too," Mother said, her eyes still on her husband's face. "Zachariah, I'm asking a lot of Lizzie, so I want to give her a gift. It'll really be from the both of us since you'll be the one to see it's carried out."

Zachariah looked puzzled, but nodded.

"You've heard what I'm asking of her. But before she takes over, I want to send her to Albert and Emma's so she can spend a day at the hospital. Two, if it can be worked out. Will you see to it?"

"Sarah! You know I can't manage without her!"

"I've already talked to Dr. Martin. He said Nadine could stay out here and tend me a couple days, and maybe Aunt Mattie could hold the household together that long. I'm sure we can bear her clucking and spitting for a day or two." Then beseechingly she added, "I will endure anything to see Lizzie get a day at that hospital." She sighed then and closed her eyes, weakened from the exertion. "Please, dear, something could be worked out. Will you see to it?"

Zachariah leaned forward and kissed Sarah on the forehead. "Yes, Mother. I'll see to it."

Under Nadine's direction, the room was soon put in a new order. The bed was pulled away from the wall and moved nearer to the window. Another chair was brought in from the kitchen so there was one on each side of the bed. With the bed away from the wall it would be easier to care for Sarah's physical needs and change the linens.

Lizzie had squared her tired shoulders and dried her face with her shirtsleeves. She listened carefully to all of Nadine's instructions, interrupting the seasoned nurse several times with questions. She didn't want to miss anything. Over an hour was spent educating Lizzie in the use of the medical supplies Nadine had unpacked, including a full description of symptoms to watch for and how to address them as they came. In the end, Lizzie was responding to Nadine's test questions without hesitation, and Nadine was smiling so broadly that Lizzie hardly recognized her.

"Dr. Martin, I'm very impressed," Nadine said as she closed the buckles of her bag. "You told me I would be delighted with your young nurse, and you were right." Then, before leaving the room, Nadine gently woke Sarah to say, "You ought to be very proud. You have brought up a very capable young lady."

Sarah smiled and looked at Lizzie with an "I told you so" look on her face.

CHAPTER FIVE

Lizzie closed the door and stood alone in the shanty, thankful they were gone. Her head ached from all the orders she'd been given. How in the world was she supposed to remember all that? What was the matter with everyone? How could they possibly think she could take care of Mother's needs and do all the other things around the house Mother had always done?

She turned and steadied herself against the door. She felt hollow inside yet bloated in the head because of all the details. Where was she to start? Father would know; he'd be able to tell her.

But she must speak with him alone. That meant getting him out of Mother's room long enough to find out what to do. And why was he speaking only Dutch? Surely he could see that it was hurting Mother. His sudden relapse into the old language was unnerving. Something about it made everything else all the more frightening and confusing.

Lizzie knew the family history. She had heard them tell it many a time. When they came to this English speaking community, her parents agreed to put their mother tongue behind them. But today Father seemed bent on speaking only Dutch, giving no thought to how unsettling it was for the rest of them. Once they had gathered in the bedroom, he spoke not another word in English. The few words he had uttered throughout the morning were directed only at Lizzie and were all in Dutch. Even when Dr. Martin and Nadine took their leave he did not bid them good day. Lizzie's heart winced remembering the hurt in Mother's eyes when he spoke.

Fortunately, Lizzie still remembered the Dutch language. In fact, she not only remembered it, she tenaciously worked at not forgetting it. She was almost six when her parents had made their new resolve. They had gathered the children around the old oak table to tell them of their decision to put the Dutch away and speak only English. It was just the five of them at that time: Father, Mother, J.C., Willie and herself. Father insisted, no more Dutch was to be spoken in the home. It was important, he had explained, that if the Van Ankum family was to become a vital part of this new community, they must be English-speaking. In establishing any business they may choose to consider in the future, (and Father seriously hoped to own a creamery of his own one day) then speaking English was critical.

Unbeknownst to her parents, Lizzie had, all these many years since, kept a separate journal where all the entries were still in Dutch. Once, several years ago, J.C. had discovered her writings.

"Hey, Lizzie, bet you don't know what I found this morning with the pitchfork." He doubled over laughing, pointing at her and teasing. "All your secrets, that's all. I haven't forgotten it either, y' know."

After that she had to find a new hiding spot for her

Dutch-written journal. She nailed up a couple short slab pieces in the far corner of the barn loft. In the corner that was always covered with loose hay. When the supply got low, she'd pitch several forkfuls over it. The tablet was assiduously hidden between the slabs, safe and secure. When she moved to Calgary for nurses training she had decided to leave the journal hidden. She wasn't likely to find time to record all her comings and goings and contemplations anyways. It would just have to wait in the loft for her until she got home on visits.

Yes, the first thing she had to do was speak with Father. Lizzie opened her eyes and lifted her heavy head from the door. She squared her shoulders, and went inside. Once she had talked with Father, then she'd tend to the house.

Doctor Martin had mentioned how Mother had become increasingly unable to get about the house the past two weeks, and it showed. Lizzie had noticed it the minute she walked in the door yesterday afternoon. The kitchen never would have looked this way if Mother were up and about. Mud had been tracked in but not swept up, the two kitchen rag rugs were caked with dried dirt, wood chips and dust lay about the stove. Coats were hung on the backs of kitchen chairs rather than on the pegs meant for that purpose. Even some of the outdoor gear: boots, bridles and gloves, instead of hanging in the shanty where they belonged, were piled high just inside the kitchen door. The wash rag and tea towels were dingy almost to the point of being slimy. No wash had even been attempted, that was plain to see.

On her way through the kitchen Lizzie checked the bread box. Half a loaf. And no more to be found in any of the cupboards. How was she going to do everything that needed doing? And attend Mother? For the first time in her life Lizzie wished she had been made to stay in the house and do "women's work." Maybe then she would have been prepared for this. All her hours of working alongside Father in the barn and in the fields wouldn't do much for her now. Somehow, though she knew not how, she would have to get all her newly acquired obligations into some kind of manageable order.

Thankfully, she didn't have too many outdoor chores to worry about. Jake had agreed to take on her chores, along with his own, when she left for nurses training. He had agreed willingly, much to Lizzie's surprise, him with his craving to get out in the world and do something that really mattered, like building bridges and roadways and such.

Jake was a strong, self-disciplined twelve year old, and he had good sense. In some ways Jake seemed almost like a man already, just a smaller version. He always held his head high, and other than the fact that he was still quite short and not at all meaty, Lizzie thought he resembled a man, particularly in his serious and steady countenance.

Many of the chores that had been handed over to him when she left for nursing school were downright easy, and were they not so mundane in nature, he might be persuaded to do them for years to come. But chopping turnips for the cows, gathering twigs and cow chips for kindling, picking rocks, and even slopping the pigs were much too repetitious for him. Mindless work, he called it. Such chores gave no room for creativity and design.

Lizzie picked up the two kitchen rugs and took them outside for a good shake. The dust and dried mud flew, some of it blowing back in her face.

How was she going to tell the family what the doctor had said? Surely, she wouldn't have to be the one to break the bad news. That was Father's place. Yes, that had to be first. She must speak with Father right away, while Mother slept. Then, once Mother was awake, Lizzie would ask for her help in lining everything else up into a workable way.

Taking in a deep breath she went to her parent's bedroom door. She poked her head through the curtain.

"Father?" she asked softly, not wanting to wake up her mother. "Can we talk?"

He didn't respond; he didn't even look her way. But Lizzie was sure he heard her.

"Please, Father, come to the kitchen. I need to talk with you."

She felt disrespectful talking to him that way, like he was a child and she was giving the orders. The blank look on his face made her wish she hadn't come in just yet, but she forced herself to go on.

"Father, please, there are things I need to know. Things we need to talk about."

"Go on, talk," he said in Dutch. "You can see she's sleeping."

"But Father!"

"I'm not leaving this room," he said firmly. "If you want to talk, talk. Otherwise, it'll have to wait." His gaze hadn't left Mother's face.

Lizzie couldn't talk about it with Mother lying there. She just couldn't. She backed quickly out of the room and ran upstairs crying. She plunged facedown onto her unmade bed and Dr Martin's words began blasting again in her ears.

"You are the hub and the anchor right now,

Lizzie."

How was she going to be hub and anchor if she couldn't even get Father's attention for a few minutes? How was she going to manage this household and care for everyone and everything in it? Surely she wouldn't be expected to do it all alone. How could she? Couldn't Father see that she couldn't?

Prostrate across the bed, she pounded her arms against the pillow and blankets, thrashing like a pair of impotent scissors until her arms could pump no more. At last her sweat-drenched body became limp and she flopped over onto her back and stared at the crack that ran the length of the ceiling.

***

It was quiet around the supper table. Not only was Mother's chair empty again, but so was Father's. Lizzie had made mashed potatoes, Father's favorite, in hopes of persuading him to come to the table and eat with the rest of them. She had worked cream into the potatoes, and some butter, and had told him so, but it had no affect on him.

"Leave me be," he said, refusing to leave Mother's side.

Lizzie had spoken to J.C. and Willie about Mother as soon as they finished the evening milking, and Willie offered to tell the children. Lizzie was grateful. As she fixed supper and set the table, he explained things to the children. J.C. sat quietly in his place, his head in his hands.

Lizzie placed a pot of goulash and a bowl of mashed potatoes on the table and sat down. Willie asked everyone to hold hands while he asked God's blessing on the food. When he prayed, he never said anything about the food at all. Instead, he thanked God for his mother and prayed for his father and sisters and brothers.

Jake was the first to respond after the prayer.

"I love her," he said, gulping back a throatful of tears. And as soon as he had said it, both girls began crying.

J.C. and Willie pushed back their chairs, each of them drawing one of the girls onto their lap. Jake sat with his head bent over his plate. Lizzie slid into the chair Rosie had vacated beside him and put her arm around his quivering shoulders.

Lizzie had no tears left. Her well had gone dry, it seemed. Nothing came pouring out of her like it was now from the others. Instead, the sense of emptiness that had begun to creep into her soul as she lay on her bed earlier now grew broader and deeper.

**

Lizzie and her older brothers agreed that daily routine should remain as close to normal as possible. In fact, how could it not? The chores still had to be done: the animals fed, the cows milked, the eggs gathered, the fences mended. Money still had to come in; therefore, J.C. and Willie would continue working at the creamery in town as well as continue to work at building up Father's cream routes.

"And school's still in session," Willie said. "I don't see how it would be good for the children to be home all day watching Mother suffer."

Lizzie, for one, was thankful for the hours the

children were away at school. She needed all the time she could find to get a grip on her new tasks.

And now there were the extra preparations needed for Aunt Mattie and Nadine's two-day stay. Father had kept his promise to Mother by asking J.C. to make the arrangements necessary for Lizzie to visit the hospital in Calgary. Lizzie would take the train to Uncle Albert and Aunt Emma's. Dr. Martin was asked to assist in setting things up for Lizzie to spend a day in the middle of the nursing world, something he was happy to do. It was all cared for and the day after tomorrow Lizzie would step into the Calgary General Hospital for the very first time. The event she had anticipated so long had lost much of its glory.

She couldn't deny that she looked forward to it, but going now with Mother so ill, and knowing it was just for one day instead of a whole term, well, it took the exhilaration out of it. Maybe she'd feel differently once she got there. Maybe the fire would return and it wouldn't matter that the experience lasted only a day.

Everyone had done their part in helping Mother give Lizzie this gift, and now she had to do all she could to make the house ready for company. She stocked the cupboards by bringing up from the cellar ample amounts of canned chicken, berries, and preserves. She churned up a large batch of butter and had Mother talk her through the bread making process. She wanted to make sure there was plenty to work with, especially if the children ended up having to fix for themselves.

"This will not be easy for the children," Lizzie warned Mother, as if she didn't already know. "Aunt Mattie is so bossy and—"

She was going to say lazy, but she stopped herself

in time, knowing Mother would scold her.

But it was true. It was hard to get excited about a visit from Aunt Mattie. Besides being bossy beyond words, she never expended a mite of her own energy in getting things done. It had always been that way. And she always had so much to complain about. Nothing and no one was ever so good that there wasn't something to complain about was what Aunt Mattie believed. And by her own admission she had never really learned to cook. At least not the way most women did. She either couldn't understand the difference between flavor and flatness, between fresh and stale, or she didn't have any taste buds. It was hard to tell. Lizzie's opinion was that Aunt Mattie just plain didn't *want* to understand. It saved her a lot of work, not understanding.

Lizzie felt bad for the children, knowing what they would have to endure while she was away, but Mother persisted.

"Come now, Lizzie, it will only be for two days. They can bear it that long. I don't want to hear any more about it. It's all worked out, and there's nothing I want more right now than to see you get to that hospital."

"I hope the girls will get enough to eat," Lizzie said, still feeling unsure about the care they would receive from their least favorite aunt.

"Just think, Lizzie," Mother cheered as valiantly as she was able. "A whole day in an honest-to-goodness nursing class!" You've got to go. I can't bear it if you don't. Besides, Aunt Emma needs your visit now. You can give her the news and comfort her."

So, everything was lined out. Lizzie would catch the train in town and travel the fifty miles to Calgary. She would stay with Uncle Albert and Aunt Emma, of course.

While there, she'd pick up the rest of her belongings. After all, she would not be attending school as planned; she would not be keeping the housekeeping job she had secured to help pay her school bill; she would not be having tea with Aunt Emma every Wednesday afternoon.

How Lizzie hated to have to tell Aunt Emma the news. How she hated to miss out on all she had planned with her precious Auntie. To Lizzie there was no one in the world as special as Aunt Emma. She was more of a friend than a relative. It didn't matter to Lizzie that there was eighteen years between them. That had never mattered. And though they visited mostly through letters now that Uncle Albert's business had gotten off the ground and expanded into the city, Lizzie still preferred Aunt Emma's company over anyone else she knew, school friends and cousins included. Lizzie wasn't entirely sure why there was such a special attachment between them, but it was there just the same.

She suspected it may have begun the day she was born. Mother had fallen from the wagon when the horses had jerked ahead unexpectedly. Labor pains began immediately, weeks earlier than anticipated, throwing Aunt Emma into the unexpected role of midwife. The baby had come so fast that Emma, Sarah's younger sister, had no choice but to play the part.

From that time onward Lizzie and Aunt Emma's relationship flourished with each point of contact. When Lizzie was five the attachment solidified further. Mother had become ill with gall bladder problems that resulted in surgery. Complications had prolonged Sarah's stay in the hospital causing Zachariah to house the children out with relatives. Lizzie ended up spending six weeks with Aunt

Emma and by the time Mother was home and on her feet again, Lizzie had to practically be pried from Aunt Emma's arms.

"I can't help but feel bad for the children," Lizzie said again at bedtime as she braided Mother's hair and wound it into a crown on top of her head.

"Never mind that! Just pay close attention so you can tell me everything you learn."

CHAPTER SIX

A bell tinkled faintly, and a brisk rapping on the door made Lizzie stir. It took her a moment to remember where she was, but when she heard Aunt Emma call her name she turned over and made her way to the surface of the smooth satin sea that engulfed her. Pink and white pillows billowed on every side and silky blankets draped the bed, reaching to the floor. Sunshine flooded the lovely room. Lizzie loved this room. It was to have been her room, had she been able to remain in Calgary for schooling.

Aunt Emma knocked again.

"Come in, Auntie," Lizzie said, patting the pillows and pushing away a puffy comforter.

"Good morning, my sweet Lizzie," Aunt Emma said, shoving against the door with her shoulder. "I trust you slept well."

The aroma of dark Dutch coffee came in ahead of Emma and quickly permeated the room.

Emma carried in a wicker tray adorned with fine china, gleaming silver and a small pot of coffee. Her eyes danced and her face shone almost as brightly as a literal sunbeam. There was no sign of the tears and sadness of last night, when Lizzie had spoken the news about Mother.

"Aunt Emma, you'll spoil me," Lizzie said, swinging her feet over the end of the bed.

"Then spoil you, I will," was Emma's response. "It's mine to do if I choose, isn't it? And I choose. So stay put and enjoy your breakfast. And I want you to eat every bite. I know you have a big day ahead of you, but if you don't mind I'll pull up a chair and visit while you eat."

"Do, Auntie, do."

There was so much to talk about—and so much of it not good. But Aunt Emma wanted to hear it all. Lizzie elaborated on the doctor's words as best she could. She told about the shock of seeing Nadine come to the house with Dr. Martin. She spoke of Father's black mood. How he had spent the first couple days hardly leaving Mother's side, and now, suddenly, he seemed to want to be anywhere else but in the room with Mother.

Delicately embroidered handkerchiefs dabbed up the tears that fell as Lizzie poured out her heart. Aunt Emma shook her head and patted Lizzie's hand when Lizzie told her about the promises she had made to her mother. At one point Lizzie was overcome by such a fit of weeping that she choked on a bite of bread.

Lizzie felt weary from telling it all again, but Aunt Emma's delicious poached eggs on rye bread, along with the stout coffee, fueled her tired body. Lizzie reached out and took Emma's hand. It was so good to be here.

Suddenly, Uncle Albert poked his head in the door.

"I hate to break this up, girls," he said, his hearty laughter filling the room, "but I've lost my secretary and

I'm offering a reward. Did she happen to sneak through here?" Uncle Albert's joviality quieted to sympathy when he saw the sad faces of his wife and niece. He quickly drew them both into his arms.

"All right, Albert, I'm on my way," Emma said. "We just needed a little time together. I haven't forgotten about the meeting."

"Good morning, Uncle Albert," Lizzie said, quickly planting a kiss on his jaw.

"Good morning to you, too, Missy. Were you able to get any rest in this mountain of goose feathers?" He let go of Emma and squeezed Lizzie so tightly her back popped.

"The best I can ever remember."

"Well then, if that be the case, up with you! Time, she is a tickin'. You haven't come to laze in luxury, I understand. You really think you're up to spending the whole day walking those sickly hospital halls?"

"Oh, Uncle, I won't be just walking the halls. Didn't I tell you? The matron of nursing herself has set it up. I get to float the hospital with several doctors and student nurses. It's more than I dreamed."

"Yes, Dumplin', you told me. What's that now? The third, or is it the fourth time you've said it. I swear, I've heard nothing else since you set foot off the train. So, up with you then! It's time to meet the day. Besides," he said taking his wife in his arms and waltzing her about the room with exaggerated shoulder movements. "I need this beautiful secretary of mine. She has acres of paperwork to do before that big shot from Toronto gets in this afternoon.

***

The students had been promised a lengthy lunch period, and Lizzie, for one, was more than ready. Not only did her feet ache, her brain was numb from all the information she had tried to gather. She had never imagined so many ulcerated bed sores, hemorrhoids, stitches, and broken bones existed in all the world, let alone all under one roof. The medical names of all these various ailments and conditions were beginning to melt together so that she was forgetting which terms belonged with which infirmities.

"That'll be all for now, class," the chief instructor announced. "I'll see you all back at the emergency desk in two hours."

The group issued a collective sigh and scattered like marbles from a pouch, each rolling quickly away and out of sight. Lizzie patted the sandwich in her pocket and turned toward the nearest exit. Oh, for some fresh air.

The right door of the large double door entrance opened easily. The sun was shining and she was anxious to spend some time in it. As she stepped beyond the protective awning, the sunlight smacked her in the face with such blinding brilliance that she missed the first step. She attempted to correct her balance but in the process twisted her ankle and stumbled forward. She reached out to brace herself against the fall, but instead of landing in a heap, as she expected, she was caught up and supported by a pair of strong arms.

"Easy does it, Miss," a man said, holding her steady before releasing her to stand on her own.

Lizzie looked up at him but the bright sunlight smote her again, driving her head downward.

"Sorry about that!" he said, moving quickly around to her other side. She turned to face the speaker and discovered the darkest brown eyes she had ever seen. The young man tipped his hat, exposing a mop of wavy coffee-colored hair. A tiny smile touched his lips, but his eyes looked truly concerned.

"You all right?" he asked, bending down and gathering up the scattered tablet pages. He offered his arm and pointed to the wooden bench that sat under a nearby weeping willow. "Come, sit a minute."

She tested the heel of her shoe, nodded, and took his arm.

"Thank you, sir. I'd be on my chin in the street if you hadn't come along when you did." She held out her hand to him and said, "Hello, I'm Lizzie Van Ankum. You know, of the Van Ankum clan to the northwest of here. And you are?"

"Pleased to meet you, Lizzie," he said, taking hold of her hand and smiling what seemed to Lizzie a teasing smile. "I'm Daniel Winslow. You know, from the Winslow clan up north." He shook her hand firmly and tipped his hat again. His broad smile took Lizzie off guard and an unexpected flutter launched from deep inside her stomach.

She laughed a funny sort of laugh that she herself didn't recognize, and cleared her throat. She had no idea who the Winslow clan was and he probably had no idea who the Van Ankum's were either.

"You're fine then?" he said. "No sprained ankles."

"Yes, I think I'm fine." She looked down at her shoe again, twisting the heel side to side. "Thanks to you, I'm very fine. Fine and dandy, as they say." Her words sounded silly, but they were out before she could fix them. For some reason, standing next to this handsome stranger, she felt light-headed and awkward. Perhaps it was the rush of adrenalin from the near fall. She allowed him to steer her toward the bench.

Spring-like temperatures had been sunning the earth in record breaking fashion the past two days, and today was more of the same. The leafless branches above them let the radiant sunbeams shine through, warming their backs. Lizzie was glad now that she had decided to eat outside rather than in the nurse's lunch room. She slipped off her overcoat and was about to spread it across the bench.

"Please, allow me," he said, removing his own coat and laying it out lengthwise. She tossed her own over the end of the bench and sat on his. He, too, sat down, leaving enough space between them that Lizzie was sure both Rosie and Anna could have squeezed in. He set his hat on the bench beside him. She hoped he was not in a hurry to go.

"It's our lunchtime," she said. "Am I ever ready for it."

She had hoped to spend the break getting to know someone on the hospital staff. A registered nurse perhaps. Even the conversation of a nurse's aid would have been sufficient. But nothing had worked out. Everyone had plans, places to go, errands to run.

"I have only a sandwich, but I'm glad to share," she offered. "If you're so inclined, that is." She hoped he was.

"Never been able to turn down free food," he said, smiling. Then reaching into his pack he pulled out an object wrapped in wax paper. "And look here! I, too, have a contribution. The minute I saw this I knew it would come in handy sometime today." They moved still farther apart and laid out the lunch items on the bench between them. He separated the carefully folded cube, and there sat a thick piece of gingerbread cake. It was covered with creamy icing and although it was slightly smashed along one side, it looked scrumptious.

"My goodness!" Lizzie cried out. "What a beauty!"

"It's settled then," he said. "We'll share." And they shook hands again. He took out a pocket knife and halved the sandwich and then the cake. Carefully he skimmed the excess icing from the blade with his thumb and forefinger, poking it into his mouth and pocketing the knife.

They ate, and they talked. Lizzie couldn't help but spill out the enthusiasm she felt about spending the day with the nurses in training. He, too, talked. But very little. He mostly just encouraged her to keep on talking.

Lizzie tried to make out his character by what she saw and heard. He seemed a very thoughtful person, and well-mannered, but also somewhat hard to read. His smile, when he turned it on, was as bright as a sunny morning. But it wasn't always on. And even when he did smile, his eyes seemed to betray an inner sadness. Perhaps not. How could she know? Perhaps it was the color of his eyes that made them so hard to read. They were black like coal. She tried not to stare and checked herself repeatedly, but his eyes were like magnets. She couldn't help herself. She had never before seen eyes so brown that they were black. There was no way to tell where the pupil stopped and the iris began. To Lizzie they seemed like gatekeepers safeguarding yet-to-be-discovered territory. Those eyes kept tugging at her even though they seldom looked directly at her. Once, while both she and Daniel were taking a bite of their respective sandwiches, their eyes met. Something leapt inside her. Immediately, she forced her eyes back to the sandwich in her hand.

Through guarded glances Lizzie gathered what she could. His shoulders were square and broad, and his back was straight. His posture reminded her of Willie's sermons to Jake about how hard work builds a man. Daniel's handshake had been very strong, unlike the city-boy handshake Uncle Albert had teased about in the past.

"Don't you be givin' your time and attention to any fellow with a handshake as limp as a dishrag," he'd said more than once. "You can tell a lot about a man by his handshake." He chuckled as he spoke. "So shake his hand first then you'll know whether he's worth looking at twice."

That didn't seem fair, thought Lizzie. Surely there were exceptions. But she didn't have to worry about that right now since Daniel's handshake was very strong— both times they shook hands.

Lizzie thought of hurrying through her portion of the sandwich but decided not to. She had still an hour and a half before class and she liked very well the turn her lunch break had taken. There was no reason at all to hurry through it. After all, he might decide to up and walk away, exiting her life as quickly as he had entered, and she would never see him again.

"Stop it!" she scolded herself. "You're not here for him. You're here to learn some nursing."

She turned slightly to face the front of the hospital. Bold blue letters proclaimed CALGARY GENERAL HOSPITAL. There it stood. The starting spot. The springboard for all she ever dreamed. And here she was, standing on the threshold of what could have been, having to acknowledge anew that the jigsaw of her life was not going to come together as she had planned. How could it? Mother's illness had changed everything.

The whole flow of my life will go a different direction now, Lizzie thought sadly. She chafed inside at the reality that after today there would be no more time and no more opportunity to pursue nursing, other than what she'd been equipped to do for Mother. Unexpected tears gathered, but she swallowed hard and drew them back inside. This was no time to start crying.

For the past three hours she had been bustling about the hospital with a mixed group of staff nurses and student nurses getting a glimpse of all she ever hoped to be and do. It was inspiring. The constant hustle was exhilarating. The place was alive with hope, yet lurking near death all at the same time. Doctor's waved down nurses, handing them charts and new orders. Nurses nodded and carried out the doctor's wishes, swabbing bed sores, bandaging torn flesh, wrapping and rewrapping swollen joints. Patients cried, some groaned and moaned, others laughed. One room was full of rejoicing at the doctor's announcement and the next was steeped in sorrow.

"It's been an incredible morning," she said out loud, sighing.

"Tell me about it," he said.

He sounded truly interested.

"Nurses are amazing, don't you think?"

He barely shrugged, looking like he had never thought about it.

"All morning I've been accompanying a class of student nurses. In all my wildest dreams, I never imagined all they do. You know what I think? I think it's the noblest calling on earth." She paused to nibble off a corner of crust. "At least that's my opinion, and from what I've seen so far today, I think I might be right. I never realized the responsibility they carry. You should see it in there! It's incredible, that's all I can say. It's beyond words."

"So, have you never been in this hospital before?" he asked.

"Never! It's been nothing more than a dream before today."

Lizzie took the cut of gingerbread he offered and hummed her delight at the taste of it.

"So, what brings you here today?" he asked. "Have you begun classes?"

"Oh, I wish! That's been my only wish for almost two years now." She paused to take a bite, chew, and swallow. "No," she went on, sobering noticeably. "Actually, being here today is my mother's gift to me. She is very ill. The doctor says she's dying. I don't want to believe it. She's very strong. I mean it. She is."

"So your mother knows of your nursing dreams, does she?"

"Certainly, she does! She's been in on it all along."

"And now she wants you to get your chance to see the real thing while she can see your response to it," he stated as though it was a matter of fact. He picked up his hat and began thumbing the rim.

"Maybe," Lizzie said. "I don't know. But she asked me to promise to be her nurse, right to the very end. I couldn't believe it when she first said it. She knows I haven't had any schooling."

She paused.

He waited. It almost seemed, for a moment, that

he was listening for something.

"The way it's looking now," she said, "I'll probably never get any more training than what I can glean today. I'm sure I won't be able to do everything Mother needs. We'll probably have to call in Nadine."

"Nadine?"

"Nadine specializes in caring for people who are dying of terminal illness. That's what it's called, you know. I learned that today. Terminal illness."

He seemed suddenly disinterested. He looked away and cleared his throat. The hat kept moving between his fingers, 'round and 'round. Suddenly, he was getting up.

"Feel like going for a walk?" he said. "There's a fine park about a block from here."

Lizzie gathered up the pieces of wax paper and crumpled them into a ball. Daniel replaced his hat, swung both coats over his arm, and took her elbow. A trash can at the entrance of the park received Lizzie's meager deposit.

"Good, the snow is gone," he said. "When I was here two weeks ago, it was still a good six inches deep right here."

"Isn't spring incredible?" Lizzie said, feeling lighthearted, almost giddy. "And summer, I can't wait for summer. Everything is better in the summer. If Mother can just make it 'til summer! Everything will be better then."

Daniel didn't respond. Lizzie looked at him and his face seemed drawn and his eyes far away. They walked on in silence.

It was a gorgeous day. The sky was bright blue, the sun was warm. Robins were pecking at the ground while smaller birds cloaked the tree tops and sang short chirpy choruses to one another. What a beautiful spot it was! What an unforgettable day! But Lizzie wanted to hear Daniel's voice again; she wanted to get to know him.

"Do you like the city?" she asked, looking straight ahead, not at him.

"It's all right, I guess. Not much peace and quiet for contemplating though. And you, do you like it?"

"Oh, no, I'm not at home a'tall in the city. I hardly know how to act. You should have seen me bumble my way through supper last night. My goodness! How many forks and spoons does a person need to dirty at one meal?"

He laughed, and Lizzie caught sight of the sparkles that flashed from his pupils.

"To tell you the truth this is only my second time ever. My father and brothers, the older ones, that is, they come in every week. But poor Jake, that's my younger brother, he's hardly been here more than me. And he resents it plenty, too, I can tell you. I'm sure if he had his way, he'd ditch his barnyard boots in a minute, and for good, if he could find some way to get off the farm."

"Tell me about Jake."

"Well, for one thing, he's twelve, wishing he was twenty. He dreams of doing important things someday. Things much bigger than milking cows or slopping pigs."

Daniel pulled his pocket watch out just far enough to see the time, then tucked it back inside. Lizzie didn't notice and kept right on talking.

"He's not at all like J.C. and Willie. They're my older brothers. Father keeps them busy with the cream routes, plus they both work at Vanderhorn's creamery in town. Those two, they love pigs. You should hear them when they get home at night. They talk and plan and figure like they've about to land the proverbial pot of gold with those pigs they've bought."

"Sounds like you have a house full of brothers."

"Just those three. Three boys. Then there are three of us girls."

"Six of you! How do you manage with your mother so ill?"

"Well, there's been a bit of a shuffle in who does what this past little while, mainly for Jake and me. The first few days were the worst—for me anyway. It was hard to accept what the doctor was saying about Mother. It still is. I don't know what it will be like if things get as bad as he says. And Mother, you should see her. She never complains. Never demands. And I know she's in pain. Her color is turning bad and she cries out."

Lizzie wasn't sure why, but she felt comfortable telling this stranger her troubles. Something about him made the words come out easy.

"It's hard to watch her. When I think about what's ahead, it scares me."

"I'm sorry for you all," he said, his voice cracking. "It must be very hard."

The path wound around a small grove of pine trees and led them to a small pond. The ice was completely thawed. Lizzie watched as a flock of geese dipped close to the water then changed direction and flew away, quacking and squawking noisily as if some of their members did not agree with the course correction. A train whistle sounded somewhere in the distance and Lizzie watched as Daniel kicked loose some small rocks. He picked up three and skipped them one by one across the crystalline surface.

"What time do you have to be back?" Daniel asked, putting on his coat and straightening his hat with the right corner tipped down just a bit. "If you have time, you could walk me to the train. The station's just over there aways." He pointed east.

"Train?" Lizzie asked, surprised at the sudden panic she was feeling. "Are you going somewhere?"

"Yes, I'm finally going home."

Lizzie heard a whistle blow. It was much closer this time. It was coming for him, coming to take him away.

She took her coat from him and swung it up over her shoulders. Tears welled up in her eyes as a sense of loss took hold of her. She didn't know what to say. They were just getting started. Maybe he didn't have to go. Maybe he could wait for the next train. Isn't that what Father had said, that people just hop the train any old time they feel like it.

"You have to go already? I—I—"

She started over. "I was hoping to get to know you better."

"I have to go. They'll be boarding soon. Tell you what!" he said, holding out his hand for another handshake. "How about this?" She put her hand in his. "I have to be back in the city briefly one month from today. Do you think you could meet me? Maybe you could come in with your father. We could meet in the exact same spot we did today, at the same entrance. What do you say? Could you?"

He hadn't let go of her hand. Nor did she want him to. A month from now? Possibly. But with Mother so ill? Surely she could come in for just the day. If not with Father, then with one of the boys. She would talk to them well ahead of time.

"Yes, I think—Yes, I'd like that," she said, not at all sure she should be making the agreement.

"Remember! One month from today," he said, and squeezed her hand before turning and running down the path. "At the front entrance," he called back to her. "I'll be waiting."

CHAPTER SEVEN

Nadine was gone and Lizzie was in charge. With no big to-do the reins were slipped into her hands and she was forced to steer the thing. She didn't sense any new power or authority rise up within her for the task, but everyone kept looking to her, calling her name, asking her the questions they used to ask Mother, and waiting for her answers. So, there she was, playing the part. She had to. There was no one else.

Four days had passed since she had assumed full responsibility for the household and the care of Mother. Mother grew weaker day by day, and every day Father stayed away from the house more and more.

Mother implored Lizzie to read to her from the Bible every free moment she had while the children were at school. It was the only true comfort Lizzie felt she was giving her mother. The physical ministrations brought little, if any, relief, Lizzie could tell that. Mother wanted never to let go of her daughter's hand while she read. When Lizzie had to turn the page or hunt for a particular reference that Mother had asked for, Mother moaned until her hand was back in Lizzie's.

Mother wept almost constantly. She made no noise about it, only tears. It weakened Lizzie to see the tears always flowing.

"Sis, please make sure Willie takes the children to church. I want them to go every Sunday he does. And you too, Lizzie. Think about it at least. I want you to go, too." Her voice quivered with urgency.

Of course, whenever Father did go to the bedroom, the tears stopped. Mother didn't want to burden him.

But Father didn't spend much time in the house anymore. Any one of them might find him dilly-dallying in the barn or sawing and hammering in the shed, morning, noon, or night. Even when all the chores were done and there was nothing to do but enjoy the warmth of the evening hours in his beloved wife's company, he chose to be out, away from the house.

It was maddening. Lizzie thought he would want to spend every possible moment with Mother. It was becoming very apparent that it wouldn't be long before she would be unable to go on. Lizzie swabbed Mother's face and body and tried everything she could think of to make her rest comfortably. The cool cloths and the lotions brought temporary relief from the surface discomfort and itching, but the internal pain became increasingly unbearable, tormenting Mother's frail body until she cried out. Lizzie mixed the black smelly Paregoric liquid with Mother's drinking water with increasing regularity and grew more and more frustrated with Father.

Why doesn't he come in? Lizzie fumed. *He should be in here comforting Mother in these horrible hours.* But instead, he left her to languish alone. It just wasn't like him. He had always been sensitive and tender toward

Mother. Why had he changed so?

Lizzie couldn't reason it out no matter how hard she tried. Then on Saturday evening, while she was filling the copper tub for Father's bath, a thought came to her. Perhaps staying outside was his way of coping. Watching the light go out in Mother's eyes was more than he could bear. Spooning nourishment through her parched lips and never seeing any change for the better was killing him inside. Being with her forced him to admit that he was losing her. And he couldn't do it. In fact, Lizzie surmised, his mind had decided to deny the whole thing. If he didn't have to watch it, maybe it wasn't really happening at all.

But can't he see how shutting Mother out is hurting her? Can't he be strong for her sake?

Fear of the inevitable was driving him into a world of make believe where he didn't have to admit anything was wrong. Unfortunately, in the process, he was losing forever the moments he had left with his wife of twenty three years, and it angered Lizzie.

"Lizzie," Mother said as Lizzie lifted the bedpan away. "Will you bring me a pencil and some of that pretty stationery Auntie Emma gave me? I want to write your father a letter."

"Sure you're up to it?"

"I want to try. If I can't finish, you can help me."

Lizzie helped Mother to a semi-sitting position then busied herself with dusting the dressers and slats of the bedstead, shaking out doilies and the braided rag rugs. She polished Father's lone pair of dress shoes, contemplated doing Mother's Sunday pair as well, then decided against it.

Mother was getting fidgety and her breathing was noisy. Lizzie offered to help, but Mother said she was almost done and wanted to finish it herself. Momentarily, Sarah Van Ankum touched her dry tongue against the seal and handed the envelope to her daughter.

"Will you make sure Father gets this today?"

Lizzie propped the letter against Mother's basin in plane view. That way she wouldn't forget. And if she did, Father was sure to see it.

She returned to the bedside and swabbed Mother's face, neck and arms with some tepid water and tucked her into a comfortable position. Then she pulled Mother's long lifeless hair up and over the top of the pillow.

Lizzie wished she had gotten a peek at the letter before Mother sealed it. No doubt, Mother was doing her best to comfort and encourage Father.

***

Lizzie stirred four spoons of yeast into a dipper of warm water, added sugar, salt and lard then poured it into the large metal bread pan. She added more warm water, several dipperfuls. She had forgotten exactly how many it should be, but it looked right. She pulled open the flour bin and added flour, one-quarter sifter full at a time, stirring between additions until the dough was too stiff to stir. She rolled up her sleeves and kneaded with both hands, adding flour when it got too sticky. Kneading, giving a quarter turn, and kneading again. Occasionally, she stopped to work the sticky dough from her hands and fingers, letting the bits fall into the large lump. Then back to the kneading. Her back ached by the time the dough was "talking back" to her the way Mother said it would when it was ready. Lizzie dumped the dough onto the table, spread some lard in the bread pan and returned the dough to the pan for rising. She'd iron the clothes next. There'd be enough time to get at least the shirts and pants ironed. The linens could wait if need be.

Jake came trudging into the kitchen: boots, mud, and all.

"Jake!" Lizzie cried, trying to keep her voice down. "If I've told you once, I've told you a hundred times. Keep those muddy boots out of the kitchen." She reached for the broom and shooed him back to the shanty.

"I just need some matches."

"I don't care what you need," Lizzie scolded. "Take your boots off first. Don't you think I have enough to do around here without following you everywhere mopping up your tracks?" She pulled a handful of matches from the matchbox above the stove and took them to him. "Here, now stay out of here for awhile, will you. I'm trying to get things done."

"Yes, Mummy," Jake mocked.

"And check on Father, will you. He hasn't been to the house all day."

"He's still out in the shed. I just took him some small-headed nails. I think he's building something, but he won't let me look."

"I wish he'd come in. Mother is starting to cry for him. Will you tell him?"

"I already told 'im four times like you said. He's liable to lick me good if I tell him again. He's mad 'nough already. Don't you hear him crashin' boards into the walls out there?"

Lizzie closed the door behind Jake and turned to wipe up the tracks. What was she going to do about Father? Something had to be done. He wasn't himself at all anymore. And he still wouldn't speak English.

Mother's heart was breaking over it. But what's a girl to do? It's not like she could scold him, or take him by the shoulders and shake some sense into his head, the way he could with her.

This morning he had asked her to bundle up a lunch for him so he wouldn't have to lose time by coming to the house to eat. It was ridiculous! The shed was just across the yard. It was absurd. And downright exasperating. But he had made up his mind, and there was no arguing with Father. There never had been. If ever your opinion mattered enough that you wanted to argue your case, you had to do it first through Mother. Then if she felt there was merit to your view on the matter, she would take it up with Father. Then he might give you an ear.

"How can he be so cruel?" she complained aloud, as if Jake were still there to hear it.

Mother is dying, for pity sake! What's he thinking? Doesn't he know how much she needs him beside her and how much she has yet to say? Can't he read her eyes and see how she longs to hold his hand and study his face?

She ripped off her apron and ran up to her room.

***

Zachariah tapped another small nail into the end of the pine box. It went in half way, then bent, chipping the wood.

"Curse you, Sarah!" he hollered, hurling the hammer against the far wall. He stormed around the saw horses that supported the box, kicking at the loose boards scattered about on the floor.

Jake had approached the shed, but waited for the racket to subside before knocking.

"Leave me alone!" Father ordered. He picked up a short piece of two-by-four and pitched it at the door.

Jake jumped back, thankful he was on the other side of the door. He turned and walked away, tucking the matches into his pocket.

CHAPTER EIGHT

The following Saturday Lizzie noticed a change in Mother's countenance. And she barely moved about in the bed. A sweet quietness seemed to have come over her and a look of settled contentment filled her eyes. In fact, she was so peaceful that Lizzie wondered if Dr. Martin would turn out to be wrong after all. Perhaps Mother was beginning to feel better. The past two days Mother had asked to see each of the children, one by one. At first, Rosie and Anna balked at not being allowed to go in together jumping onto Mother's bed as they did every other day and at any time they pleased, but with the weather warming up, mud soup to fix, and a recently emptied grain bin to pretend was a playhouse, Lizzie was able to divert their attention and keep the house relatively quiet.

Jake blew into Mother's room like a refreshing breeze relating every tidbit of news he picked up from school, plus, he kept her updated on the growing head-count in the barnyard.

"Mother, you should see Tomboy! She's in foal for sure this time. Even I can tell. Father was right all along. I made a bet with J.C. He says she'll come due on the twentieth, on Sally's birthday. I say the fifteenth. What's your guess?"

Mother smiled. She enjoyed knowing what was happening outside her four walls. Tears spilled over with each thought of what she was missing. She would never see the colt, she knew that. She would never again hear the soft mooing of the cows as they comforted their calves. And she'd never get to meet the new neighbor Jake was talking about just now.

". . . That's what folks are sayin'. She's a widow lady and she's inherited ol' man Bannister's place. Can you imagine that, Mother? How's she ever going to make a go of it, when a man couldn't even do it?"

"What do you know about her?" Mother asked.

"Not much. Has a couple kids. 'Bout my age, I hear. I'll find out more on Monday if they come to school."

"Make sure you give them a kindly welcome. It's not easy moving to a new place, especially these days. We need to make sure she feels cared about and at home here. I'm going to pray for her. She'll need God's help for sure. You pray for her too, Jake."

"Sure, I will," he agreed cheerfully. "And another thing, the pig pen is so full that I doubt—"

"Jake," Mother interrupted, reaching for Jake's hand. "I want you to pray with me right now for the widow lady. What's her name again?"

"People call her Widow Bannister, that's all I know."

"We need to pray that God will bring her all the help she needs."

They joined hands and Mother prayed that God

would have mercy on the lady and protect her. And that He would provide for her every need. Jake followed with a short prayer of his own.

Mother drew Jake close.

"Jake," she said, tears flowing freely. "I don't know how to tell you how much I love you, how proud I am to have you as my son. I'm so thankful for the way you've pitched in and taken over the outside chores so Lizzie can take care of me."

Cheek to cheek, and with their arms wrapped around each other, they hugged, tight and long. Jake cried, too. It was hard to hold back the tears when Mother was crying so.

J.C. and Willie visited with Mother simultaneously by the light of the lantern. J.C. laughed and joked, robust and so much in love—Sadie the center of all his talk. His sweetheart's love made his heart sing and his singing heart made Mother smile. For J.C. seeing Mother's smile made the whole world right again.

When the conversation quieted or turned a more serious direction, J.C. jumped from his stool, kissed Mother on the forehead and bid her goodnight.

Willie lingered on, drawing out her expressions of faith and bubbling over with his own. As fellow pilgrims, they journeyed together along the road of faith and every day discovered new things to talk about. Willie held the Bible close to the light and probed eagerly as he expounded different passages. Mother lay with her eyes closed, joy radiating from her countenance as he read and talked. They recited favorite memorized Bible verses together, Mother merely mouthing the words when her strength was gone. They sang a hymn of praise. Mother's sweet soprano notes failed quickly, but Willie's smooth tenor stayed strong, moving from one song to another, even long after Mother drifted off to sleep. When Lizzie came in to prepare Mother for the night, Willie gently kissed Mother, one cheek then the other, and soaked in a long look at her precious face before backing out of the doorway.

* * *

Jake carefully backed out into the night, easing the creaky door closed. He was tired of being chased away from the shed. There was stuff in there he needed. Besides, he wanted to know what Father was hiding in there. Father's daily devotion to the shed was starting to work on Jake's nerves.

"I'm gonna find out what Father's up to," he confided to Betsy as he stripped her teats dry during the evening milking, "even if I have to wait 'til the middle of the night to do it."

Again today Father had hollered at him when he tried to get into the shed when all Jake wanted was a few scrap boards.

Just scraps, that's all. He didn't need anything special, no special length or width, just something he could nail together to make a ramp for the older chickens. He had figured out how to help the aging hens that were having trouble making the jump over the doorsill of the henhouse.

Blackie, the cattle dog, moved alongside Jake toward the shed, his tail swishing the backs of Jake's legs. There was no need for a lantern; the moon shone as bright as a candle from heaven. The semi-darkness cast eerie shadows on every side, the kind that would have sent

Rosie and Anna squealing, but he wasn't afraid. Every shadow represented something real, he knew that. The only reason it looked different at night was because the sun was on the other side of the world. So what's to be afraid of?

Jake lifted the latch and carefully scanned the shadows as the shed door creaked itself open. He peered inside, surveying the darkness as best he could before stepping over the threshold. There it was. The project Father had been working on.

"So that's it," he whispered, seeing the casket. So now he knew. But why was Father being so secretive about it? It's not like it was the first casket ever to have occupied Father's work bench. Father was a master wood worker and had made several in this very spot.

Then the reality of it hit Jake. This was Mother's casket. Mother would soon be in this box. Something inside him wanted to run, but he fought against it and stepped closer, running his fingers along the smooth wood. Father must have been working on the finishing touches for the lid was set in place. Jake shivered at the thought of closing Mother up in a box. A box without the slightest window for light to come in. The hair on the back of his neck stuck out. He smoothed it down with a sweaty palm and took in a deep breath. He felt around the box for the handle and gently began to lift the lid.

WHAM! The lid flew into the air and crashed to the floor. It wasn't the crash of the lid that sent Jake running but the fact that someone was inside the box. At the very moment he had lifted the lid a strong arm pushed the lid off flinging it to the floor.

Jake ran as hard as he could, first to the barn, then through the barnyard and at last to the house. His heart was beating so hard he could feel it in his gums. He stood inside the shanty trying to catch his breath, and trying to reason out what he saw. Or what he thought he saw. But by now his mind was playing games with him, making him think that whoever was in that casket may come after him. He kicked off his boots and hurried through the kitchen and up the dark stairway to his bedroom. He moved his mat from its place against the wall and placed it quietly between his brothers' beds. Their steady snoring comforted him and eventually brought calm to his tattered nerves. Then he realized that in his hurry to get out of the shed he had not closed the door of the shed.

Meanwhile, out in the shed, Zachariah pulled himself from the casket and carefully replaced the lid before going to dig again in the yard on the backside of the house.

CHAPTER NINE

Zachariah's hands shook as he adjusted the patchwork quilt and tucked it snugly under Sarah's chin. His eyes were red from holding back the tears. Perspiration speckled his shiny scalp doubling as adhesive for the few remaining strands of graying blonde hair he combed over the top. He swiped his shirt sleeve across his forehead.

With ragged weariness he dragged the chair next to the bed and sat down, bending close to Sarah's face. She was asleep. He remembered Dr. Martin talking about her coloring. He was right. Each day she looked worse. Zachariah brushed a wisp of dark hair from her forehead, then changed his mind and made it into a kiss curl instead, patting it softly to make it stay.

"Where's the good news now, Sarah?" he whispered in Dutch. He knew she would scold him if she heard him talk that way but what did it matter. Nothing mattered anymore. And even though he felt a twinge of guilt in speaking his mother tongue, doing so brought immense comfort. Like salve to an open sore.

He remembered the promise they'd made each other. To put the Dutch away and speak only English. And he remembered the day they made it. It was the day they took possession of the farmhouse. At that time the house consisted of three rooms: the large porch-like shanty, the kitchen, and a bedroom. They had argued for weeks before they both agreed that putting the Dutch behind them was the right thing to do. He, in particular, felt it was crucial to make every opportunity available to their children in this new English speaking community. They must put the old ways behind them, including the Dutch language, and welcome the new.

From childhood, both he and Sarah had learned English as well as Dutch. Their own parents, both from Holland, had insisted.

"In this new country," he remembered his own father telling him, "You must put English first. If you want to get along and make a good life for yourself, you must. Don't do what I did."

Sarah hadn't liked the idea of abandoning the Dutch heritage and resisted it vehemently, but Zachariah had won out.

"Think of the children," he had reasoned. "They'll be in English school. Eventually, they'll have to do business in this English community. I don't want them losing out on account of being Dutch."

So, at last she had given in. He was the head of the household and he had felt it was the right thing to do. She had had to trust him with it.

So together, on the day they pulled their wagon of belongings onto their newly acquired piece of farmland, Zachariah and Sarah had made the resolve, and until this fiendish thing came crashing down on their heads neither of them had ever broken their promise.

Sarah stirred slightly and turned her face the other way without opening her eyes.

His dear sweet Sarah. How could this be happening to her? She of all people!

"It should be me that suffers, not her," he muttered under his breath, his jaw tightening. He lifted her hand gently and examined it, stroking the sides of each finger and gently squeezing each fingertip. Sarah was not only his wife, she was also his best friend. The only person on earth he could talk his heart out to, in the good times and in the bad. She was his source of hope. She was to him like a well that never ran dry. Had been for twenty two years. She had been his tower of strength, especially the past couple of years. She was always finding a reason to hope and sing and plan. Even in the worst of times. He bent and kissed the palm of her hand.

Exhausted, he leaned forward, laid his head on her arm, and closed his eyes. The digging had wearied him. And his own desire to demonstrate strength left him deflated. Why couldn't she be buried on the farm? This was her home. She should be allowed to be buried at home.

"Oh, Sarah," he mouthed silently. "Can you see anything good ahead? How will your God come through for you this time?" He made no audible noise. His lips moved, but no sound came from them, English or Dutch.

He didn't understand Sarah's hope in God—he'd never really tried. But one thing was sure. From the day Sarah made her mind up to go with God, as she called it, she was never the same. He couldn't figure it out, but somehow, for Sarah, God became the center of everything.

"It's kind of like he sits on the throne of my life," she said one day, trying to explain it to him. "Truly Zach, it's like for all my life I've been in charge of me—*my* plans, *my* thoughts, *my* energy. But now, *He's* in charge. It's much better this way."

To Sarah God was "ever-present," "ever-able," and "ever-willing" to do the unimaginable for all those who called upon his name. From the moment she first believed, she knew no such word as hopeless, and she refused to let him fall prey to despair.

"God is God," she would say. "And as long as he is, there is no room for self-pity or despair. So, don't you be going all hopeless on me." And she meant it.

Zachariah kissed her arm repeatedly, his lips barely touching the skin.

"Help me, Sarah," he whispered, tears now washing down his face and his voice cracking. "What will I do without you? I can't. . . I need. . . .I. . .

He dropped face first onto the covers and wept, his chest heaving hard as the pent up fears broke through.

I need my Sarah back.

***

During the night Lizzie got up and added wood to the stove then went to check on Mother. Father lay asleep across her abdomen, his lower body still sitting in the chair.

"Mother," Lizzie whispered, touching Mother's face. "Do you need anything?" But Mother didn't stir. Gently Lizzie moved strands of limp hair from her mother's forehead and patted her cheek again, more firmly this time. Still there was no response from Mother.

Lizzie cried out, startling her father.

He sat up, teetering slightly, then stood to let Lizzie get closer. Lizzie reached for the rag in the basin and touched the damp cloth to Mother's face. Still Mother didn't move. Lizzie dropped the rag onto the pillow and covered her gaping mouth with both hands.

"Is she breathing?" Father's question was barely audible but it rocked the room, springing Lizzie into action.

She leaned an ear to Mother's mouth and pressed her fingers into the wrist of the hand that lay on top of the covers. She couldn't hear anything. She couldn't feel anything. She swiped her hair back around her ears and twisted to listen with the other ear. She felt for the pulse in Mother's neck, first one side of the throat, then the other. Nothing! Nothing? Why wasn't she breathing? Lizzie held her palm against Mother's cheek, then forehead. She felt warm. Well, kind of warm. She leaned over and felt Father's face with both palms. Her shoulders fell. No, maybe Mother wasn't that warm after all.

Father turned and walked out of the room, cursing and pulling the curtain to the floor, string and all.

Lizzie burst out crying, covering her mouth once again. She stood there looking down at Mother's still face then collapsed to her knees beside the bed.

"Oh, Mother!" she cried, not able to take her eyes off Mother's face.

Lizzie loved that face. It was a beautiful face. True, it wasn't the plump, enthusiastic face she had grown up with or the excited face that had seen her off to nursing school barely two and a half weeks ago, but still, it was the most beloved face on earth. Gently she cupped Mother's face in her hands and kissed both cheeks.

She wasn't sure what she should do next. She should probably wait for morning then send word to Dr. Martin. She stood up and went for Mother's brush. She hummed a night-time lullaby as she fixed mother's hair. Then she rinsed Mother's face and hands, laying her arms gently beside her body under the covers.

"It's customary to completely cover the body and face once death has arrived," she remembers an instructor saying that day at the city hospital. But she couldn't do that. She couldn't cover Mother's face. The thought of it made her gag. She pulled the blankets neatly up to Mother's chin then smoothed out the whole bed. She gave no thought to Father, where he had gone, or where he would sleep, or anything else. She dragged in the mat she'd been sleeping on in the big room the past few nights and laid it on the floor under the bedroom window. She would stay with Mother 'til morning.

CHAPTER TEN

Rosie and Anna slipped off their shoes and tip-toed down the stairway to the kitchen, hoping to get a peek through the kitchen window. The rest of the family, along with a crowd of friends and neighbors, were gathered outside around a pine box near the garden. The girls had been told to stay out of the way, and out of sight. But they were determined to get close enough to blow Mother a good-bye kiss.

"Absolutely not!" Father had shouted when Rosie asked to see Mother in the coffin. "I won't have it."

Rosie had pleaded, bawling like a calf freshly separated from its mother, but to no avail. Father stubbornly refused to allow the girls to see their mother once she stopped breathing. Rosie's cries had sent her into a fit of coughing and still Father was unmoved. He ordered Lizzie to keep them away from Mother's coffin and out of sight during the funeral. They were not to be seen at all, by him or anyone else.

"But she's our mother too," Rosie protested to Lizzie. "It's not right that we can't say good-bye, too."

Lizzie squatted down and pulled the girls into her

arms. "I'm sorry, girls. But what Father says goes, you know that."

They cried on her shoulders, Anna's wet face rubbing against Lizzie's neck, and Rosie's coughing eventually quieting into wheezing.

Now, through the slim crack in the door, the girls could see Mrs. Foster reclining in their father's chair at the table, wolfishly devouring a large piece of chocolate cake. An unexpected squeak from the door caught the woman's attention, sending the girls scampering back upstairs.

Earlier in the day, even before Uncle Albert and Aunt Emma had arrived, Lizzie dressed the girls in their Sunday dresses, tights, and shoes. She put their hair up in braids just in case they did get spotted. If sweet little Mrs. McCradey caught sight of them, even just one of them, Lizzie knew there would be a big to-do until the girls were allowed to come down. Lizzie could already envision the childless neighbor carrying on over them.

"Oh my poor babies, my poor sweet babies." She would insist on having her way, and there would be no peace for anyone: not her husband, nor for Father, until she be allowed to pull the girls into her arms. Lizzie could imagine Mrs. McCradey covering them with hugs and kisses, smoothing their sleeve ruffles and skirt gathers, and reworking their hair.

"She's our mother, too," Rosie mumbled again to Anna from the upstairs window.

All they could do was watch as family and friends moved closer around the box. Anna let go of the curtain and reached both arms around Rosie's middle, leaning her head against her sister's throat. Rosie leaned against the narrow window sill so that her shoulder pinned the curtain open ever so slightly. Then she closed her arms around Anna, pulling her little sister close and feeling the tickle of Anna's hair under her chin.

A cold drenching rain began to fall midway through the eleven o'clock service, forcing everyone to pull their collars up and their hats down.

"See Anna, God's crying too," Rosie said.

Young Pastor Stebbins, a recent Bible school graduate and pastor of the local church, conducted the service. Due to the rain Pastor Stebbins hastened through the reading of the twenty-third Psalm and closed the gathering in prayer. He omitted the hymn he had planned to solo. After the final amen he announced that refreshments would be served inside and everyone was invited to partake.

"That's the way Sarah would have wanted it," Emma whispered to Albert as they made their way indoors. "No one ever goes away from this house hungry."

The service had been conducted at the farm, next to Sarah's beloved garden. Once the crowd dispersed the coffin would be taken by wagon to the new cemetery beside the church and buried in the hole that had been prepared. Sarah had asked to be laid to rest in the picketed area next to the garden where premature twins had been buried three years ago. But it was not to be.

"I'm sorry, Sarah," Dr. Martin had said. That's not permissible anymore. New county ordinances won't allow you to be buried at home."

So, in the end, Sarah's funeral was not exactly as she would have wanted. She would be buried in the cemetery next to the church property, away from her precious family.

With Aunt Emma's help Lizzie had prepared dozens of open-faced buns, some of cheese, others of egg salad, and some of butter and gooseberry jelly. Several ladies brought desserts, for which Lizzie was extremely grateful. She still did not possess a teaspoon's worth of confidence in her own baking abilities, especially when it came to pastries and desserts.

The mourners quickly made their way out of the soaking rain and into the warm house but Zachariah stayed behind, clinging to the carrying rail of Sarah's pine box. He had not moved during the service, nor had he looked up. Statue-like he clenched the rail, his eyes still looking only at the box. As loved ones and neighbors moved away from the casket, several placed a hand lightly on his shoulder, but he acknowledged no touch. No tears fell from his eyes.

His face was fixed and his eyes were empty; he was clearly unmoved by the words of comfort that had been spoken during the pastor's brief message and untouched by the condolences of loved ones and friends. He saw no one and heard no one. And all who stole a glance at him feared for him.

J.C. received hats and coats inside the shanty door, and although many were dripping wet he layered them on pegs and nails and saddle horns. Condolences were spoken in hushed tones.

Willie headed for the kitchen intending to help Lizzie but was interrupted by Aunt Emma.

"Willie, where's your father?" she whispered, straightening his tie. "He needs some nourishment. And he needs to warm up before he catches his death out there."

Willie turned around and made his way outside

again, forging ahead through the incoming flow of friends and neighbors. When he found his father still gripping the coffin rail, rain pouring from the brim of his best felt hat, Willie put an arm around his father's shoulders.

"Dad, you've got to come in now. You're soaking wet." Willie gave a gentle tug, but Zachariah stood in place as heavy as stone. Willie bent forward a bit to look into his father's face.

"Father, come to the house," he said, speaking up a bit.

Zachariah didn't stir.

"You can't stay out here. You need to warm up and get something to eat." As Willie spoke he placed his warm hand over his father's ice-cold fingers and pried them gently from the rail. Immediately Zachariah began to tremble and took his son's arm, leaning into him as they turned and walked to the house.

Willie glanced back toward Pastor Stebbins and nodded, signaling him and the three others to load the casket into the wagon and pull it away.

Feeling his father's weight against him brought a fresh surge of tears to Willie's eyes. He had never seen Father in such a state, so unsteady, so unaware and unresponsive to everything and everyone. These past couple weeks had turned Father into a stranger. He no longer ran the farm or pursued the creamery business. He never talked about anything, not even his seeding plans which had to weigh on any farmer's mind this time of year. He hardly ever acknowledged the youngsters. Neither of the girls had been invited onto his lap for sips of coffee and bites of his bread since Mother was confined to bed, and he ignored all of Jake's challenges to tying knots and drawing blueprints.

It hurt to see Father shutting down and drawing away, acting so weak and hollow. They had lost Mother. Would they lose him, too? Willie leaned his head against Father's hat.

"Heavenly Father," he prayed silently. "Have mercy on Dad. He's falling apart and none of us know how to help him. Please, God, for the family's sake, help him."

CHAPTER ELEVEN

Jake lumbered through the shanty and into the kitchen swaying with the weight of his load, his arms piled high with split wood. "Why's there never anybody around to open the dang door for a kid, especially when his arms are full an' all?"

"You can't bring all that wood in here," Lizzie scolded when she saw him coming in with another armload. "You've already put more in the box than it can hold."

"You asked for wood, so you're gettin' wood."

"Jake, you know better than that! What am I supposed to do with all this wood?"

"Burn it. Isn't that what you usually do with it?"

Heat rose into Lizzie's face and she stiffened. "I mean it, Jake! Don't you dare put that wood down in here! I don't have room for it."

"So it's a dare, is it? All right, I accept." He gave a crooked smiled and dumped the load at her feet.

She jumped back and yelped as a slivered edge jabbed into her shin. Jake pivoted on his heels and stomped from the kitchen.

"You come back here this minute!" she yelled, stubbornly taking her stand, her hands on her hips. She stood firm.

He'd be back. He just needed a minute to think through what he had just done. His conscience would get the better of him and he'd be ashamed of himself. Then he'd be back to pick it up.

Lizzie waited. He'd pace around in the shanty long enough to let her know he was really mad about it. But he'd be back, preferably with an apology. She didn't like the idea of having to pry that out of him. Mother would have insisted that he apologize, so she better be prepared to do the same. Surely, it wouldn't come to that. She held her ground, awaiting his return. But when she heard the outside door slam shut, she knew he wasn't going to come back and fix it. Her strength gave way and she crumpled to the floor, crying into her apron.

Rosie and Anna came bursting through the kitchen door, Rosie panting and doubling over trying to catch her breath.

"What's the matter with Jake?" Anna asked. "Is he mad or. . ."

Seeing Lizzie crying Anna ran to her. "What's the matter? Why are you crying?"

"It's all right, girls," Lizzie said, sitting up and pushing several wilted strands of hair back from her cheeks and forehead. The girls helped her get up, each brushing the shavings and wood particles from her apron and skirt. Lizzie spit onto her fingertips and swiped away the blood that had surfaced on her leg.

"I'm all right." She pulled Mother's yellow edged handkerchief from the apron pocket and blew her nose. "Everything will be all right." She tucked the handkerchief into the waistband of her apron, squared her shoulders and said, "Anna, you load me up, will you? We'll pile this bunch in the shanty. Rosie, you sweep up the mess for me, ok? Take your time."

Anna lifted one piece at a time into Lizzie's outstretched arms, and Rosie went for the broom.

Lizzie was so thankful for these two cooperative girls. They listened and obeyed when she spoke to them. If only Anna were a little older, or Rosie a lot healthier, things would be so much easier. But at barely five years old Anna could hardly be expected to slop the pigs or chop turnips, the two chores Jake loathed the most. Up until Lizzie had headed to school these had been two of Lizzie's chores. If Anna were older, she'd gladly do them. But, as it was, Anna had not so much as gathered the eggs alone.

Not that it was entirely Anna's fault. Mother was really to blame. Any time one of the older children suggested Anna go "choring" with them Mother had always said, "What's the hurry? She's still a baby." The children would groan and say she was missing out on all the fun. She, too, begged Mother to let her go.

"No, Anna," she'd say, pulling Anna close to her skirt. "There'll be plenty of time to learn all that outside work."

Lizzie thought Mother overdid it somewhat with Anna, especially in light of how badly Anna longed to pitch in and do things.

"No children! I want Anna with me," Lizzie remembered Mother saying. She's going to learn cooking and baking. You never know, if she doesn't become a teacher, which I truly hope she will, then maybe she'll open up a bakery in town."

"Oh yes, Mama, I will," Anna would cheer. "I'll do it all. I'll teach and bake, and cook all day long. You'll see."

Anna probably would do it all—someday. But for right now Lizzie had to figure out how to lighten the load on Jake. For sure, it wasn't going to happen through Anna.

But Rosie wasn't the answer, either. Ever since birth she'd been frail. She hardly owned an ounce of strength, even yet.

"Yer 'bout as sturdy as a snowflake," Jake had yelled at her yesterday, angry that she wouldn't go get the cows for him.

Dr. Martin said it was asthma, and warned that they could expect it to slow her down all her life. But he was particularly pleased with the progress she had made the year she turned six. Before that no one knew for sure if she would make it from one week to the next.

Now at eight years old, she could walk and play at an easy pace without any visible discomfort, but she paid dearly each time she tried to run and skip. Heavy lifting was definitely out of the question. For Rosie there would probably never be any carrying or hoisting of slop pails, water pails, or anything of the like. The exertion could kill her.

Lizzie stood in the shanty, arms loaded, trying to decide what to do with the excess wood. There was just no room. Finally, she had Anna unload her, piece by piece, just outside the door. That was close enough that Anna could haul chunks to the kitchen as needed.

"Yes, that's it!" Lizzie said to Anna. Suddenly, like a match striking flint, an idea lit Lizzie's thinking. The wood pile was not very far from the house, and the split chunks were not excessively large. Surely that was not too big a chore for a five year old.

"From now on, Anna, you're in charge of bringing in the wood."

* * *

"Mother, how on earth did you do it?"

Lizzie often asked this question or questions like it. And even though her mother was not there to hear the questions, let alone answer them, Lizzie asked them anyway. Presently she was bent over the washtub.

"These collar rings are impossible to get out," she said as if having a conversation with someone. She bore down heavily on the shirt, pumping it with all her might against the washboard. Again and again she dipped it into the wash water, now almost cold, but it didn't look any better. She scrubbed longer, determined to loosen the dirty ring, and somehow, in the process, also rub Daniel's face from her memory. Her thoughts kept returning to that day at the city hospital and the young man who caught her up in his arms.

"What good does it do thinking about him?" she mumbled. "None! Where's it getting me? Nowhere!"

She was better off to forget him. Forget she had ever met the man. Just like she had to forget about nursing. She gritted her teeth as if that might add some power to her scrubbing.

How did Mother get the whites white, that's what she wanted to know. Since she took over washing the clothes, Willie's Sunday shirts, as well as the sheets and white aprons, were getting dingier by the week. And the dark rings around each shirt collar were only getting darker. They looked as though they'd been washed after the barnyard clothes, not before.

"And another thing!" she said. "How was Mother able to hum her way through wash day?" Lizzie's head ached from the pressure of her teeth gritting against each other.

She lifted the shirt to examine the collar again. It wasn't good, but she wasn't about to spend all morning on the shirts. She needed to get out to the garden yet today.

With the clothes finally secured to the line, and the dirty water dumped, Lizzie went for the shovel and hoe. If she spent a little time on the garden spot each day this week, by Saturday it should be readied and the girls could help with the planting. She would hoe the rows and they could drop in the seeds.

CHAPTER TWELVE

Sunny days and warm spring temperatures eventually pushed winter's final threats aside and life burst forth all over the farm. Smoky, the largest of the barn cats, gave birth to five healthy furballs, each of whom, within a couple weeks, were as eager as the older cats for a spray of warm milk.

"Please, Lizzie, please," the girls begged. "We only want *two* for house cats."

"No! Two is two too many. Now don't ask again."

"But why? Look how beautiful they are." Anna and Rosie each shoved the kitten they were holding toward Lizzie's face.

"Girls! Out with them! I said no, and I meant it." But the girls wouldn't hush up about it until J.C. put his foot down on Lizzie's behalf.

All four sows delivered successfully once again, bringing the pig population to thirty four. J.C. and Willie shook hands and exchanged winks each evening as they surveyed the overcrowded pig pen.

Two springs earlier they had come up with the idea of raising hogs. Every penny needed for the venture had come straight from their own pockets and it was they who stood to profit most by the yearly swell in numbers. Father held no interest in pigs but had allowed them to work it however they wanted as long as it didn't interfere with their commitment to the milk farmers.

"You get to pick the one you want for butcher," the boys promised Lizzie, just as they had promised Mother the previous year. She got the pick of the litters, but she hadn't tagged it yet. She'd wait until closer to butchering day to see what the summer slopping produced in them.

A bright purple patch of crocuses covered the picketed square where the twins had been buried three years ago. That knoll always bloomed first, but now the entire meadow between the house and the pond was also dappled purple and white. Every day Anna picked handfuls of each color and at night Lizzie helped the girls pull apart the petals, laying them out to dry on used butcher paper and sliding them under their beds. In her last letter, Aunt Emma had promised to visit the farm for her birthday in June (which had been her custom for years), and the girls had in mind to surprise her with a basketful of fragrant color.

Six more calves had joined Daisy's set of twins. Five heifers and one bull calf, and there were more to come. Had Father not cloistered himself away he would have whooped and hollered over the increase. But as it was, he wouldn't even go out to take a look.

Instead, he insisted on being left alone. What little he did eat was eaten in his bedroom. His trips to the outhouse were as far as he got from the house. He refused to take part in any of the chores or family routine. He rarely even spoke. And when he did, it was in stern

Dutch, making Rosie cry and Anna hide behind Lizzie.
He didn't go out to the barn. J.C. and Willie divided his
tasks between themselves and took over outside much the
same as Lizzie took over inside.

"I don't get it," Jake complained at supper last
night. "It's stupid!"

"Jake! Don't talk like that," Lizzie scolded. But
inside she agreed with Jake. In Mother's final days Father
did all to avoid the bedroom, but now that Mother was
gone, he wouldn't leave it.

Lizzie peeked in on him periodically each day
only to find him curled up in bed or sitting in the wooden
chair on Mother's side of the bed. Day was no different
than night. While passing through the kitchen to use the
outhouse he didn't so much as stop at the water pail to
dipper up a drink of cold water. It was worrisome.

He was slipping away from them, Lizzie could
feel it. He had crawled into a self-made box and was
dragging its corners in around himself. She missed the
father he had been. She missed hearing his deep satisfied
sigh after a long thirst-quenching guzzle. And his wink
telling her all was well on the earth. She felt closed off
from him now, and the hardest part was that he seemed to
want it that way.

"I don't know what to do," she cried, pacing the
kitchen floor. If only Mother had told what to do with
Father. At times Lizzie wanted to holler at him and order
him to get into his overalls, get out of the house, and give
her some space. But about the time she would storm into
the bedroom with her courage summoned and ready, there
he lay, looking pathetic and splintered, like a mirror that
had been stomped on and abandoned. And her well
rehearsed lines jammed up in her throat like bottlenecked

logs and she slipped out of the room without spilling a breath of her intention.

Days passed without his bed being made up. Mother would not have liked that. Lizzie didn't like it either, but it was hard to find a time when he wasn't in it. Everyday she tried to make conversation with him, but he wouldn't talk back. No matter how she tried, she couldn't get a reasonable response. Often he rolled over and turned a cold shoulder to her presence in the room. Other times he acted like she wasn't even in the room at all.

At night, when the house was still and the children asleep in their beds, she could hear his crying and groaning through the floorboards.

Some nights she crawled out of bed and pressed her ear flat against the floor trying to make it out. The agony of his sorrow reached up through the cracks and took hold of her heart and she lay crying along with him, her tears soaking into the bare wood floor.

"How can I help you, Father?" she whispered. "I don't know what to do. If only I knew how to ease your pain." Her body shook with sobbing as she mouthed words her father would never hear. "Please Father, don't shut me out. I want to help you. I want to comfort you."

She gave up calling him to meals and simply took them to him, placing the tray on the bed beside him. His eyes were red and strained, and at times glassed over, and his chin hung to his chest. Other than the potatoes he barely touched the food, but his coffee cup and glass of water were always empty. Lizzie was thankful for that. At least he was taking liquids. Dr. Martin had drilled her on the importance of liquids to the body, and that day at the hospital she had observed for herself the results of dehydration. She was relieved she didn't have to force the fluids down his throat, but it frustrated her that he wouldn't eat more.

This morning as she made up his tray, her mind was in a mood to scold him.

"What are you trying to do, Father?" she rehearsed at the stove. "If you don't watch it, you'll end up sick yourself. Is that what you want? To die, and join Mother? Well, you better make darn sure you know what you're doing, because if I understand Mother correctly, it's not like you can just waltz into heaven anytime you want. There are conditions. You have to *know* God. You have to *believe* in him."

"I don't want to hear about God," Father had yelled at Willie just days after the funeral. "He makes people hate him by what he does."

Lizzie knew Father didn't share Mother's belief in God. It was not that he was ever mean about it. In fact, he made no argument when Mother voiced her opinions about God, and had never discouraged her from reading the Bible aloud, or Willie for that matter. But he had never claimed to believe, and had never exhibited the peace that Mother and Willie had found. If Father had put his faith in God since Mother's death, Lizzie was sure she would know it. People change once they know God. Mother and Willie were evidence of that. And if Father did believe, he'd have hope. He'd be able to cope, wouldn't he? If only she could persuade him to go out to the barn for awhile, maybe he'd begin to see that spring had come, that hope was still alive, that life goes on.

***

Tomboy's time was near. She looked ready to burst, and Jake made sure everyone remembered that this colt was his. Father had promised.

"You should see her!" he exclaimed, reaching for his chair and unlacing his boots. "If she don't have that colt today, I'll milk Two-bit for a month. I mean it! And you won't hear me complain once 'bout her kickin' and tail switchin'."

From the time Jake came in from the barn he was bubbling over the top, like a bucket of Daisy's best milk. It had been weeks since Jake was happy about anything. This morning he was acting like his old self, all carefree and full of anticipation. Tears of relief welled up in Lizzie just listening to him. It was good to see him showing some joy again. She was tired of striving with him over everything. Maybe he had come to terms with the way things had to be.

His exuberance had the girls laughing and chattering like a couple of chickadees. Lizzie decided to take advantage of his cheery disposition and asked him to bring in a couple extra pails of water before heading off to school. Surprisingly he agreed, and yodeled his way through washing up for breakfast.

Jake's sudden enthusiasm made the kitchen glow. If only Father would come to the table and have a part in it. It would do him good to hear the children laughing.

"Glad to see our old Jake has come back to us," Lizzie said, smiling and dishing hot oatmeal into eagerly surrendered bowls. The girls giggled and pestered, begging Jake to tell all the names he had picked out for his colt.

"I've got some in mind all right, but I'm not tellin' yet," he teased as he sugared his porridge. "Anyways, there's more important things for a man to be thinkin' 'bout. Today..." he began then caught himself.

"Well...today's going to be a mighty fine day."

What happened between yesterday and today to turn Jake around, Lizzie wondered. His switch in attitude was remarkable. But something in his tone sounded a bit strange, almost suspicious. She didn't know what to make of it. Apart from the possibility of a colt being born, Lizzie knew of nothing extra-ordinary that might happen today. The coming of the colt seemed hardly enough to explain this transformation.

"And why do you suppose today will be so good?" she queried with cheer in her voice.

"Uh, I just know, that's all."

She glanced at Jake, and just as she did, he made a face and stuck out his tongue. He did it so quickly that no one noticed but Lizzie.

Anger ignited and instantly Lizzie's neck and cheeks developed a fiery blush.

Did he just mock me? Why would he?

Lizzie turned to the stove, unwilling to confront Jake. He was up to something. She appraised the events and conversations of the past few days, wondering if she had missed some clue as to what was going on in his head. Dipping the corner of her plain white apron into the water pail, she dabbed her hot face. She must bridle her accusing thoughts. Perhaps he hadn't made a face at all. Maybe her eyes were playing tricks on her. She was tired, after all. Now her imagination was running wild, making things up.

But no, there was something in that look. And considering his recent behavior, she couldn't help but worry.

"I don't know you anymore, Jake!" she had called after him as he walked away from her last night. And she no longer knew what to expect from him. When she asked for compliance, she got defiance. When she requested cooperation, she got an angry outburst. If she asked for silence, she got a racket. He was dynamite with a fuse no longer than a nose hair. Often he would run off before she was even finished speaking.

Thankfully, he always came back, and when he did, he was cooled down and peace and quiet ruled again until she made another request of him. Then, without warning, the fire would return, the flame of his fury aimed directly at her.

Not that she blamed him. She didn't like playing mother any more than he liked her doing it. And she hadn't exactly kept her dander down either.

They were both thrust into roles too tight for them. Pushed into garments that didn't fit. Their wretched circumstances had them both throttled, igniting the worst in them both.

During the night, unbeknownst to Lizzie, Jake had made a decision. He had opposed himself over it most of the night, considering the potential consequences, but by the time the rooster crowed, he had squared it away with himself and had drawn up a plan.

"It's time I pull up his boot straps and start acting like a man," he resolved. And he knew just how to go about it.

But no one must know. Not even Lizzie. Especially not Lizzie! And this Lizzie would want to know. She acted like she had to know everything about everyone, every single minute of the day. *Where are you going? When will you be home? Are your chores done?* Well, not this time. She knew too much already. Yesterday he had slipped and asked how old she thought the widow Bannister was. Now he was sorry he had opened his mouth. If he wasn't careful, Lizzie would piece things together.

Ever since Mother died, Lizzie seemed bent on exercising Mother's authority, and he was sick of it. What's more, she seemed to see right through him—just like Mother had. J.C. and Willie were no help. They insisted that he answer to Lizzie for everything. Well, not this time. This was his private business, and as long as she didn't know about it, she couldn't ask questions or make demands.

Today was a new beginning. He was no longer a boy, and he would prove it, one way or the other. He knew Lizzie wouldn't like it, but she'd just have to live with it. He wouldn't be coming home with the girls after school, but he wasn't about to tell it now. He would walk with the girls till they could see the house, then he'd hightail it over to the widow's place.

***

"You're almost home now," Jake told the girls a half mile from the house. "So get on home. I've got things to do."

"But Jake, what about your chores?" Rosie asked, stopping in the road.

"Go on home. I'm not coming."

"But what should we tell Lizzie?"

"Tell her whatever you want, I don't care. I've got important things to take care of. Maybe it's time you girls learned to do some chores instead of playing with dolls and mud pies all day long. Anyways, the chores can't be that important if Father doesn't even care. You don't see him out chorin' anymore, do ya'?"

Rosie started crying. "Jake, don't talk like that."

"I'll talk however I want. I'm practically a man now, ya know. And stop being such a bawl-baby. People get sick of it! Leastways, I do. Anyways, it ain't like I'm doing something wrong. Now get on home!"

He turned and ran across the road without so much as a wave, jumped Mr. Rudyk's log fence and ran full tilt across the open pasture. Rosie cried harder, begging him not to go and covering her eyes with her hands. He ran anyway. When she peeked through her fingers and saw him still running, she cried louder and called his name over and over. Anna stood silently, a frown forming on her perfect little brow. She watched her brother become a tiny speck moving across the field. Finally she turned, took hold of Rosie's coat pocket, and pulled her sobbing sister toward home.

CHAPTER THIRTEEN

Willie smiled to himself and whistled a tune about pussy willows as he and Father inspected the fences. It was high time Father got out of the house. Willie had planted himself in his father's room, refusing to leave until Father agreed to get dressed and go outside. It took over half the day, but it was worth it. And what a day for it! The sun was bright and warm, and the April breeze invigorating. Maybe a long walk in the fresh open air would pull Father free of the black cloud that had swallowed him. When Willie wasn't whistling, he was talking.

"See this. Here's another bad spot. And this one's new since J.C. and I were out here last week. Looks like animals took it down, don't you think?"

Zachariah shrugged.

"Two or three new posts should be enough to make it sound. There's still plenty of barbed wire. We checked supplies yesterday."

Zachariah didn't speak a word, but Willie didn't mind. He believed that just walking the land was doing his father's grieving heart a world of good. "We'll try to get it done right away. Then we can move the steers over here."

Father nodded and cleared his throat a time or two, but never did say anything. Occasionally, he kicked a willow post testing its stability, but his arms stayed stiff against his sides and his hands never came out of his coat pockets. Willie opened and closed the gates letting Father through first. When they crossed to the new field, Willie stepped on the sagging strand of wire fencing and Father stepped over it easily.

The fences were holding up pretty well for the most part. The wooden crisscross fencing surrounding the home quarter had suffered most from winter's bully fist.

"We'll start fixing fence next week," Willie told Father. "Once that's done it'll be time to get the new field turned."

It felt so good seeing Father outside again that Willie couldn't keep from smiling and whistling. It was good seeing Father raise his head and look out into the distance, even if the frown never left his brow, and even if he didn't loosen his shoulders and let his arms free.

"That's going to be a mighty fine field," Willie said, more in the mood to talk than whistle. "And what a gift from God! I can hardly believe old man Bannister let you take it over. And for just a dollar! I'm still scratching my head over that one."

Father remained quiet while Willie rambled on.

"But, I guess it was his land to do with as he pleased. Word has it that he left his home quarter to some relatives. I hope they'll manage better than he did, poor man. Did you ever see a man with so many troubles?"

When they got back to the house, Father was first to reach the door. He sighed with fatigue as he pushed against it.

Lizzie had put on a fresh pot of coffee and was hoping she could talk Father into sitting at the table for awhile.

"Umm, that coffee smells good," Willie said, removing his coat and boots. "If you're up to it maybe we can talk over our seeding plans." As Willie hung up his hat he mentioned that he planned to go to church in the morning and asked Father if he'd like to come along.

Zachariah let out an agonizing moan and rushed headlong at his son. Rising to his full five feet ten inches he took hold of Willie's shirt front and pushed him against the wall. His steaming face went nose to nose with Willie.

"God may be your helper," he snarled. "And he may have been your mother's helper, but he's no helper to me. Do you hear? What's he ever done for me, ay? Tell me that!"

Zachariah pushed away from Willie, kicking his muddy boots hard against the shanty wall and throwing his coat to the floor. He turned and stormed back outside in his stocking feet.

Lizzie overheard the angry words. Quickly, she dusted the flour from her hands and peeked out the kitchen window. She was relieved to see that Father was wearing his thick wool socks.

Willie, too, went to the window and took a quick look before reaching for a cup.

"It's all right, Lizzie. He'll be all right. You go ahead."

Willie had offered to stay in the house awhile and keep an eye on things as soon as they got back from checking the fences.

"Go for a walk," he had said. "Take Princess for a ride. Do whatever you want; you deserve some time to yourself."

Lizzie didn't know what she'd do without Willie. She would have unraveled ages ago, of that she was sure. Every week, and now almost daily, he found some way to lighten her load. It was almost as if he could read her mind—especially since the funeral.

"Come here, Lizzie," he had said this morning, taking her hand and pulling her from her spot near the stove and almost dragging her into the shanty. He had seen the tears running down her cheeks as she broke old bread into a pan for bread pudding.

"Lizzie, you're missing Mother, aren't you?" He took her by the shoulders and looked squarely into her face. "You need to remember how much she loved you. And I can tell you, she'd be proud of you." Then he pulled her close and stroked her hair in much the same way Mother used to do. She pressed her sobbing face into her brother's chest and clutched the back of his shirt in her fists.

How did he know? She hadn't said anything. But somehow he understood that this time her tears were tears of loneliness. Not frustration, or heaviness, or self-pity. She needed Mother's touch, her voice, her love. And somehow Willie knew.

And he noticed things. Things no one else noticed, like when the cook stove reservoir was dry or the shoes needed polishing. Every night he praised her for the scrumptious supper, even if it was the rabbit stew she loathed to fix, or the mush the children fussed about eating. He offered to help with the dishes just at the times she was so angry she'd rather throw them than clean them. He seemed increasingly able to sense what she needed, and *when* she needed it. It baffled her, and she wanted to ask him about it, and thank him—but not today. If she didn't get out of the house, and soon, the butter would fly.

"Thanks, Will," she said, slipping off her apron. She had measured out the flour and other dry ingredients for biscuits, but hadn't poured in the milk. Good. It could wait. She stepped into a frayed pair of overalls that hung on a nail near the door and tucked her skirt inside. Then, with tears already gathering, ran to the barn and scaled the log wall.

"What's to become of us, indeed?" she muttered, echoing the very question Mother had asked the day Dr. Martin announced the bad news. She pulled herself through the loft opening and went to the southwest corner. Pushing open a spot between two bails she eased her way into the wedge. She settled in, resting her arms along the bails like they were arms of a giant chair. Sucking in deeply, she filled her lungs with the sweet straw air and exhaled slowly. As her shoulders loosened and fell, unexpected tears also splashed from her lashes and ran down her face. "Oh Mother!" she cried.

Lizzie hadn't been to the loft in weeks. Her last visit was the day before she travelled to Calgary to begin her training. She was flying like a kite that day. Mother had helped with the packing and with time to spare had handed Lizzie a small package to open in the loft. It was a small booklet, its pages empty, each one waiting to receive Lizzie's thoughts and ponderings. Lizzie had confessed to Mother last summer that many of her diary writings were still in Dutch. Mother had said that she was glad to know that. The gift was Mother's way of reminding Lizzie to keep it up.

"Oh Mother, if only—" Lizzie cried now as hot tears dropped from her cheeks into her lap. "Why did you have to go?" She licked at the salty flow trickling into the corners of her mouth. "I don't know how long we can go on like this. Father's not the same as he was. You wouldn't even know him. I don't think you'd like him. And something's really wrong with Jake. You should see how we are. You *can* see, can't you?"

She tried to muffle the cries stored up in her soul, but she couldn't. Her shoulders shook and wailings escaped her lips that she herself did not recognize. "Oh Mother, I don't know if I'll be able to keep my promise. I'm not you. I don't know how to be you. I can't give the family what you did. I want a life of my own."

She was trapped and she knew it. Sealed like jam in a jar with no one to unscrew the lid. Bound like a bail of hay; the wire tight and getting tighter. She snapped up a loose piece of straw and clenched it between her front teeth, then made a quick swipe across her wet cheeks with her sleeve.

"Look at me! Here I am hiding in a pile of hay, instead of setting broken bones. I'm stuck here, and I can't do a single thing about it."

"Let *me* help you," Lizzie heard someone say. Quickly, Lizzie looked up and around to see who had spoken. She saw no one. She jumped up, spit the straw from her mouth, and looked down into the barn. She had heard a voice; she could have sworn she did. It wasn't just her imagination. Imaginations don't speak loud enough so you can hear them. Anyways, it sounded like Willie.

"Willie, you in here?" she called. There was no answer. She called again but heard nothing other than

Samantha's lazy breathing. Samantha had given birth to a set of twin calves during the night and had been left in the barn to rest. She was bedded down comfortably and gave no more attention to Lizzie's call than a switch of the tail. Lizzie listened closely, holding her breath for several seconds, but she heard nothing more than the dull grind of Samantha's teeth as the lower jaw rocked methodically against the upper, milling away at a mass of regurgitated hay. Apart from Samantha, all was still.

Lizzie returned to her spot between the bails, sat down, and covered her legs with loose straw. She laid her head back against a large support log and closed her eyes. Instantly, her mind went back to that day at the city hospital and the young man from up north.

How could she have been so dull-headed? Why hadn't she paid better attention to what he had said? She wasn't even sure she remembered his name anymore. Daniel? Daniel Windsor? Or was it Samuel? What was the matter with her anyway? What had possessed her to be so self-absorbed that she had not taken note of a single thing he had said. She let out a lamenting sigh, trying hard to revive the memory of him. But about all she could remember was his handsome face and compelling eyes. Those eyes! So dark and deep, like wells of rich chocolate. And that head of hair! She'd never seen anything like it. So thick, and dark, and wavy. So different from her blond, straight-haired brothers. Seeing it again in her mind's eye she imagined running her fingers through it. Yes, the man's eyes and hair were both firmly imprinted upon her memory. But apart from those two features, she was losing hold of him.

She tried again to recall other details. His clothes were dark, a deep blue. Or was it a dark gray? Probably wool. Was there anything else? She tried her best to relive the moments they had spent together. His hat was in his hands most of the time, that she remembered. He kept thumbing its rim over and over. Around and around it went in his hands.

Was that all? Was there nothing else to hold onto? She wished there were more, and her heart stung afresh at the thought of missing their scheduled meeting at the hospital's front entrance.

If only she hadn't been so stupid, so assuming—to think that all would go as planned. Especially with Mother as sick as she was.

"Why didn't I get the name of his town at least," she growled, flicking one piece of straw after another from her lap. "If only I had listened more closely to what he said about his north country."

She crawled deeper into the straw, scolding herself. Maybe he had said something that could have led her in his direction, but she hadn't listened well enough to catch it.

"Well, I'm sure I said plenty to lead him in my direction. I know I did. I babbled on and on, for pity sake. He could have found me by now, if he had wanted to."

She sat up straight, her body reacting to a cold new possibility. Maybe he didn't want to find her. Maybe he had no desire to get better acquainted with her and had no intention of meeting at the designated time and place. Maybe it was all her doing. She couldn't remember now if it was he who had suggested it, or she. But certainly, they had both agreed. Surely she wasn't wrong about that.

The barn door creaked below, and Willie hollered. "You in here, Lizzie?"

Lizzie didn't answer, but held her breath instead.

"Hey, Lizzie, guess what! Sadie and Sally's folks are here. You in here, Lizzie?"

Lizzie wanted to pretend she wasn't there. If she held real still and didn't stir then no straw would fall through the floor boards, and he would go looking somewhere else. But she couldn't do that—not to Willie.

"I'm here," she called out, sighing and pushing the straw away. She mumbled to herself, "I shoulda' known it wouldn't last."

"Sorry, Sis," he shouted up. "I didn't know they were coming, honest! They bought one of those green Fordor Sedan's. Come take a look."

Like I care what color it is, thought Lizzie.

"I think I know what they're really up to," he said, laughing. "They want to size me up, see if I'm a fit beau for their daughter. Do you think I'll make the grade?" Willie sobered as he watched Lizzie climb down. "Sorry you didn't get more time to yourself."

Lizzie knew he meant it. Willie wouldn't bail out on purpose. Anyway, it was just like Sadie to want to surprise the heck out of him.

Lizzie reached the barn floor and shook the straw from her overalls.

"I'll make it up to you, Lizzie," Willie called as he ran toward the automobile. "I promise. The girls are making rope dolls at the table."

Lizzie walked slowly toward the house, feeling gypped. She watched as Willie hopped into the back seat of the shiny green vehicle with its black fenders. With a honk of its horn they were off. He called out the rear window saying he wouldn't be gone long.

She supposed she should start something for supper. What would be something good to go with the biscuits? Potatoes again? Yes, that's something Father might eat, and the boys would expect potatoes. What else? Turnips? No, she was tired of turnips. Carrots? Yes, carrots. Creamed carrots! That sounded good. She hadn't fixed creamed carrots in awhile. What about meat?

"Why must we always have meat?" she grumbled, kicking a small rock across the yard. "That's the hardest part." Stubbornly, she decided that tonight's meal would have no meat. "I'm sure it's not a crime to have supper without meat once in awhile."

"What do you think, Rosie?" Lizzie asked as she pushed through the door to the kitchen. "What do you say to having supper without meat tonight?"

"It don't matter to me, Lizzie," Rosie said, biting off a loose thread. "But what will Father say about it?"

"Father won't say anything," Lizzie barked. "And you know why? Because he doesn't care about anything anymore. He hardly eats what I fix anyway. So I'm sure he won't notice if the meat's missing." Lizzie picked up the armload of clothes she had taken off the line earlier and made her way to the sitting room. Father was probably able to hear what she was saying, but she didn't care. Rosie called after her.

"Ya, but what about J.C. and Willie?"

"I don't care! Maybe it'll make them see I wasn't put on earth to wait on them hand and foot. Maybe it'll make them hurry up and marry those twins and I'll have two less mouths to feed." A smothering thought suddenly flitted across her mind and she added, "And those girls better not think they can move in under this roof."

CHAPTER FOURTEEN

"Where have you been, young man?" Lizzie drilled, cornering Jake the moment he stepped into the dark kitchen. She held her candlestick toward him, her eyes surveying his filthy clothes and her nostrils flaring to decipher the origin of the stench he brought in with him.

Pigs!

Each of the past three nights, the minute she heard him coming in, she had quickly smothered the wick and hurried upstairs. And by the time he got through the shanty and into the kitchen, she was back upstairs, listening to his every move. Each night he stopped at the stove, poured a little water into the dishpan and washed up before climbing the stairs to his room. But Lizzie couldn't stand it any more. She'd had enough of this mystery.

"What are you trying to do? Scare me to death?" She was whispering, but there was nothing soft in her voice. "And don't look at me like that," she ordered when he rolled his eyes. "I'm mad, and I have a right to be. You go traipsing off to who knows where, 'til all hours of the night, telling no one, leaving your chores to me, and I'm not supposed to get fired up about it?"

She placed the candle dish on the table and faced him.

He spread his feet as though bracing to take her on, but said nothing.

"I'll tell you this, Jacob Van Ankum," she said with the hand on her hip rising just long enough to poke him in the chest with the index finger. "It's got to stop."

His frigid eyes punctured her confidence and she stepped back. He untied the double knot in a new blue handkerchief tied around his neck and stuffed it into his right pants pocket. Lizzie hadn't seen that hanky before. It was the only thing on him that wasn't caked with dirt.

"I know you think the whole load landed on you, but it didn't," she continued, slipping into a chair at the table. "And what did couldn't be helped. They're all chores you can handle. You know the girls can't do them. And I can't do everything myself."

She paused, hoping he'd say something, but he didn't. Well, so be it. She had enough words for the both of them.

"And another thing! I want to know where you've been. It worries me sick not knowing if you're alive or dead."

"You know I wouldn't be dead," he said, pulling out a chair and dropping into it.

"How am I supposed to know that? When you disappear without a word, and no one in the family has seen you, how am I supposed to know?"

"You don't need to know everything. You're not my mother." He slapped father's dusty chore-doing hat onto the table and watched it slide across the smooth wood and drop off the other end.

"You don't come home after school, and then you sneak in after dark. Jake, four days now this has been going on, and I want some answers."

He bent down, rolled up his mud caked pant legs and unlaced his boots. He didn't offer any of the answers Lizzie was looking for.

"I'm tired of covering for you, Jake. And I'm not going to do it anymore, that's all there is to it. Either you give me some sensible answers or I'm going to let the boys in on what's going on."

She waited for a response but he said nothing. "When are you going to understand? I need your help around here."

Maybe she should tell him that she loved him and that Father loved him and that Mother would have done anything to spare him this extra work if she could have, but Lizzie doubted he was in the mood to hear any of it. She wasn't sure she believed it herself. Did she really love him? Lately, she felt more anger than love. And what did Father feel toward Jake? Anything? Did he care about any of them anymore?

"There's more people in this world needin' help than just you, Lizzie," Jake said at last, not looking at her.

Lizzie detected a flicker of tenderness in his voice. Then instantly his voice bulked up and his lips thinned.

"And what about Father? It's not like he's helpin' anybody. He can't even get himself out of bed. He stays in his room day and night carin' about nobody but himself. So why dump it on me?"

Lizzie stood and threw up her hands in exasperation. "So you're not going to do your share. Is that what you're saying?"

She moved to the chair beside Jake and lowered

her voice. "There's nothing I can do about Father. You know I've tried. We all have. And if J.C. and Willie were home more hours of the day, I would gladly put more on them. But as it is, Jake, it's you and me. And I've just got to have more help from you."

Jake stood up, unbuttoned his shirt and pulled the tails free of his britches. "I'm tired, Lizzie, can I go to bed now?"

"First I want you to promise me you'll come home after school and do your fair share of the chores. And promise you won't go running off anymore."

He walked the few steps to the upstairs door looking more like an old man than the twelve year old he was, and paused with his hand on the latch. It was plain to see he was exhausted. She wanted to tell him to get cleaned up before crawling into his freshly washed sheets, but he looked so beat she couldn't.

"I'll try to do better with my chores," he said, pulling the door open and looking up the stairway. "But I won't promise to stay home once they're done."

***

Before dawn Jake pulled his weary body from his narrow mat on the floor. He had collapsed onto the bed without removing his dirty clothes. Quietly now, he reached for a wool quilt and worked it into lumps under the covers, then quickly exited the room. J.C. and Willie were both still asleep, but with the roosters already tuning up they wouldn't be that way long.

He needed to get the deed done and get back home from Widow Bannister's place before anyone realized he was missing. He'd get back before breakfast and no one would know the difference.

Squealing pigs dashed this way and that as he ran about the pen determined to nab just the right one. Nothing less than the fattest piglet would do. If he could get his hands on it, that was. He darted frantically, slipping and sliding in the muck and even getting a hold of its tail at one point, but the critter's slimy hide kept Jake from gaining a firm grip. In desperation he lunged at the thing hoping to overtake it by the sheer weight of his own body, but the stout little glutton curved quickly to the left and Jake landed face down in the mud.

Pulling out the new blue handkerchief and wiping pig waste from his face, he reconsidered his options. Probably just as well. That hefty little piece of meat was likely too heavy to carry all the way to the widow's place anyhow.

His next victim was secured with relative ease, but as he hoisted it skyward, it squealed with such blood curdling urgency that all the sows came to their feet. Jake released his prize and hopped the fence until they settled down.

He eyed the nervous pen full then glanced anxiously toward the horizon. The sun, though still beneath the horizon, was tossing up soft yellow rays, lightening the eastern sky. If he didn't succeed, and soon, there'd be no time to get the thing settled at the other end. He pulled his hat down tight, and with renewed resolve decided to try for the skinny little oinker presently nosing around in the empty trough at the far end.

"No one will miss you, ay, little feller," he said as he lifted it into the air by its hind feet. "Two chickens last week, and you, little piggy, today." He hurried across the field, carrying the terrified runt.

CHAPTER FIFTEEN

Lizzie hadn't really wanted to go to church, but because she was beginning to feel guilty about always turning Willie down she went along. She was glad she said yes for she was thoroughly enjoying the two mile ride. She rode alongside Willie at the front of the wagon. What a big umbrella it was that hung over the earth, she thought. So big and bright and blue. This morning there wasn't a hint of a cloud to be seen anywhere. Nothing obscured her view as she looked to the four corners of the earth. The Rocky Mountains stood far off in the distance silhouetted against the royal blue heavens. A gentle breeze stroked Lizzie's cheeks turning them the color of the wild roses that would grow along the ditches come summertime.

Willie turned the team into the church yard and reined them to a halt at the rail. Lizzie remembered the last time she had been inside the church. Mother had insisted that the whole family attend the Christmas Eve service. The weather had turned out in her favor and even Father could not get out of going.

Lizzie had no good reason for not going to church

with Willie on a regular basis. It was just that she had other things she'd rather do.

She scanned the building's exterior and admitted that it looked very inviting. She particularly liked the steep peak of the roof and the double front doors. They were low and wide, and were presently flung open as if to beckon the whole world inside. Willie secured the reins and jumped from the wagon, and before Lizzie's feet had time to touch the ground, Pastor Stebbins was beside the wagon greeting her.

"Welcome, Lizzie," he said, holding out his hand to her. She caught sight of the wink he shot at Willie. "Welcome! I hope Willie told you we have a guest speaker today. I think you'll be very encouraged by what you hear."

"Thank you," she said quietly, glad that her glove concealed the sudden moisture on her palm.

"I'm *so* glad you've come," he went on, his handshake lingering. His smile was exuberant, reaching into every corner of his good-looking face. "I've been praying for you everyday. For all of you."

Lizzie didn't really know Pastor Stebbins very well, but she thought he seemed a bit nervous. Possibly he was just overly excited about this morning's guest speaker. The pastor had called on Mother and Willie several times over the past couple years. Lizzie hadn't liked sitting in on their conversations even though Mother often invited her to stay.

Lizzie had not noticed the redness in the pastor's hair before, nor his height. He must be at least as tall as Uncle Albert, maybe taller. She realized she was staring and turned her eyes away. In doing so she saw the new cemetery Jake had talked about. She could see two mounds of dirt and knew one of them must be Mother's.

Suddenly Lizzie wanted to be alone. She wanted to run to Mother's grave and tell her about how everything was going wrong. Mother should be told how unfit she was for the job and that every week some new piece of the family puzzle was falling apart. Nothing was working out as it should.

She needed to tell Mother the truth. That she wasn't able to comfort Father, and that she was failing miserably at steering Jake in the right way. She didn't know how to be the example she should be to the girls. She wanted Mother to know these things. She wanted her to know things were not getting better; instead, they were only getting worse. She wanted Mother to know she needed out. After all, Mother was the only one who could set her free.

"Please, excuse me," she whispered, her voice cracking and her eyes fixed firmly on the grave site.

The pastor released her hand. She brushed him lightly with her shoulder as she slipped around him. He watched her until she passed through the low picket gate then he turned to greet the others. Willie had Rosie and Anna by the hand with his Bible tucked under his arm. Smiling, he assured his pastor that their prayers were working. Stepping up the shallow steps to the church door James Stebbins cast another look in Lizzie's direction before following Willie and his little sisters inside.

***

Lizzie shifted uncomfortably sitting so near the front. It was a rotten trick, she thought, but Willie had insisted that the back benches were for mothers with babies. It seemed to Lizzie that the seats in the back should be saved for visitors. That way they could get familiar with the goings-on without feeling like they were being watched by everyone. It wasn't so bad during the singing and opening prayer, but now that the visiting preacher, Brother Lemont, was talking, she could swear she felt his breath on her face.

"Did you know?" he was saying just now. "Do you realize that God is the master designer, the divine engineer in your life? That's right, there's nothing about your life and the circumstances of your life that God doesn't care about. He has a hand in it all."

Lizzie tried desperately to give her attention to the speaker, but both body and soul wanted to be outside with Mother. She had barely gotten to Mother's grave when three girls came to the gate, announcing that the singing was about to begin. She hadn't had two minutes alone with Mother. She would have stayed where she was and not gone in to the meeting at all, but Ella, a school mate Lizzie had never liked, threatened in her usual taunting tone to send Pastor Stebbins out to fetch her.

"Wherever God has put you," the preacher was saying. "In whatever situation you find yourself, pour yourself out in whole-hearted devotion to Him, in that very thing and in that very place."

He gathered up his well-worn Bible, closing it around the index finger of one hand and leaving the other hand free. One long lanky arm swung loosely by his side as he walked off the low platform and down the center aisle searching the eyes of the congregation. "Yes, in the very circumstance you are fighting against right now. God is fitting you for things that you may know nothing about as yet."

What? Lizzie turned her attention fully toward the speaker. *What did he say?* She shifted in her seat to look at him.

"Hear me now, friend." His voice became very soft, and Lizzie felt the weight of his appeal. His gentle eyes connected with hers. He held his Bible up in the air. "The Bible says," he proclaimed, maintaining eye contact, "'Whatsoever thy hand findeth to do, do it with all thy might'."

But I have no might left in me, she argued under her breath. Troubled, she turned back to the front and lowered her head. She closed her eyes tight, determined not to let one tear slip down her face. She wasn't sure why she suddenly felt like crying. She hadn't felt the tears earlier when she stood at Mother's grave, but something about this man and the manner in which he spoke drew them near the surface.

"You might be thinking," the speaker went on to say. "'Preacher, I don't like where I'm at. I don't like the spot God has me in. I have no strength for it'."

He paused a moment. Lizzie was anxious to hear what he would say next, but she didn't look up. She didn't want him looking her in the eye again.

"And I'm here to tell you, friend, you're right," he said. "You can't do it alone. You need God's help."

When he returned to his place at the front, Lizzie looked at him, and again their eyes met. She looked quickly down to her lap, but was sorry she did for the tears she had successfully held inside rolled off her cheeks. And she was sure he saw it.

"Perhaps you think you came to church today because a friend invited you. Or maybe you came because you heard there was a new voice in the place this morning. But believe it or not, the real reason you are here today is because God is drawing you to Himself. Yes, God! The Creator of heaven and earth. The maker of all mankind. He wants you to know something, every one of you." His free hand swooped wide to include everyone in the room. "God wants you to know that he loves you and that he has a plan and purpose for your life. And it's a good plan."

Obviously, this man doesn't know what sickness and death can do to good plans, Lizzie mumbled to herself.

"Are you in a hard place right now?" he asked softly, an elbow on the feeble lectern in front of him. Lizzie couldn't keep from looking at him, wondering how he could know so much about the hard place she was in. "Are you overwhelmed by the miseries of life?" He leaned forward, resting both elbows on the wooden stand and tenderly surveying the group. "I believe some of you are."

Lizzie fidgeted in her seat, feeling drawn to the speaker, yet angry with him at the same time. She wanted to challenge the man with her burden and see if God could do anything about *that* predicament. She straightened her back and glared at him. He seemed to be waiting, expecting something from her.

"I want to invite you," he said at last, looking at her, then out to the others as well. He spread out his hands to include everyone. "I want to ask you to open up your heart's door and let God have his way in your life. That one act will make all the difference for you. You can start down a new road today. A road of peace with God and joy in living out His plan. Please, please, all who will. Come. Come to the Savior today."

He closed his Bible and stepped back from the stand. Pastor Stebbins joined him at the front and suddenly a small white-haired lady began playing softly on a mouth organ. Several people began making their way to the front. Lizzie had to move her legs to the side so a large man could squeeze by in front of her.

Lizzie wasn't sure what was going on. Why were the people so quick to get out of their seats and accept his offer? Didn't they have questions for him first? Didn't people get to ask questions or challenge his statements? Why was it suddenly over? And without any discussion? It seemed he had barely gotten started. There was still so much to talk about. Why did he stop talking just as she was starting to pay attention?

She looked at Willie. He smiled at her and mouthed something, but she couldn't make it out. She sighed and looked back to her dress. The woman on the mouth organ played a soothing song several times through as the pastors prayed for the people who knelt at the front. Someone had opened the doors allowing the sun to come beaming inside. Lizzie stood, and keeping her eyes down followed others who were heading to the door.

The warmth of the sun on her face washed her questions away, and she pasted a smile on her face for those greeting her. Several voiced delight in her coming, saying they hoped she would come back again next Sunday. With people so anxious to visit she couldn't get back to talk to Mother. She'd have to come back later.

She made her way to the wagon. Standing alone she watched the others laughing, hand-shaking, and talking. She didn't know all of the people, but she did recognize several neighbors.

Nosy old Mrs. Foster was there. That was one

person you need encounter just once to remember for a lifetime. Lizzie turned away, hoping the woman was too busy gathering bits of information to notice her. Lizzie wondered if Mrs. Foster was a regular at church or one of those the preacher had referred to as one being "drawn by God." Lizzie knew of no one who could so quickly and thoroughly gather up community news, scramble the details, and scatter her new revised version around as the "gospel truth."

The young people who had called her from the cemetery earlier now began clustering around Lizzie at the wagon. They were very friendly and Lizzie could tell they were trying to make her feel at home. They had just finished official introductions and were joking about Willie and Sadie getting married when Pastor Stebbins tapped Lizzie on the shoulder.

"Lizzie, I would like to personally introduce you to our guest, Brother Lemont."

"I'm very pleased to meet you, Lizzie," the visitor said, stretching a long thin arm in her direction. Lizzie could feel the kindness and gentleness of the man coming through his handshake. "I'm so sorry to hear of your mother's death. Pastor Stebbins told me of your loss."

The man's face was the picture of tenderness and concern and his voice like a soothing melody, much quieter than it had been during his sermon. His eyes reached deeply into her soul. She looked down.

Where was Willie? Wasn't it time they started home? She had dinner to fix. Perhaps Father was up and looking for everyone. That wasn't likely, and she knew it.

"Pastor Stebbins tells me you have a real desire for nursing," the man said, quickly regaining Lizzie's attention.

"Well. . . I . . . I did have," she stammered. "But I don't see much hope for it now."

Anna came running up to them, jabbering like a blue-jay. She took hold of Lizzie's hands, pulling and pleading for her to come meet someone. Rosie too joined in the song.

"Girls, please," Lizzie scolded. "You're interrupting! Where are your manners?" Immediately both girls fell silent, clinging close to Lizzie, one on each side.

"I'm very glad to have met you, Lizzie," the middle-aged man said. "And I'm delighted to hear of your interest in medicine. I have just come from the great northern region. The homesteaders and mill workers up there are begging for nurses and doctors. So, coming to be with your pastor this week, and hearing of your desire, well, it just blesses my heart to hear that God is preparing souls to serve in this way."

Pastor Stebbins caught the look of confusion in Lizzie's eyes and interrupted, guiding the visiting minister toward an elderly couple getting into their Model T. Looking back over his shoulder, Brother Lemont said, "It was good to have you in church today, Lizzie. I hope you'll be back for the evening service. I'd like to talk further about the medical needs up north."

She would have liked to talk to him, too—had her training gone as planned. But what was the use now?

The girls tugged on Lizzie's skirt gathers and led her toward the charcoal colored Model T that was parked center of the three vehicles remaining in the church yard.

"Guess what," Anna whispered, laughing and skipping. "We met the queen. Didn't we, Rosie?" Rosie's ringlets bobbed in the affirmative. Lizzie sighed; not at all sure she was in the mood for their ridiculous chatter.

"Anna, don't be silly! The queen doesn't live around here."

"Just take a look for yourself. You'll see."

As they approached the driver's side of the automobile, a lovely face looked out the window and smiled. The woman swung the door open and stepped out graciously. The girls were right. She did look like a queen. Her dress was black with white at the collar and sleeves. The drape around her shoulders was a light colored fur. Atop her head was a large-brimmed felt hat with a veil that screened her forehead and eyes. Her shiny cinnamon-colored hair was groomed neatly into a loose bun at the back.

"So you must be Lizzie," the lady said, her olive-colored complexion beaming. She extended a white-gloved hand toward Lizzie. "I've heard so much about you, and I've been anxious to meet you. I'm Mrs. Bannister. I've inherited the Bannister homestead not far from your place."

"How do you do?" Lizzie said, shaking the lady's hand.

"Your sisters are absolute dears. They've been so sweet to my children. Here, children," she said, turning and leaning into the automobile. "Come out and meet Lizzie."

Two children, a boy and a girl, looking to be close to Rosie's and Jake's ages squeezed out of the back seat and each offered a shy handshake. Neither of them said a word, but their eyes were full of admiration. Lizzie had heard the girls talking about these children often, how kind they were, how well-mannered.

Mrs. Bannister introduced them as Frankie and Isabelle. Frankie was in second grade and Isabelle in fourth. They were enjoying school very much and had been made to feel very welcome, especially by Jake and the girls.

Jake! Lizzie couldn't imagine him doing much to make them feel welcome.

Lizzie saw Willie coming their direction and hurried to excuse herself and the girls, saying they needed to get home to their father. Mrs. Bannister suggested that perhaps Lizzie could come over for tea sometime. Lizzie thanked her and hurried the girls to the wagon.

It's not likely I'll have time for tea any time soon, she muttered under her breath as she hurried away.

CHAPTER SIXTEEN

Lizzie pushed away the covers as soon as the rooster's morning call began. She had not slept well. How could she? In fact, how could she do anything but fret and fuss now that she knew Mrs. Foster was coming to visit. Yesterday, over Sunday dinner, Rosie told of overhearing Mrs. Foster whisper to a group of older church ladies that she planned to pay poor Lizzie Van Ankum a "surprise visit."

"Poor pathetic thing," Rosie had heard her say. "Someone needs to keep an eye out."

"Well, Mrs. Foster," Lizzie stewed out loud, pulling up a pair of Willie's hand-me-down britches. "If that's the way you want it, have at it. Spy all you want. You won't find anything juicy enough around here to pass around to the rest of the community."

And Lizzie meant it. She would turn the house upside down if she had to. She'd leave no corner untouched. There was no way she would give that nosy busybody something to tantalize the neighbors with. She'd have the place shining and dust free, if it was the last thing she ever did. She tiptoed down the dark stairway, feeling her way.

The door to the kitchen made a long dry squeak as she opened it.

"Shh!" she commanded. But the heavy door replied with another annoying creak as it closed behind her.

She lit the lantern that hung near the door, then crossed to the stove. She opened the lid, stoked the remaining embers, and reached for some kindling. The bucket was empty. There wasn't so much as a single stick.

"Jake!" she said, scowling. "When are you going to—"

Then she remembered. She had turned that chore over to Anna. It wasn't Jake's fault there was no kindling at hand. She picked up the empty pail and headed to the cellar below the shanty floor. Recently, she had cleared out a spot down there so that she could teach Anna how to split kindling. Hanging the lantern on a spike near the cellar door Lizzie quickly descended the rough ladder and gathered up just enough to get the fire going. She'd have Anna bring up more later.

In her hurry upwards Lizzie tripped on the third rung and lost hold of her supply. The bucket ricocheted from several touch points before rolling end over end into the darkest corner, twigs and shavings scattering thither and yon. In an attempt to catch the pail on its way down Lizzie flung out to the right. But in doing so she lost her grip on the ladder and tumbled to the dirt floor. Her shoulder scraped hard against the rugged shelving that carried the few remaining preserves, canned pickles, and berries from last year's harvest. She landed in a heap, her shoulder burning, and her heart pounding.

"Slow down, you Dodo," she groaned, spitting the

taste of dirt and sawdust from her mouth.

Lizzie dug into her right pocket and pulled out a handkerchief. Gingerly she reached around to dab at the shoulder. In the shadowy light she could make out the blood smears. She spit on the handkerchief and dabbed again. It was bleeding but not badly. The shirt was shredded at that spot, another item to throw onto the mending pile. She got up carefully, brushed off the dust and dirt, and tested for other damages. Then, more cautiously this time, gathered together another pail of wood scraps and ascended the ladder.

She opened the damper on the stove and poked at the remaining bed of cinders, glad now that she had added wood during the night. The nights were still quite cold, and she was finding that it was well worth the effort to get up during the night to add more wood instead of starting with everything stone cold in the morning.

She crisscrossed the tiniest sticks first, watching as the heat ignited the tender fuel. The sticks crackled and curled and spit, surrendering to the growing flame. Several larger pieces were added from the wood box. She replaced the lids of the firebox, shook the ash tray's contents down a bit then took the ashes outside and scattered them over the garden spot.

The morning air was crisp and clear, chilly for sure but at the same time imbuing her with energy. The sparrows were singing their cheery morning greetings to one another. Lizzie was glad someone had something to sing about. She hurried back to the house and started in on her list of chores. The shanty took priority.

Making a good first impression was of utmost importance in cases such as these, she knew that, and since the shanty had not been scrubbed in many many weeks, it needed a thorough going over. She intended the job done and the floor dry before anyone was up to track across it.

Lizzie attacked the most obvious clutter first, hanging up bridles, rearranging coats on their nails, and knocking dried mud from the boots. She swept up the surface dirt then brought in a pail of hot water, a scrub brush, and a mop. The spruce floor whitened up beautifully as Lizzie poured out the soapy water and scrubbed vigorously on hands and knees. She started near the outside door and worked her way toward the kitchen.

Though she hadn't spent much time keeping house, at least not in the way Mother had, she was satisfied and sat back against the kitchen door, surveying her efforts with pleasure. She wanted to linger and enjoy the sight but knew she couldn't. There was too much yet to do. She rose quickly, carried the pail of muddy water outside and tossed it to the left of the house.

The kitchen felt toasty. Lizzie opened the upstairs door and also pulled back the curtain to Father's bedroom so the heat could spread through the whole house. She expected to see Father lying curled up on the bed as usual, but he wasn't there. She didn't have time to investigate.

She went back to the stove, stretching her back. Soreness was reaching around the scraped shoulder and across her lower back. She gathered up the two small braided rugs from the kitchen floor and took them out for a good shake. They were hung over the backs of the kitchen chairs and would be returned to their places once the floor was swept. But first…the cake.

The cake must be baked now if she expected to have it iced and ready by the time her visitor arrived. Lizzie washed her hands and pulled open the flour bin.

How she would have loved to show Mrs. Foster that she was plenty capable, but this was no time to try anything fancy. She wasn't about to waste Mother's delicate dessert recipes on Mrs. Foster. A simple yellow cake would do.

By the time J.C. and Willie were up and making ready for the morning milking, the rooster had long since crowed himself hoarse and a sweet vanilla aroma permeated the house.

"Mornin' Lizzie," J.C. said, almost stumbling into the kitchen. "How's a fella supposed to think about chores with his mouth watering to his chin?"

Lizzie looked at him, smiling. He winked and headed out to the shanty.

Mr. Van Ankum, too, was up and putting on his boots before Lizzie realized that he actually intended to follow the boys to the barn.

"Father, do you want some coffee before you head out?" she asked, unsure what he was about to do. It didn't seem likely that he was actually going to get out to choring, so sudden like.

"It's made and ready," she added, smiling and holding up the coffee pot so he could see it was so. It felt strange to see him shuffling about, even if he was feeling his way as much as seeing it. She wasn't sure if he really knew what he was doing or where he was going. She wished he would just sit at the table for a few minutes. Just long enough to be sure he was thinking clearly.

His fingers were fumbling with the buttons of his coat. His eyes were red, unusually so, and his face tight with determination. She had to look away.

"No, Sis," he finally said. His voice cracked. Once the last button was secured he added, "I'll have some when the chores are done." His eyes met hers squarely, connecting, and she knew he was all right. He was not only all right. He was back. "I've got to get out and help the boys."

His legs seemed weighted, but he dragged them across the room.

"There'll be porridge and biscuits ready when you come in," Lizzie announced tenderly.

Seeing Father up and pushing into the ordinary morning routine concerned Lizzie, especially as she observed his fingers shake their way into a pair of gloves. But as she watched him gain strength with every step toward the barn, her worry turned to jubilation.

"And he was speaking English!" she giggled out loud. "I wonder if he noticed that." She sat at the window facing the barn and watched him until he disappeared into its opening. Father was up and moving! He was looking and actually seeing, and all of his own accord. She suddenly felt light and giddy.

She clapped her hands and jumped up and down. She started to the stairway to wake up the girls, but reconsidered. Instead, she tip-toed a figure eight between the stove and the table, raising her hands to heaven like she'd seen Mother do when she was praising God. Lizzie pulled out her handkerchief, waved it over her head, and mouthed Mother's words, "Hallelujah! Hallelujah!"

She felt a little guilty borrowing Mother's praise words. But she couldn't help it. Father was alive! Up, and alive! She could see it in his eyes. She could see it in his shoulders. How could she not sing and be glad!

She hummed her way through breakfast preparations, woke and readied the girls for school, and made lunch sandwiches. She set the baked cake on the corner cupboard and had just finished filling the lunch boxes when Father and the boys came in.

Laughter and conversation splashed about the breakfast table much like a bubbling brook waters the ground around it. Zachariah did almost no talking. But J.C. and Willie rattled on and on about one thing and another, their talking turning spasmodically into fits of laughter. The last time they had carried on so, Lizzie couldn't remember. Their hilarity even brought a smile to Father's face a time or two. Jake joined in like he was his old self and the girls giggled as though they were being tickled.

"I'm sorry to spoil the fun," Lizzie interrupted at last. "But Mrs. Foster is coming today, and I've got to get this house ready." She brought the dishpan over to the table and began gathering the breakfast bowls and loading up the silverware the others were handing to her. "Boys, in case you haven't noticed, the shanty's clean and I want it to stay that way. Don't leave things laying around in there. And don't spill any milk. Girls, I want you to get all the beds made before you head to school." Lizzie thought of giving Jake a job or two as well but decided not to risk it.

"What's to get all strung up about?" J.C. teased, trying to revive the laughter. "She's just a little old lady.

"Strung up, ay?" Lizzie's brow hardened and her face turned stern. "Do you realize how she talks about people? Well, I'll give her nothing. Do you hear me, nothing! She wants to gather details so she can report to the whole world how pitiful we all are. You can bet on it. She's certainly not coming to gather a *good* report, you know that! And in case you didn't notice, there's nothing little about her."

"Now, Lizzie," Father interrupted. "Don't be too hard on Mrs. Foster."

All eyes turned to their father. He drained what was left in his coffee cup and pushed it to the middle of the table, wiping up a spot of cream with his sleeve. "Her coming is what made me take a good look at myself."

The whole family was speechless. Waiting. Hungry for more. And Father didn't disappoint them.

"Last night when I heard you tell the children she was coming—well, I panicked. I knew I couldn't be holed-up in the bedroom with you out here doing your best to show her we're making out all right."

He pulled out his handkerchief and shook it loose. "It got me to thinkin'." He cleared the phlegm from his throat. His voice sounded almost rusty from lack of use. "Time has been a blur since . . . since . . ."

He spit into his hankie, determined, it seemed, to have the words come out. "Well, you know, since Mother passed on." He wiped the handkerchief across his mouth then wiped both his forehead and the back of his neck before emptying his nostrils into the large dingy-white square. He snorted back some tears and coughed his throat clear.

"I been workin' it out all night long. And she's just the spur I've been needin'. So really, you might say, I owe her."

Father was talking again, and every word in English. Every eye stayed on him, and every voice was still, wanting more.

None of them had heard him up pacing the kitchen floor through the wee hours of the night. Nor had they seen him wadding up blankets and wool socks and throwing them wildly against the bedroom wall. No one was awake to see him outside in the dark with a shovel, digging and digging until he collapsed onto the muddy mound, and finally, in outright exhaustion and surrender, submitted to the present realities: Sarah's death—his emptiness.

"Well then, Mrs. Foster," Lizzie finally declared, taking in a deep breath and brushing together the last of the breakfast crumbs. "If Father says you are welcome, then welcome you are!"

Anna squealed her approval, clapped her hands above her head and ran to Father.

"Oh, Father! Oh, Father!"

He opened his arms to his little one and she climbed onto his lap. She nestled her face into his chest. Rosie too, slid off her chair and went around the table to Father. He embraced her as well and squeezed her onto his lap alongside Anna.

CHAPTER SEVENTEEN

Lizzie hated to rush this special moment with Father, but she had to. All this time around the table would make the children late for school. Mr. Vanderhorn would wonder what was keeping the boys. And she had to get busy. She couldn't let Mrs. Foster catch her unprepared. Someone had to take charge and get things moving, and like it or not, she knew it was hers to do.

Before long Lizzie had Jake hoisting the girls up onto Molly's broad bare back and swinging himself in line behind them. Rosie had their butter and jelly sandwiches tucked safely into her large skirt pockets. A small bag of oats dangled from Jake's belt. Lizzie watched as they made their way down the lane. What a morning it had been! Father's return had been exhilarating for them all. Lizzie had received nothing but obedience and cooperation from all three of the children as they readied for school.

With a final "good-bye" she went inside. Breakfast must be cleared away first. Then she would tackle the other items on her list.

Lizzie filled the dishpan with water, put it on to

heat, and brought in the broom. Things must be done quickly, and perfectly. She had no intention of giving Mrs. Foster even the tiniest morsel to gossip about.

She cleared off the center of the table: the sugar, the cream, the butter and jelly, and wiped the table. She stacked the dirty dishes on the cupboard nearest the stove then swept the kitchen floor.

"I'm proud of you, you sweet Rhodies," she said, referring to the exceptional efforts of the Rhode Island Red hens. The warmer daytime temperatures had the chickens laying more eggs than Lizzie knew what to do with. She decided Mrs. Foster would get a dozen. *That should get me some points,* Lizzie thought, then felt guilty for thinking such a thought. She moved the basket of eggs to the end of the pile of dishes. They would be washed last, once the dishes were done.

She reached for the stack of breakfast bowls with one hand and gathered up the pot holders with the other. But as she did, the bowls caught on the lip of the dishpan and flew out of her hand. The whole lot of them slid across the stove like a company of ice skaters and dropped off the other end. It happened so fast that it did no good to reach for them, but she tried. Every last one broke to pieces as it hit the floor. Bits of glass and porcelain scattered everywhere and both pot holders landed in the hot dishwater.

"Dang it!"

She ran for the broom, kicking at a kitchen chair as she passed by.

"I don't have time for this!" she whined through gritted teeth.

She shook the particles of glass from the rag rugs and hung them once again on the backs of chairs. The room was swept, again. The splashed water was wiped up, and with a deeper level of concentration the remainder of the dishes were washed, dried, and put away. Once the eggs were washed Lizzie packaged up Mrs. Foster's dozen, tied them with string and set them on the shelf near the door.

She'd have to speak to Father tonight about replacing seven porridge bowls. She had dusted the furniture on Saturday as usual, but couldn't let it go at that. It must be done again. She checked the big room. Sadie and Sally had visited the boys on Sunday afternoon, and it showed. Popped corn! Crumbs! She dragged the large braided rug onto the front step then flung it over the railing. She walloped it with the broom then pulled it back inside.

Lizzie hurried upstairs for a quick peek at the bedrooms. Some people have a way of gaining entrance, even into every private place. And if anyone could do it, Mrs. Foster could, if she took a mind to. Lizzie was determined to have no embarrassing surprises for the woman to gloat over.

Lizzie found nothing significant enough to fuss over in either of the bedrooms and went to change into something more lady-like. She chose the cream colored house dress with the large leaf design.

It was a bit summery perhaps, but no matter, wearing it made her feel good about herself, and she desperately needed that today.

While posing in front of Mother's full length mirror, the one she had laboriously dragged upstairs after Mother's funeral, suddenly, Lizzie noticed her hair.

For pity sake! She grabbed the brush from the dresser top. What a sight she was.

She hadn't taken time to brush her hair earlier. There was too much on her mind and too much to be done. And, of course, no one in the household made any mention of it. Not that she would have appreciated it if they had.

She brushed it well now. A full one hundred strokes. Just as mother had taught her, and had always done with her own. Lizzie added a few extra for good measure then she twisted the golden strands into a rope-like bun, set it low along her neck, and pinned it. She felt she looked more like a woman with her hair that way. Maybe that was a good thing, today. She took a step closer to the looking glass, examining her face. She had never liked her lips. They were much too pale. And fuller than they should be. Certainly fuller than most of the other girls she knew. Her nose was tipped up slightly but she didn't mind that. At least she wasn't cursed with a nose like a hawk's beak. She noticed a tiny line across her forehead that she hadn't seen before. She spit on her fingertips and massaged it, but it didn't go away.

She stepped back from the mirror, twisted this way then that, examining her full-length profile. She hoped she wasn't finished growing, especially in certain parts, but she suspected she was.

She could hear horses and a wagon coming into the yard and peeked out the bedroom window. Her visitor was early.

"Wouldn't you know it?" Lizzie mumbled, running downstairs. She grabbed the rag rugs from the chairs and laid them in their places. She straightened the chairs around the table, tied on Mother's Sunday apron, and headed to the door, pinching color into her cheeks.

Mrs. Foster had made it to the step and was

reaching up to knock when Lizzie opened the door. Mrs. Foster's only son, Herbert, smiled ruefully and waved then circled the team around in the yard and left.

"Come in, Mrs. Foster," Lizzie said, pasting on a cheery face. She was being a hypocrite and she knew it, letting on like she was pleasantly surprised and gladdened by the visit when inside she was anything but. But for Father's sake, and for the family's, she would act the part of a perfect hostess. After all, as Father had said, the woman did deserve credit. It was she who had prodded him back to reality. Indeed, she did deserve Lizzie's warmth and hospitality. Lizzie smiled bigger, saying, "How nice of you to come for a visit."

"I told that boy o' mine over and over," the woman said breathlessly and heaved her weight over the shallow doorsill and into the shanty. "I must get over to see Lizzie, I must. But, I regret to say, he's too much like his poor departed father, that one."

Mrs. Foster huffed heavily as she peeled off her coat and gloves. She handed them over at last to Lizzie and settled her short heavy body onto a nearby stool to remove her overshoes.

"It was not until yesterday morning would he agree to bring me over," she said. "Men! Young or old, they're all the same. I get so exasperated I could haul off and hit him. 'Give 'em time, give 'em time,' was all he would say. Like time is some special potion, for pity sake! I doubt you'll find that in the Bible. No, I always say, women need company more than they need time. Any woman on God's good earth would agree, I'm sure. So, finally on Saturday, finally, he gave in and promised to bring me over come Monday."

Lizzie hung up her visitor's coat and offered her

hand to Mrs. Foster. With a grunt the woman hoisted to her feet and shuffled behind Lizzie into the kitchen.

"Please, have a seat," Lizzie said. "I'll put on some coffee, or would you prefer tea?"

"Oh, coffee is fine dear, perfectly fine." Mrs. Foster was panting. "Don't go to any special bother now. Whatever you're having is fine with me."

"I'll put on a fresh pot of coffee, and we'll have some cake."

"Umm! Cake even. My, my!" Mrs. Foster adjusted her chair to face the doorway to the big room. "Sounds wonderful, dear. See! Poor Herbert; he doesn't know what good things he misses, staying away from his neighbors."

Lizzie pulled the coffee pot to the front, added fresh water and gathered together the teacups, saucers, forks and spoons before remembering that the cake was not yet frosted. *Dang!* And she had no substitute on hand. No pudding. No sweet sauce. Nothing but cream. She had hoped to do better than that today.

Next time she'd know better. Refreshments must take priority over redusting.

Mrs. Foster read the pink in Lizzie's cheeks as pleasure in having company and set about reporting on all her aches and pains, her worries about the weather not staying warm long, probably another big blizzard coming along before spring was here for sure, and how sorry she was for not getting over to see Lizzie sooner. Lizzie busied herself setting the table and watching over the coffee. Mrs. Foster talked, non-stop.

Every move Lizzie made was furtively scrutinized, and likewise, the whole interior of the house. Everything within the woman's field of vision fell prey to inspection, her keen eyes conducting their notorious white glove inspection. She paused between sentences only briefly now and then to take in a deep breath, or heave a plaintive sigh.

"I can't tell you how much I miss your sweet mother," she was saying as Lizzie set a plate of cake slices on the table and sat down. "What's it been now? Five, six weeks, since she was laid to rest? Yes, indeed, I truly do miss her. As well I should. She was the kindest sort of woman, you know. And to think, I was the first to welcome her when she and your father moved onto the place here. Wasn't much to this property back then. Just an old abandoned shack, did you know? Before your folks came, some young city boy thought he'd try homesteading. But it was too much for him. Had no wife, no animals to speak of, nothing.

"Yes, I've known your mother a good long while. I remember thinking when I first met her how she hardly looked old enough to have three children and a fourth on the way. But like I said, that was several years ago. Then after Jake, came Rosie, and Anna after that." With a long dismal sigh she added, "My, how the years go by." Then, with a pause so slight that Lizzie did not have a chance to offer cake, she went on, "And you, my dear, how old are you now? Seventeen? Eighteen?

"Uh—" Lizzie faltered. "Uh—my birthday is—

She flushed as the realization came over her. "Actually," she admitted, swallowing loudly. "My seventeenth birthday has passed me by."

Lizzie had not once thought of her birthday. Not until this very moment. Nor had she thought of Father's. His, too, had gotten overlooked. Lizzie's mind replayed the previous days and weeks and realized that Father's birthday had been the very day of Mother's funeral.

Sorrow and agony and isolation had swallowed up his special day and hers as well.

Mrs. Foster eyed Lizzie, squinting slightly as she assessed the girl. Lizzie felt the woman's eyes boring into her soul. She reached for the cake and passed it to Mrs. Foster.

"Please, Mrs. Foster, have some cake. And here's some cream, if you like. I'll check on the coffee." The older women's zest for talking was outdone only by her lust for food, and any who knew her also knew that much conversation could be avoided once eating became an option.

Mrs. Foster secured a large corner piece, moved it to her plate and immediately cut into it. When Lizzie returned with the coffee her visitor was inhaling the thing without the aid of a fork. She didn't look up until her finger tips had picked up every crumb. Lizzie began to pour coffee into Mrs. Foster's cup.

"Not too much, dear," she said, motioning Lizzie to stop pouring at half full. "I enjoy a good bit of cream in my coffee, don't 'cha know. It enhances the flavor considerably."

Lizzie stopped pouring as directed, filled her own cup and took the pot back to the stove. When she returned to her place at the table, her knee accidentally bumped the table leg.

"Oh, forevermore!" Mrs. Foster yelled, an impatient look piercing Lizzie. The coffee had spilled over the brim and splashed into her saucer.

"I'm so sorry," Lizzie said. "I'll get a rag."

"Never mind! It's fine." Mrs. Foster picked the cup from the saucer, lifted the saucer to her lips and slurped up the spillage. "No need to make all that fuss over a little spill."

Mrs. Foster was panting, winded apparently, from the episode. But shortly she reached for the sugar and added two heaping teaspoons to her cup. She stirred the sugar in thoroughly, then selected a second piece of cake.

"You have no idea how I ache for you, my poor dear," she mumbled through her crumbs. "You're in such a sorry situation here. Of all in your family, yours is the worst plight of all, I fear."

The woman took a long slow drink of coffee. Lizzie did the same, grateful for the moment of quiet.

"Take your father," the woman said, licking her lips. "Grant it, he's taken a mighty blow. But still, well... he's a man. His work will keep his mind occupied and his hands busy. A man's work can become his companion, don't 'cha know. Take my dear departed Harvey, God rest his soul. Didn't have much need for my companionship those last years of his life."

Lizzie fidgeted in her chair, uncomfortable with the direction the conversation was going. She didn't really know Mrs. Foster, not the way one neighbor typically knows another, but the woman's reputation went before her. And ever since she had walked in the door she had lived up to everything Lizzie had heard about her.

Did she really think she was speaking words of comfort? With each new sentence the woman uttered Lizzie's muscles tightened further. At present her throat felt too tight to swallow the bite of cake she had taken.

The woman leaned back in the chair oblivious to Lizzie's discomfort. She pulled a handkerchief from her bosom and mopped around her mouth.

"Yes, dear. And your older brothers, too. I'm sure they won't be long in getting married and finding their own way in the world."

Lizzie pulled the cup to her lips and sipped, thinking that perhaps some movement might act as a distraction and shift Mrs. Foster's attention in another direction. It didn't work.

"It's a pitiful shame," the woman continued. "And I say it from my heart. You have received the bitterest blow of all." She tucked the handkerchief back into deep cleavage, picked up her fork and began collecting crumbs that had fallen around her plate. "Now, the little ones— they have you. And if you are as attentive to them as it appears you are to this house, they'll be looking up to you as "mother" before you know it. Probably already do."

Lizzie felt hot. She rubbed the palms of her hands against her apron under the table. The room was tightening around her. The air seemed thick and stale. It was hard to breathe.

Mrs. Foster didn't see the wall going up between the two of them. Her opinions continued to roll off her tongue, interrupted only by large gulps of coffee. And she had no difficulty speaking through a mouthful of crumbs.

"You see what I mean, don't you, dear? I can see that you do. I've discussed it with several of my dear friends and they agree wholeheartedly. You are very much needed here now, and will be for many years to come. It's such a shame that someone as young and pretty as yourself must sacrifice her whole future to meet the needs of the others. I say it again; it's a pitiful shame."

Lizzie hoped the woman was winding down for there was a full two seconds of silence. But not so.

"And don't you see what will happen?"

You wicked woman! You want to see me squirm, don't you? You like it that I'm stuck here? Lizzie pulled her cup to her lips but was sorry she did when her gulp echoed through the room.

"Think of it!" Mrs. Foster went on. "Your father will not be able to spare you. Not as long as the younger ones still need a mother. You'll be depended on every day, all day, for who knows how many years, just as your father has been depending on you since your mother was first confined to bed. And the sorry part is that by the time the youngsters are grown, all the suitable young men will have given up on you and married others." The woman reached over and patted Lizzie's arm. "Don't you see it, Lizzie? "Life will be nothing but loneliness and labor for you, you poor sweet girl. Life can be so cruel, I say. And no one will know it better than you, I'm afraid."

Does this woman never shut up? Lizzie felt a sudden urge to attack the incessant buzzing. Her head was spinning. She wanted to cover her ears and scream her lungs out, company or not. There must be something she could do to stop this noisy hornet. She turned in her chair and went to the stove, pulling up the corner of her apron and drying her forehead and temples.

"I see only one hope for you, my dear," the woman said. "Yes, now that I think of it, this is probably your only chance." Lizzie was afraid to ask the woman to elaborate. Nothing she had said so far held the least bit of comfort or hope.

"You know, Lizzie, I have been a good neighbor for many years. In fact, I'd say I've been such an attentive friend that I believe I could bring a fair measure of stability to this household."

Horror stuck Lizzie at the heart and she almost doubled over. *What! Is she saying she is the answer to—*

"I'd be here to care for the children and feed your

pa, and you'd be free to follow your dream."

Lizzie gagged, coughing into her apron.

"Would you care for another cup of coffee, Mrs. Foster?" She choked the offer out, still facing the stove. "There's plenty."

"Yes, dear, just a little more. You make a very good pot. And the cake is extremely nice. One more piece will do me." Mrs. Foster helped herself. "Fresh cake! I say, who can leave it alone?"

Obviously not you!

Lizzie heard an automobile come into the yard, coughing its way to a stop.

With pot in hand Lizzie rushed to the window and fairly squealed, "Oh look! It's Pastor Stebbins." Immediately Lizzie's shoulders relaxed and her lungs freely drew in air. Though she hardly knew the man, at this moment she wanted to hug him.

He had been very kind to Lizzie, to the whole family, as he had helped with Mother's funeral arrangements. And since then he had stopped by the house several times. But Lizzie, each time, had excused herself, thinking the pastor had come to visit Willie, who was, undoubtedly, his hungriest convert. Willie couldn't get enough. He gobbled up everything Pastor Stebbins would share with him about God and Jesus and the Bible.

Typically, when the pastor stopped by, the two of them, he and Willie, would spread their Bibles wide on the kitchen table and talk the evening away, all the while flipping the delicate pages from one passage to another. It was plain to see that Willie admired Pastor Stebbins. He had even confessed to Lizzie that he wanted to be just like him someday.

Right now Lizzie was doing some admiring of her

own. His timing was perfect.

Lizzie hurried to invite him inside. *Please, please don't refuse,* she cried inside. She didn't want to beg, but another minute alone with Mrs. Foster and she would hit the ceiling. And that's exactly what the old bat would love to see. It was one pleasure Lizzie wasn't about to give this nosy neighbor.

"Good morning, Pastor," Lizzie said, almost pulling him inside. "Please come in. Mrs. Foster has come to visit and—well, please stay." Panic lined her voice and she knew it, but she didn't care.

"Thank you, Lizzie," he said, smiling. "I'm glad to." He hadn't intended to stay, he explained, just needed to drop off the Dutch Bible Willie had loaned him. But seeing Lizzie shaking, how could he not? She looked as ruffled as a bantam hen. He took off his thick sweater and placed it over several others that shared a large peg and set his hat atop them all.

"I can't stay long, mind you. The Finlay's have invited me over for the noon meal. I can never turn down dear Mrs. Finlay's liver and onions. Can that lady ever cook!"

Greetings were cordial between the minister and Mrs. Foster. He had taken the chair Lizzie indicated and was quick to initiate conversation. He inquired about the health of Lizzie's family and also gave due attention to Mrs. Foster. His presence brought life back into the room and Lizzie smiled as she served up another round of coffee. Pastor Stebbins declined cake saying he didn't want to spoil his appetite.

"Speaking of neighbors, Mrs. Foster," the pastor interjected as the older woman pondered aloud about how in the world a pretty widow could manage alone on the old Bannister place. All that work and with no husband to carry the load. Mrs. Foster had taken a breath and opened her mouth to say more, undoubtedly about the widow, but was sufficiently diverted and nodded him to continue. "I haven't been out to see old Pete Donnelly in a while. His place is just the other side of yours. I'd be happy to give you a ride home?"

"Well—no," she said. "I told Herbert to fetch me, and I've been having such a good visit with Lizzie. Do you know I could not get him to bring me over until today? Blast the man! He's worse than his pa."

"It would be no trouble," the pastor said. "I'm already going your way."

Mrs. Foster secured her handkerchief again and wiped around her mouth, shaking it freely over her plate. Her eyes squinted in a far-off, thoughtful sort of way. She was obviously weighing her options.

"Well yes, now that I think it over, I believe I will take you up on your offer." She didn't say it out loud, but she concluded it was the perfect opportunity to share her observations regarding Lizzie's pitiful situation. Such an opportunity may not come along again in weeks, and who better to hear it than the local burden bearer.

With considerable effort Mrs. Foster rose to her feet. She thanked Lizzie and apologized for not staying longer. "But," she reasoned, "there's no need to use up Herbert's precious time when I can get home this other way."

Lizzie waved from the doorway as the automobile rattled around in the yard and drove down the lane. Then suddenly, remembering the eggs, she stomped her foot and slammed the door. Weary and deflated, she returned to the table and buried her face in her arms.

Why, she wondered after several peaceful moments alone, why did she still imagine herself dressed in white, moving from bed to bed, tending the sick and injured? Why couldn't she let it go? If only she could forget about school. Forget about the hospital. Forget about nursing altogether.

Mrs. Foster living under this roof? Never!

And Daniel's face? Why did it have to keep popping up? If only she could forget him. She wished she could. No, that wasn't exactly true. She didn't want to forget him, not really. She should, perhaps. A part of her wanted to. But a different part wanted to see him again, even if just for one last time. Maybe, if she could explain why she had not met him as promised, maybe it would be easier to let him go.

She slammed her fist down on the table near her head.

"Blasted woman!"

CHAPTER EIGHTEEN

Early the next morning, out of the blue, even before the children were off to school, Uncle Albert arrived at the farm saying he wanted to show Zachariah a new creamery that was starting up in Calgary. To Lizzie's amazement her father didn't argue and agreed to go with him. Uncle Albert said they would be back by bedtime.

"You'll bring Aunt Emma too, won't you?" Lizzie cried. He would have had to have been blind to miss the begging in her eyes.

"Child, are you suggesting I give that sweet secretary of mine some time away from the office?" Uncle Albert laughed. "Why, the place will fall flat on its nose if she's not there."

"Ah, Uncle, please. I need to see her." That was no lie. "And the girls need her." Lizzie was willing to do whatever begging necessary to get her auntie out to the farm, even if for a very short visit. She needed Aunt Emma right now. There were so many things she needed to tell, and to ask.

Lizzie could not find any written instructions for most of Mother's best recipes. She was getting tired of fixing the same things over and over; plus, the children were begging for their favorite dishes and desserts, especially that cream-filled pastry Mother had often made. Lizzie wanted to try new things; she wanted to improve her cooking and baking skills. And Aunt Emma was just the one to give this much-needed guidance.

And Mother's clothes and things? What was she to do with them? Now that Lizzie could get at the bedroom, she needed to know what Aunt Emma thought. But it wasn't only that, she needed the warmth of Aunt Emma's embrace.

"Besides—" Lizzie pleaded, placing a hand on her uncle's arm.

Uncle Albert, in turn, laid a large hand on Lizzie's shoulder. "I know, child. How about this? You fix up a nice big supper for us all and I'll have your pa back by then. And fix up a bed for yer Aunt Em and me. Does that suit your fancy?"

Lizzie squealed her delight and flung her arms around Uncle Albert's neck. He squeezed her tight and twirled her around, her feet circling a good foot from the floor.

As soon as they drove off Lizzie's mind and body shifted into high-gear. Dilly-dallying was not an option if she was going to get Father's bedroom cleaned and ready, plus have a big meal prepared in time for their arrival.

Within minutes Lizzie had it all planned out. Uncle Albert and Aunt Emma would stay in Father's room. That had always been Mother's way. Company always got the best bed in the house. There was only one problem. Father's bedroom was filthy! She'd be ashamed if Aunt Emma saw it as it was, much less had to sleep in it.

Lizzie set to work. The room was stripped. Bedding. Rag rugs. Dirty clothing. Everything that could be moved was hauled into the other room. It was all dumped onto the floor and sorted through. Even the straw mattress was taken from the room. It was drug out to the shanty, cut open and filled with fresh straw. After the sheets were soaked and washed and hung out to dry, the hardwood floor was swept and scrubbed. While the floor dried Lizzie filled the wash tub and washed Father's clothes, starting with the whites and ending with his dark work pants. The wool blankets and the patchwork quilt were draped over the Caragana hedge and beat without mercy. The pillows were plumped and laid in the sun.

Lizzie didn't take time to sit down for lunch but chewed on some carrots and a raw potato she had brought up from the cellar. She chose a good looking ham from the ice house. Fried ham was Uncle Albert's favorite. And she decided this was the perfect time to make Mother's scrumptious bread pudding with rum sauce. In order to do that though, she'd also have to get more bread baked. But that she could handle.

"Don't disappoint me today, Jake," she whispered as she peeled the potatoes and set them to the side in a pan of cold water. She'd ask him to fetch the cows after school even though that was one chore she was trying to relieve him of. Surely he wouldn't put up a fuss, not with his bridge-building uncle coming for supper.

Carrots were peeled as well and set to wait in their own kettle of cold water. Lizzie used every last slice of bread on the bread pudding, baked it, and set it on the table to cool. By the time the girls walked in from school Lizzie had the makings of the evening meal well planned out and had only to mix more bread dough and put

Father's room back together.

Jake didn't come home with the girls as hoped. She waited half an hour but at last had to recruit the girls. If everything was to be ready by supper time she'd need help.

"Girls, I have a job for you," Lizzie called toward the garden spot where they were playing. The girls quickly abandoned their rusty pans and stirring sticks, shaking out their skirts.

"I need you girls to get the cows for me. Think you can do that?"

"All by ourselves?" Anna asked eagerly. Lizzie picked their coats from the pegs, pulling Anna's coat sleeves right side out.

"Anna, how many times have I told you? Pull your coat sleeves through once you take it off? Yes, by yourselves."

Anna began hopping and skipping around the separator, singing, "We're getting the cows today, we're getting the cows."

"Anna, stop! I don't want any silliness."

Why did Jake have to be so irresponsible? He was here this morning when Uncle Albert came. He knew what was going on. And still he did not come and do his share. Why can't he show some respect? You'd think of all days to be home this would be it.

Actually, Lizzie was as frustrated with herself as she was with Jake. She had gotten carried away cleaning Father's room and now without Jake's help everything was piling up on top of everything else.

The girls had gone with her to get the cows the past two days and had done so many times last summer, Rosie dilly-dallying at her own careful pace and Anna way out ahead, more like a shepherd leading sheep than a farmer herding cattle.

When it came right down to it, Lizzie felt more comfortable with having the girls get the cows than she did with leaving them home alone to bake the bread. Neither of them had any experience with a hot stove, and at present the stove was very hot. Once the pudding was baked and a new batch of dough put together she had built up the fire. But then, absorbed with her cleaning project in the bedroom, she forgot to turn down the damper. Now the windows and doors were flung wide open doing their best to cool the blazing furnace. This was not the time to turn the kitchen over to the girls.

It was much safer to send them for the cows. They knew the path well, and what's more, the cows knew their way home. A bark or two from Blackie and the cattle would start moving toward the barn out of sheer habit.

"Now Rosie," Lizzie said sternly, taking her sister by the shoulders. "I want you to take it slow. And I mean all the way. It's still early, so you have plenty of time."

The girls buttoned their coats, and Lizzie held their rubber boots as they wiggled their feet into them. Anna was still bobbing around in circles.

"Blackie will do most of the work. Just make sure all the calves are coming along. Anna, now settle down. Don't be acting silly. I don't want Rosie sick over this."

"I won't," she promised, singing her answer.

Lizzie called Blackie and walked halfway to the barn with the girls before letting go of their hands.

"Go on now. I'll be watching for you, and I'll have the barn door open."

Lizzie didn't feel completely at ease about sending them off alone, but what choice did she have? There are only so many things one body can do in a given space of time, and not knowing whether Jake would come home or not, well, what else could she do? Besides, the cows were only half a mile away.

She went to the kitchen, cut the rising dough into loaves and slapped out the air before stuffing it into pans. She had planned to make a cinnamon swirl loaf for tomorrow's breakfast, but now, with the unearthly heat in the kitchen, and all she had yet to do in the bedroom, she wasn't in the mood to do anything special.

She had to hurry. The bedroom must be put back together quickly. What if Uncle Albert returned early? She glanced out the kitchen window. "Good girls," she whispered. They were taking it slow. Blackie was between them, wagging his tail in large lazy swoops. She checked the stove then went back to the bedroom.

She flung a clean sheet over the fat mattress. Its fresh aroma filled the room. The breeze had been perfect for whipping out most of the wrinkles. They weren't exactly wrinkle free like they would have been had Mother been in charge, but Lizzie was satisfied. The bottom sheet was tucked as tight as she could stretch it. The top covers were tucked in only at the foot. She plumped the pillows again and laid the heavy wool quilt over the foot of the bedstead on Father's side. That's the side Aunt Emma would sleep on.

Lizzie retrieved the chair and dresser scarves from the big room where they'd been laid during the cleaning of walls, floors, and furniture. Then she gathered up the items she had tossed into Mother's basin. She dumped the contents of the basin onto the bed and examined the bowl. Just that one chip. Otherwise, it was perfect. What a gem it was! What a treasure! Such a delicate leaf design. All those tiny roses and all in Mother's favorite colors.

Over the years Lizzie had come to love that basin.
And handling it now made her feel as though she was
touching Mother. She reached around it with both hands.
It felt good in her arms. Mother used to hold it that way
sometimes. She'd get a far-away look in her eyes and
hum a tune Lizzie never learned.

Lizzie had never seen Mother use the basin for
any practical purpose, like washing dirty faces or mixing
cake batter—ever. Mother had never used it at all, at least
not that Lizzie could remember. But she did occasionally
bring it down and set it on her lap when she was telling
about her home in Holland.

Lizzie walked it to the tall dresser and carefully
set the basin in its spot, wondering if that's where Mother
would want it to stay? Probably. If there was a better
place for it, Lizzie couldn't imagine where. And since
Mother had always kept it in that spot, then that's where it
should stay.

She gathered the pile of small things she had
collected throughout the room and laid them out on the
bed, sorting through them one by one. Father's cuff links,
six in all, two pairs that matched, two singles that didn't.
Three expandable arm bands, all gold-colored. Several
buttons of varying sizes and colors, each needing to be
sewn back onto shirts and trousers, no doubt.

When she had gone through Father's clothes for
washing this morning, she had pulled everything from his
two top drawers and sorted through them. She was
looking for anything that needed washing or mending.
She hadn't thought to check for missing buttons.

She had never really rummaged through Father's
things before now and wasn't sure if he would want the

various items set on his dresser top, or the window sill, or if he had some other place he liked to keep them.

She considered pulling out the bottom drawer of his dresser, a dresser he had built for himself years ago when the children were toddling around the house getting into places they had no business being. In all her life Lizzie had never opened Father's bottom drawer. Mother referred to it as Father's stash, and Lizzie had never once had any reason to look inside.

Mother had her own special drawer in her dresser, but it had been opened wide to the children many times. It held all her favorite things. A piece of Aunt Emma's wedding cake was there, still wrapped in pretty parchment and blue ribbon. Poems and rolled-up Bible promises. A tea set from her childhood. Mother's gallstones were also in that drawer, wrapped in a white handkerchief trimmed in green.

Lizzie reached for the chiseled knobs of her father's bottom drawer, but then drew back, feeling uneasy about opening it. Was it right to go into Father's private place? But, on the other hand, if she looked, she might find the missing armband and the other cuff links.

Not only that. She might find Mother's letter. She wished she knew what had become of the letter mother was so anxious for Father to read. She wished Mother had let her help with it. Lizzie had often wondered if there was something in the letter that contributed to the dark mood that fell upon Father during those days and weeks. Not that her mother would have said anything unkind. That was not likely.

Lizzie remembered how guilty she felt when the letter had disappeared before she had a chance to give it to Father. She had gotten carried away with chores and forgot to make sure Father read it on the day Mother had written it. She had promised that the letter would get into Father's hands that day, and she had failed to make it so.

Father had possibly not gotten to read the letter at all and that bothered Lizzie. She had put it out in plain sight for him to see, but she knew very well that he was not seeing even the plainly visible at that time. Mother had given her the responsibility of it and she had failed. She never knew for sure that Father had seen it, and she had never been able to bring herself to ask him about it. If Father had found the letter, it may be in the drawer.

She reached again for the knobs, and this time gave the drawer a tug. It barely moved. She tugged again, but it felt stuck. She pulled harder, and worked it side to side. Still it would not pull free. Something inside seemed to be jammed the wrong way, keeping it from coming open. She sat on the floor, braced her feet against the legs, and pulled again. Still it opened barely a fraction of an inch.

"Father probably hasn't even been able to use this drawer," she grumbled aloud.

Should she get determined and force the thing, she wondered. She got up, sat on the bed and eyed the drawer, considering how best to pry it free. A troubling question surfaced just then. Had Father jammed it on purpose? Quickly, she pushed the drawer back in, even with the others. She had better leave the thing alone. That's when she remembered the bread.

She ran to the kitchen. The loaves were fat and high, more than ready for the oven. But remembering her promise to have the barn door open she hurried into a pair of rubber boots and ran outside. She would open the barn door first, then she'd put the bread in.

Four happy kittens danced about her feet as she pushed on the barn door. She squatted, stroked their fluffy coats and tickled around their ears. Suddenly, she thought she heard a voice calling, somewhere off in the distance.

She listened. Yes, it sounded like someone screaming. She stood up, looking in all four directions, and listening. She thought of the girls and instantly fear ripped through her. She ran to where she could see the open pasture.

Oh no!

Rosie was running toward home, taking a few steps then bending over, then running again.

Lizzie scaled the barnyard railing and ran across the field to Rosie as hard as she could.

"Rosie! Stop running!" she yelled as she ran. "I'm coming!" She scanned the horizon. Where was Anna? Where were the cows? A pain stabbed her in the chest, stealing away her air. Her head was pounding.

Rosie, you've got to stop running. Where's Anna?

Lizzie slipped in the mud and hit the ground on all fours.

She scrambled up and hurried on, wiping her muddy hands against her mud-soaked apron as she ran.

Oh God, where's Anna?

Finally, Lizzie reached Rosie. Rosie was doubled over, crying and trying to catch her breath.

"Rosie, what happened?" Lizzie cried. "Where's Anna?" Lizzie gripped Rosie's shoulders and shook her hard for answers.

"Tell me, Rosie, where's Anna?"

"I'm trying. . ." Rosie said, wheezing heavily. "Anna climbed up. . .and. . ."

"She climbed up and what?" Lizzie demanded.

"I think she broke her head."

"What!"

"She fell on her head."

"Oh my God!" slipped from Lizzie's mouth. Rosie covered her ears. "Where is she, Rosie?" Lizzie yelled, pulling Rosie's hands from her ears. "Tell me! Where's she at?"

"At the far gate."

Lizzie turned and ran. She took several long strides and tripped once again before kicking off the rubber boots. She hated those boots. Willie's hand-me-downs were always way too big. If only she had put on her running shoes.

"Please God, don't let her be hurt," she cried over and over as she ran.

Lizzie cut across the field and headed for the far gate. She could see a hump of color by the gate post. It wasn't moving. Tomboy was standing nearby, her velvet muzzle trimming the new grass. Finally, Lizzie reached Anna and dove to the ground to get a look at her. She wasn't moving. She was in a heap, and her hair was spread like a veil across her face.

"Anna!" Lizzie called, brushing the butter colored strands away from her little sister's face. There was a large knot on her forehead. "Anna!" she cried again, shaking the child's tiny shoulder. "Can you hear me?"

Lizzie bent close. Anna was breathing. Lizzie felt for the pulse in her neck. It was strong and steady. Carefully, Lizzie put her hand under Anna's head and the child stirred.

"Anna, are you all right? Can you hear me?"

"Yes," Anna whimpered. "But my head hurts."

"Shh now. Let's get you home first. Then we'll

look at it."

Lizzie gathered Anna into her arms and headed home. When they got back to the spot where she had parted with the boots she set Anna down to walk on her own. But immediately Anna's small body swayed and her knees buckled. Lizzie caught her before she hit the ground and drew her up into her arms once again. She'd have to fetch the boots later.

The smell of rising bread met them at the kitchen door.

Oh, no! The bread!

Lizzie attempted to wipe the worst of the mud from her feet as she crossed the rag rugs on the kitchen floor. Rosie was sitting at the table crying into her arms. Lizzie asked her to bring a dipperful of cold water to the bedroom.

Lizzie crumbled to her knees beside Father's bed, feeling as though her arms would drop off as she unloaded Anna. Mud from them both smeared onto the clean blankets and pillows.

"All right," Lizzie said, breathing heavily. "Let me take a look." Lizzie pushed the messy hair back from the child's forehead.

"Ouch!" Anna cried, as Lizzie picked hair from the oozing wound.

"Rosie, please, the water!" she called sharply. She examined Anna's arms and legs and asked, "Do you hurt anywhere else?"

"No," she said, yawning. "Can I go to bed now?"

"Oh no, you don't." Lizzie knew that was not a good idea. She didn't know the medical explanation for why it was not a good idea, but Mother had always insisted that they not go to sleep following a blow to the head. "We've got to keep you up awhile. Besides, you don't want to miss seeing Aunt Emma, do you? Come now, sit up. And tell me what happened."

Lizzie helped Anna into a sitting position, mud contaminating still more of the bedding.

"Are you sure you're all right? You're not feeling dizzy, are you?"

"No. My head just hurts."

"Where does it hurt?"

Anna's finger met with the large knot before she intended it to, and yelped.

"That's it, though?" Lizzie asked. "Nowhere else?"

"No."

Lizzie stood up and gently drew Anna to a standing position. She waited a moment to be sure she was steady then led her to the kitchen and set her on a chair.

Rosie brought the water to the table. Her breathing was rough and her face looked as gray as ashes.

"Rosie, come sit," Lizzie said.

Rosie returned to the table and laid her head on her arms. Her breath rattled as it went in and out.

"I want to know what happened out there," Lizzie said to Rosie.

Anna stretched her arms out on the table and carefully laid her cheek to the wood.

"Oh no, you don't," Lizzie said, turning her attention back to Anna. "No sleeping for you, little lady."

Lizzie went for a rag. She swished it around in a dipper of cool water then carefully swabbed Anna's lump. She stroked the dirt from her face, neck and ears in the process. She swirled the rag around in the dipper again before folding it into a square.

"Here, hold this on your bump. It'll make it feel better."

Anna obeyed.

Lizzie untied and replaced the muddy apron, washed her hands and arms, and turned to the bread, peeling the deflated dough from the table. The loaves had not been able to wait. They had gotten so full of air that they had spilled over the edges of the pans and collapsed onto the table.

She dumped the contents of each pan out onto the table and gathered the full batch together once again. Gently she squeezed and reshaped the dough into new loaves. They'd probably turn out tough, but so be it. Anna was home, and alive, and in one piece. And that's what mattered.

The cows weren't home, but that would have to wait. She'd bake the bread first, then she'd get the cows. She sat down at the table and pulled Anna onto her lap.

***

Not long after dark Aunt Emma burst from the car like a stone from a slingshot, heading straight for Lizzie.

"Lizzie, my dear," she cried, hugging her niece with all her might. "How are you? How I've longed to see you. Let me look at you." She stood back, holding Lizzie at arm's length. "Oh, Lizzie," she said, "How good it is to be here."

"Yahoo!" Uncle Albert hooted as he ducked through the doorway. "Didn't I tell you we were at the right place? I could smell that ham a mile down the road.

Lizzie laughed and hugged Aunt Emma again. The girls heard the commotion and came rushing downstairs. Each in turn was taken up into Uncle Albert's large arms and spun around.

"Whoa, Uncle," Anna squealed. "You're making me dizzy."

"Since when?" he laughed, letting her down. Then he noticed her bump. "My goodness, child! Who clobbered you on the head?"

Anna giggled. "The ground cobbered me, that's who." Everyone laughed at her mispronunciation of the word.

At the supper table Willie and J.C. riddled their father with questions about the Calgary creamery. Jake, too, had his share of questions. But his questions were not about creameries. They were about the new roads Uncle Albert was constructing east of the city toward the Rocky Mountains.

Lizzie and the girls told of the excitement of their day, each telling their own version of Anna's mishap. Anna admitted that climbing the fence post and trying to mount Molly from there was not a good idea. Rosie praised Lizzie for saving Anna's life. Lizzie's slant on the story focused more on the size of the oozing bump, the steps she had taken to reduce the swelling, and her worries about not knowing what would have been the right thing to do if Anna had passed out again.

After supper Aunt Emma went upstairs to play with the girls before tucking them into bed. Lizzie cleaned up supper dishes and served up another bowl of bread pudding to the men. While they discussed all the angles worthy of consideration regarding expanding Father's creamery business, Aunt Emma helped Lizzie tidy up the muddied bedroom. Following Anna's mishap Lizzie had baked the bread, fetched the cows, wiped the mud from the kitchen floor, and gotten supper fixed and on the table, but she hadn't made it back to Father's bedroom.

Jake had come into the house for supper at the same time J.C. and Willie had pulled into the yard for milking. Uncle Albert and Aunt Emma had greeted him with warm enthusiasm, asking all about how the chores were going, how he enjoyed being the man around the place while the others were at work, etc. It made Lizzie mad. He had timed his entry perfectly, making it appear as though he had been out in the barnyard doing chores. She was the only one who was the wiser. What really irked her was that he didn't seem to mind in the least letting them think that that was exactly what he was doing.

She had measured him only a small bowl of bread pudding. He eyed her for it. But she set her chin, and he knew better than to ask for more.

"Serves you right," she wanted to say out loud, but didn't.

Lizzie and Aunt Emma sat up late, talking and sipping tea. As the candle light flickered across Aunt Emma's face, Lizzie recognized how much she looked like Mother. It was hard to take her eyes from her dear auntie. If only she could keep her here always. There was so much her aunt could teach her and explain to her.

They were up into the wee hours of the night, first talking, then writing out recipes and darning socks. Aunt Emma demonstrated how to knit and gave Lizzie some practice time while they discussed Mother's personal belongings, the ones in her special drawer.

"Leave them be for now," Aunt Emma advised. "I have a feeling your mother would have wanted you children to have these things someday. So let's not worry about doing anything with them right now."

"But I'd like to take the dresser upstairs," Lizzie said. "J.C. and Willie share a dresser, but Jake still has no good place for his clothes."

"In the morning we'll ask your uncle to help us move it up. But let's just leave your mother's things in the bottom drawer as they are? Jake won't need four drawers, will he?"

Lizzie didn't like the idea.

"No, we better find a different spot for them. I don't trust Jake with them."

Aunt Emma leaned forward, questioning Lizzie with her gaze.

"You don't trust Jake. Why's that?"

Lizzie lowered her head and looked away.

"Is there a problem, Lizzie? Jake was always such a joy to Sarah."

Lizzie hesitated.

"Come now, dear, don't hold it all inside. Please let me help."

It didn't seem likely that Aunt Emma could do anything that would help, not unless she was willing to haul him away. Lizzie liked that idea. She'd be better off without him. And he'd be better off without her.

"It started after Mother died," she whispered. "Everything's changed since then."

Lizzie felt like a tattle-tail spilling it all out on Aunt Emma, but she did it anyway.

CHAPTER NINETEEN

Shirttails and sheets slapped at Lizzie's arms and face as she fought to secure them to the clothesline. Spring winds blustered and blew and though her feet were spread and well planted, full-muscled gusts tipped her side to side and threatened to carry the laundered goods across the countryside. As the basket emptied she stepped one foot inside of it to keep the remaining whites from being transported away or flung across the muddy yard. Lizzie didn't mind the wind, but today she had hoped to have a little sunshine to go along with it.

Dark, low-hanging clouds tumbled across the sky, threatening rain. They boiled and thundered against one another until the whole firmament billowed forth like smoke from an incinerator. The sunbeams that showed themselves earlier, when she had first pulled out the washtub, lacked the might to break through the heavy veil.

Lizzie lifted her face to the wind. It struck against her cheeks and slashed at her hair.

"Blow if you want to," she called out. "You're not keeping me from getting these clothes on the line."

She enjoyed wrestling against the power of the wind. She always had. Struggling against its invisible strength made her feel alive with challenge and determination. Her hair flew free. It felt good to let it fly like that. But presently the wind was forcing her hair forward and around her face so that she couldn't see to fasten the whipping shirt tails. She shook her head and lifted her chin, hoping a gust would release the hair from her eyes, but it remained plastered against her face. She let go of the clothes line, bent forward, and thrust her hair back with both hands. Still, when she reached back to the wire, the shiny yellow tresses curled around her face once again.

The wind was exhilarating. Something about it made Lizzie yearn for freedom. She wished it would carry her away; to a far different place—a far different circumstance.

If only it *could*. She would run back to the hospital and its bustling nurses with their pure white uniforms and thick, crisp aprons and hats. She, too, would be in white; white from head to toe.

But when? When would her time come? Would it ever? Maybe when Anna turned fifteen or sixteen?

I can't wait another ten years!

With a scowl Lizzie grabbed hold of her loose hair and twisted it tight in the back and tucked it up inside itself.

"God engineers everything in your life," the visiting preacher had said. "Everything!" He said that God was fitting her for things she knew nothing about as yet. He was looking right at her when he said it, so she knew he was speaking to her.

But what did it mean? And why should she put any stock in what he said anyway? He was a stranger. True, he was a preacher. But does that automatically mean he knows everything there is to know about God? And about her future? When Mother had read from the Bible it said that God would give her the desire of her heart. That particular scripture was one of Mother's favorites, and she read it to the family often. Many times she had used that Bible verse to encourage Lizzie to follow the desire of her heart and pursue nursing wholeheartedly.

Lizzie suddenly felt the need to look it up for herself. She hurried to fasten the remaining tea towels to the line and jumped from the clothes stand.

At the kitchen table she searched through Mother's Bible. It seemed like the passage was somewhere in the middle of the book. She flipped through the fragile pages, but to no avail. It was nowhere to be found. She looked through the pages near the front of the book, then the pages near the back, still she couldn't find it. If only Mother would have put a special marker at that spot. Lizzie had no idea where to look. But she needed to know. She needed to know if the preacher was right, or if Mother was right? They couldn't both be right.

***

"That's not the way Mother used to read it, is it?" Lizzie asked Willie once the girls were tucked into bed. "You read it, Will." She had not been able to find the verse on her own and had to wait for Willie to get home.

He smoothed the pages of his new Bible with both hands and read from Psalm thirty-seven, verse four.

"'Delight thyself also in the Lord; and He shall give thee the desires of thine heart.'"

"See, that first part," Lizzie said. "I don't remember Mother reading that. Do you?" Lizzie asked.

"What? About delighting yourself in the Lord?"

"Ya, that part."

"Sure she did. And Pastor Stebbins brings it up often as well. He says we all love to hear about how God will give us what we want, but we don't want to hear about getting it God's way."

"I don't remember Mother reading that part." Lizzie leaned back in her chair, disappointed with Willie's interpretation.

"Maybe you were only hearing the end of it because that's the part you liked. You had your plans. Everything was going full steam ahead. And you liked that."

Lizzie sighed and closed Mother's Bible. What did it mean, then? That God may not give her the desire of her heart? That becoming a nurse may never happen. The preacher made it sound like God had a plan for her life. The Bible verse said plainly that God would give her the desire of her heart. If only that first part of verse four wasn't there. It made the whole thing sound conditional.

"Listen to the next verse," Willie said with an enthusiasm that reminded Lizzie of Mother. "This is good. Look: 'Commit thy way unto the Lord; trust also in him; and he will bring it to pass.' See that, that's encouraging, ay?"

What's so encouraging about it? Lizzie wondered, leaning forward, her elbows on the table and her head in her hands. It all sounded like a bunch of 'ifs'. If you do this, then such and such will happen. If you do that, then this other thing will happen. If *you* do this, then *God* will do that. The whole thing was getting complicated. When Mother had read it, it sounded so simple, so uplifting. God would give her the desire of her heart, and that was that.

"I'm going to bed." she said, pushing away from the table.

"Ah, come on, Sis. Don't you want to talk about it some more?" Willie missed the conversations he and Mother used to have over the Bible.

"I'm too tired."

"I think I'll read awhile longer. Can I pray with you before you go?"

Willie was practice-praying these days. Every time she turned around he was offering to pray about something. He prayed a blessing over supper every night and breakfast in the morning, and had openly offered to pray for anyone in the family if they should ever feel the need of it. Rosie and Anna both confessed their need of it almost daily. Just before supper Anna had gotten over-zealous on the plank teeter-totter Father had built years earlier. She had bounced so hard that Rosie went flying off the other end. Immediately they called Willie to pray for Rosie's sore arm. Even lost frogs were prayed for.

Lizzie bowed her head and closed her eyes, awaiting Willie's voice in prayer. She jumped slightly when he placed his hand on her head. She peeked at him quickly with one eye, but his head was bowed and he seemed to be waiting. For what, she wasn't sure. She waited silently.

The snap and crackle coming from the loaded fire box brought forth a measure of comfort and she drew in a deep breath, letting it out slowly. Still she waited.

Nothing.

He didn't expect her to pray first, did he?

She stirred uncomfortably in her chair, wondering what to do. She couldn't get up and leave, not with his hand still on her head. She crossed her legs and smoothed her skirt. At last he spoke and his smooth tenor voice spilled softly into the room. As he prayed for Lizzie, she sensed a covering of peace and protection fall over them all. Her shoulders relaxed, and she let out a heavy sigh. If only she could feel it on the inside as well. But her heart was too troubled. She had to find out what the preacher meant by his comments. Until she did, she felt she would never experience the inner peace Willie was seeking from God on her behalf.

CHAPTER TWENTY

Rebecca Bannister deposited Frankie and Isabelle at the schoolhouse then set out for the Van Ankum farm. Several weeks had passed since she first met Lizzie. She had liked the girl the moment she met her and was anxious to get to know her better. Spring rains had finally subsided and the mud had dried enough to make the trek a very doable thing.

The recent warm days were making her restless to get out of the house and become acquainted with her neighbors. She had sensed Lizzie's reserve that day in the church yard. If the two of them were to become friends, Rebecca knew it was she who must take the first step.

When taking on her brother-in-law's homestead she had not realized just how much time she would spend wearing boots. But, she admitted, it was a small price to pay, especially now with Jake's help. He was such a blessing. She hardly had to go out to the barnyard at all anymore.

"Thanks, but no thanks," was the impression she got from Lizzie regarding her invitation to tea. And yet there was something in the girl's eyes. Almost like a cry for help of some sort—something. Friendship, perhaps. Or comfort. Something.

She may have completely misread the girl, but how would she know unless she got acquainted with her. Over the past few weeks she had managed to chisel enough information out of Jake to believe that his sister needed something, something perhaps she could provide.

Anyway, it was time she got out and met more of her neighbors. And Lizzie was as good a place to start as any.

The warm touch of the morning sun on her shoulders made her smile, and she breathed in deeply as she went along. It felt good to stretch her stride out as far as it could go. She seldom had opportunity for long walks since coming to Alberta's farmlands. But now that the mud had dried and the children felt comfortably at home alone on the property she hoped to take a good long walk at least once a week.

For the most part she walked the high side of the ruts. Then, occasionally, she stepped down into a rut and took a few steps toe to heel just for fun. She adjusted the sling full of goodies hanging diagonally across her upper body and followed the ruts leading west.

Last night before going to bed, once Jake had finished his sixth cornbread muffin and headed home, she went to work. She clipped the stitches of an old flour sack and restitched the thing into a carrying bag. Cutting a piece of cheese cloth into pieces, she bundled up pieces of dried meat and fruit leathers. She poured several spoons of tea leaves into a small pouch, then cut the large pocket off a seldom used apron and filled it with some wild flower seeds she had harvested last year near Vancouver.

"Lizzie loves flowers," Jake had said one day

when she asked to know more about Lizzie. "She used to plant every kind of wild flower Mother would allow space for in the garden. But what she really cares about more than anything else in the world is nursing. I bet she won't even get married like most girls. Leastways, I've never heard her talk about boys like other girls do. But, I don't know. She's not the same anymore. Even the nursing, she ain't excited 'bout it like she used to be. Doesn't get excited 'bout much of anything anymore, 'cept when she's mad at me."

Mrs. Bannister quickened her pace until she was almost running. Hopefully Lizzie would not mind a visitor, especially first thing in the morning. If the girl did seem to mind . . . well, she'd just have to jump that crack when the time came.

***

Lizzie dipped her head forward into the dishpan and scooped handfuls of warm water over her long hair. Times for personal hygiene were somewhat easier to come by now that Father was out of the house again. The days and weeks were taking on a much more workable routine. She swished her hair around in the bowl, scratching the scalp with determined fingernails. She dunked the dipper into the nearby water pail and shivered as the cold water ran over her head and down around her face and neck.

Suddenly, she heard a knock on the door.
Who in the world?—

Quickly she squeezed out the water and wrapped a towel around her wet head. Flipping the towel's long tail backwards and tucking it in at the nap she glanced around the room, hoping things weren't too much out of order.

If that's you, Mrs. Foster, I'll ring your neck for you. She rolled her eyes, took a big breath, and lifted the latch.

"Good morning," Mrs. Bannister said brightly, her smile meeting Lizzie like a fresh bouquet of roses. "I'm sorry to come unannounced," the widow rushed to explain, feeling now she should have forewarned the girl "and you in the middle of, well, of washing your hair."

"Please, Mrs. Bannister, come in." Lizzie opened the door wide.

What a time to be caught, and by the "queen." Well, so be it, Lizzie thought. *Better she than that spying Mrs. Foster.*

Lizzie seated her visitor at the table and excused herself to brush out her hair. When she returned the lady was pulling out and laying on the table several items from her pack. Mrs. Bannister had removed her hat and sweater and hung them on a chair.

"Jake tells me you love to plant flower seeds," the woman said as Lizzie came through the upstairs door. "There's still plenty of time for planting these ones. Look here. These in this bundle." She was holding up a small sack. "These are all wild flowers. Don't ask me what their names are because I couldn't tell you. But I promise, you'll love them."

The lady pushed back a lose strand of cinnamon colored hair that had worked its way free of the low bun, then reached back into her bag.

Lizzie watched her graceful movements. The poise and gentility with which she moved was captivating. As was her British accent. She should offer the lady a cup of coffee and serve up a biscuit, but she couldn't take her eyes off the assortment on the table and the lovely fingers handling each item.

"Thought you might like to plant them even if you don't know exactly what you're getting. That way you will be surprised and blessed."

Surprised and blessed. She sounded like Mother. Mother would have had the coffee pot on by now.

"Uh, would you care for a cup of coffee? You've had a long walk."

"Yes, Lizzie, I'd love some. But perhaps a dipper of water first, if you don't mind."

Of course, Lizzie thought, scolding herself. *I should have offered that the minute she stepped in the door.* Lizzie quickly took her a glass of water, then went to prepare the coffee. Reaching into the top corner cupboard she pulled out two of Mother's favorite teacups and their matching saucers. She would give Mrs. Bannister the set without the crack.

"I've heard that there are some beautiful wild flowers up north. Brother Lemont was telling me. You remember him, don't you?"

Lizzie remembered all right. Never had one preacher's comments made her so curious about what the Bible had to say. After questioning Willie, Lizzie had set out on her own, when no one else was home, to find out if the Bible could confirm what the man had said. If God really did have a plan for her life, she wanted to know what it was. Hopefully, it would not be too far off from the plan she had for herself. Maybe it was just a matter of timing.

Within minutes Lizzie was sharing with Mrs. Bannister her dreams and hopes, even though now they seemed as good as dead. At one point Lizzie started crying and Mrs. Bannister reached over and squeezed her hand. That's when Lizzie recognized that she was talking too much. Her visitor hadn't come over to hear her troubles.

"What about you, Mrs. Bannister, how are you making out on your place? Is it hard?"

"In some ways, yes. But I love it here. And Jake!" she said. "How I love that boy."

She went on and on about Jake, as if she really knew him. But how could she? Lizzie wanted to ask, but decided against it.

"Well, Lizzie, what was it you had hoped to accomplish today?" Mrs. Bannister asked as Lizzie poured another cup of coffee.

"Well, I was going to do the ironing, but it can wait."

"Good. I was hoping I could do something useful."

Lizzie tried to argue her out of it, but she wouldn't give in.

"No, I mean it. I want to help, and I'll be very let down if you don't let me."

So they set to work. Lizzie sprinkled and rolled the articles, piling them on the table, and Mrs. Bannister ironed, handling the flat irons easily and knowing exactly how long to leave the three different sizes on the heat. Lizzie folded and stacked the perfectly pressed pieces, anxious to hear the boy's comments when they saw the difference in their shirts. She showed Mrs. Bannister the drawer where she had stuffed the ruined shirts and linens. They had become rags for mopping and dusting. Lizzie asked if there was any hope of salvaging any of them. Mrs. Bannister admitted they would best be used as rags.

"Here, Lizzie, have you tried doing it this way?" Mrs. Bannister asked. She proceeded to show Lizzie a new way to press the shoulders and a new way to fold the shirts so they wouldn't show so many wrinkles.

Since Mother's illness much of the family's clothing had taken on notable differences. Brown scorch marks branded many of the shirts, and had permanently damaged the Sunday table cloth and other linens. The gathers in the girls' dresses looked more like pleats while the boys Sunday pants had lost their sharp crease.

Lizzie was surprised to see how completely at home Mrs. Bannister seemed to be, helping herself to coffee when her cup went dry, leaning her elbows on the window sill as she looked out over the yard, and pulling out an additional chair on which to stretch out her legs when the ironing was finished.

Even after a couple of hours it was hard for Lizzie to keep her eyes off her guest. There was something exceptional about the lady. Such poise! Such dignity and grace! Indeed, she did seem like a queen. And yet, she was so kind and easy to talk to, not at all superior in her attitude toward Lizzie.

Three and a half hours later Lizzie was reaching high for one final wave as Mrs. Bannister disappeared beyond a grove of poplars. Pleased at how the morning had been spent Lizzie returned to her work in the kitchen, but somehow the house felt forlorn and cold without her new found friend to share it.

CHAPTER TWENTY-ONE

"How will we tell her?" Willie asked, massaging his clean-shaken jaw. "Her hands are full already, and if we both get married at the same time, she'll be . . . well, it'll just be too much, that's all. Besides, it's not fair."

"Remember, the pigs will go with us," J.C. reminded his brother. "That'll lighten the load some around here."

J.C. was sure they could work it out and fidgeted with excitement. Yesterday afternoon the four of them, he and Sally, and Willie and Sadie, had packed up a picnic basket, laid out blankets beside the pond, and lazed in the sweet summer sunshine. The idea of a double wedding had giggled its way forth from the girls about midway through the afternoon. The idea seemed preposterous at first, like something that happened only in storybooks, and the boys laughed at them. But the more they talked and hashed over the possibility of it, the more excited they all became.

"Lizzie is a very capable girl," J.C. said, getting up from the table and pouring both he and his brother another cup of coffee. "She's done a lot better than I thought she would, not having had much experience in the kitchen an' all."

"I know she's capable," Willie sighed. "But what about *her* plans?" He circled his cup round and round in the small puddle of coffee that had spilled onto the table. "I just don't like it that the rest of us can run off whenever we're ready to go, do whatever we want, and Lizzie gets stuck here, never getting any closer to her dream. We run full tilt ahead and she gets left in the dust."

That was true and they both knew it. And Willie in particular couldn't stand by and let it happen. They sat quietly, slurping their drinks and pondering.

"Think she'd be open to the idea of the girls moving in here?" J.C. asked, sobering somewhat.

"Are you jokin'? Another two mouths to feed, more clothes to wash? I wouldn't do that to her for anything. Come on J.C., you got to do better than that."

"Think about it a minute. Don't you see what I'm getting at?"

J.C. jumped from his chair just long enough to turn it backwards to the table and straddle the seat. Excited, he drew the chair close to the table and laid his palms on the table, spreading them across the surface as if flattening out a blueprint.

"Think about it. After the weddings . . .I mean, wedding . . . " he laughed again at the thought of it. "Look! Instead of moving out like we figured to do, Sadie and Sally could move in here instead. It would save us moving the pigs, and we'd still be here to help with the milking and field work. We've been worrying about how we could each afford our own place. Well, we could both stay put until we saved up enough. I, for one, want to stay close anyway, so maybe I could build a little house right here on the home place. That way there'd always be help with the outside work. This could work, Will. It could."

Willie leaned back in the chair, his arms folded, watching J.C. and waiting, as if for something that hadn't surfaced yet.

"And how is this helping Lizzie?" he finally asked. "Isn't that what we were talking about? Finding a way to get Lizzie out of here?"

"Will, come on!" J.C. said. "I can't believe I have to spell it out for you. Here's how it would be. The girls move in here with us after the wedding and Lizzie will be free to go back to school. Rosie and Anna will have themselves two mommies. They love Sadie and Sally, you know that. And Sadie and Sally would love it here. That's a darn-fer-sure. The household chores would be carried by two instead of one. You know how they both love cooking, gardening and all that other woman-type work.

"Here they'd be walking into a fully equipped kitchen, not living with apple crate cupboards and milking stools like they'd have to be putting up with 'til we got the pig business going, or the new creamery, or whatever we finally decided was the most profitable way to go. And they wouldn't have to give up each other's company. You've heard 'em moanin' about being separated. What could be better? The whole thing's perfect, I say."

A light was beginning to spark in Willie's eyes.

"Well, what do you think?" J.C. probed. "Don't just sit there like you're alone in the room."

Willie got up and walked over to the window. "Well, it's definitely the first possibility I've seen so far for getting Lizzie back to school."

"That's right."

"We wouldn't have to move the pigs. And our

being close could ensure Father the time he needs to develop the cream routes. "

"True!"

"And there's plenty of room for two more people in this house."

"Sure there is! We'd have to put up a wall in the bedroom," Willie said, a grin widening across his face. "There's no way Sadie and I are sharing a room with you and Sally."

They laughed. J.C. roared so hard he almost tipped his chair over backwards.

"We'll figure something out." he said, standing up. "We can hang some sheets if we have to. We can shoo Jake out to the shed for the summer; he won't mind. By fall—yesiree, by fall, things could be downright cozy around here."

Willie went back to massaging his smooth chin, wondering whether or not this was truly a good idea. "When shall we tell her?"

"The sooner the better, I say." J.C. stood up, snatched his hat from a nearby chair and went for the door. His face fairly glowed with pleasure.

CHAPTER TWENTY-TWO

Lizzie sighed as she leaned on the end of the hoe surveying the seven rows she and the girls had weeded. The garden looked beautiful. The soil around the young turnip plants was rich and dark, and for the moment, weed-free.

"Lovely!" she called to the girls. School had been out now for several weeks. Having Rosie and Anna home every day was turning out to be an outright blessing. They had become pleasant little helpers and were willing to try any chore she gave them. Lizzie made sure she also gave them plenty of time for play. She even managed to spend a little time each day playing along with them. Sometimes it was "school", sometimes "house." Presently, however, the two of them were on their knees at the far end of the garden, Rosie weeding the carrots, and Anna in the peas.

"This is fun!" Anna called back. "I want to do it again tomorrow."

"I'm glad to hear that." Lizzie wiped her forehead with her shirtsleeve. "How about you, Rosie? How you doing?"

"I'm going to be the best darn weed picker you

ever saw."

"Good girl!" Lizzie laughed. "But don't say darn. Mother didn't like that word, remember?"

Some of the words that Mother had disallowed were working their way into the family's vocabulary. Lizzie found it hard to enforce certain rules when Father went around breaking them right in front of everyone.

Lizzie moved from the turnips and started hilling up the potatoes. All twenty rows were in bloom all together. Mother would have been proud. Lizzie hoped to get five rows hilled each day for the next four days. Then next week, she'd harvest the peas. And before long the beets would be ready for pickling.

***

"Girls, please," Lizzie pleaded some weeks later. "Go play in the shed. I can't play right now."

"Ah Lizzie, come on." They sounded like a couple of magpies.

"I mean it, girls. I can't do another thing 'til I get these pickles put up."

They whined and moaned but obeyed, gathering up the rusty pans and wooden stir sticks they had brought inside with them.

"It's more fun when you play, too," Rosie added, her shoulders slumping as she walked to the door.

"I will girls, but not right now. Here—" Lizzie tossed two oversized beets into Anna's dented milk pail. "Take a couple beets to add to your mud soup," she said. "They'll give it good color." She held the screen door for them as they carried their supplies outside.

Lizzie hadn't gotten to the beets as soon as she

had hoped and now most of them were the size of her fist, some much larger. They would all need to be chunked for sure. She doubted that there was even one that could slip through the neck of the sealer whole. At least Mother wasn't there to see it. Mother's beets were always picked and pickled when they were the size of walnuts, certainly no larger than crab apples.

Where had the summer gone? It seemed she had barely covered the seeds over and now, already, the garden was producing at such a rate she could hardly keep up. The peas had been the first major harvest. With help from the girls they had been managed easily. She packed the sealers and manned the water bath while they shelled.

"Yummy, these are good," Anna had said, sucking the juicy pods.

"I told you you'd reap the benefits of your labor," Lizzie smiled. "Here, come put some in my apron." She held the pocket open. Anna dumped a handful in and Lizzie also enjoyed chewing as she worked.

The lettuce had been a refreshing side to supper meals, but was now growing bitter and going to seed. The potatoes and onions still had a ways to go, thankfully. The carrots, as far as she could tell, would turn out as long and lovely as the ones Mother had produced last year.

Lizzie was sorry now that she hadn't planted more. But by the time she had dropped the carrot seeds into the ground her back was so stiff that she couldn't face the thought of hoeing another couple rows. She had convinced herself that they had planted plenty and tossed the remaining seeds into the air and watched them blow away in the wind.

"Mother usually plants more than this," Rosie had warned, making Lizzie bristle at the time.

"Maybe so," Lizzie replied. "But as you see, I'm not Mother."

Lizzie carried the large cooker to the stove, poured in a milk pail full of beets, and covered them over with water. She brought in the wash tub and set a slop pail nearby. Once they were cooked, the peels and ends would go to the pigs and the beets themselves back into the hot water until they could be cut and packed into jars. She was not sure that was exactly how it should be done, but it seemed the only workable way. Rubber rings and sealer lids sat in a pan of hot water at the back of the stove.

"Too bad canning has to be done in the summer," she complained. "The house is hot enough already." But there was no use belly aching about it, it had to be done. She had certainly never heard Mother complain about all the food the garden produced.

If only she had spent more time helping Mother with the canning in the past. Then things would go more smoothly. More quickly, that was sure. True, she had helped some, with berry jams a time or two. And she always helped during chicken butchering season. But her part in the process was to scald the birds, pluck the feathers, and gut them. And all of that was done outside. So when she came into the house, there they'd be, row upon row of sealers stuffed full of chicken, and she hadn't asked a single question about how it got to be so.

Often Lizzie had come into the house and discovered the table loaded with jars of canned strawberries, blueberries, or vegetables from the garden. She had usually done most of the picking, or at least a good portion of it, but Mother had always done the canning, all alone, as far as Lizzie knew.

Lizzie heard a rapping at the door and shouted

over her shoulder, "I said I can't play right now. Now don't ask again."

"Sorry. Is this a bad time?" Pastor Stebbins said, poking his head inside.

Lizzie winced. *Of all people! Why was he here now?*

Jake had warned her that her bossiness would catch up to her one day. But the pastor of all people! What a time for him to come calling. Well, she'd just tell him Willie wasn't home. Then he'd go away and let her get back to her work.

She hurried to the door, drying her hands on her apron.

"I'm sorry Pastor, but Willie's not home today."

"Actually," he said, looking a little sheepish. "I was hoping *we* could visit. That is, you and me."

"Uh! Uh! Well, I'm in the middle of canning," she stammered.

"I'm sorry, if this isn't a good time . . . I mean, well, if later would be better." He too was stammering. "I certainly don't want to be a bother."

"No, Pastor, please. I didn't mean that." She definitely didn't mean *that*. "Please, come in." She pushed against the screen door and he stepped inside.

"You sure? If another time—"

"Yes, please come in! But I have to warn you. The kitchen's a bit of a mess."

He recognized the aroma. "Umm, smells like beets."

She led him to the kitchen, indicated a chair and he sat down. But within moments he convinced her to tie an apron around him and let him skin the beets while she chunked. He looked funny in an apron, she decided, but

194

not altogether unattractive.

His efficiency at the stove brightened the prospects of a productive day. He moved about the kitchen like he'd been doing it all his life. He brought laughter with him and that was as welcome to Lizzie as the extra two hands.

"What does a 500 pound mouse say?" he asked.

"I don't know," Lizzie said. "I'm not good at riddles."

"This isn't a riddle. It's a joke. Come on, try. What would he say?"

Lizzie tried to think, but it was hard. The beets in the large pot were boiling over and needed her full attention. She shrugged, "I don't know. What does he say?"

"Here, kitty, kitty, kitty."

Lizzie laughed. "That's silly."

"Of course it is. It's supposed to be. Here's another one. What's the difference between a plum and a rabbit?"

Lizzie shook her head and smiled. He was truly being silly. But she liked it. This was a side of him that didn't come through during his Sunday morning sermons.

"I give up. What's the difference?"

"One of them is not purple." They both laughed.

Lizzie was surprised at how competently he moved the tubs from here to there, nursed the fire, and handled the hot sealers. How at ease he seemed as he mopped his face with the apron. Once, before they had worked out a pattern of movement between the stove and table and cupboard, they reached simultaneously for the small dipper and collided, knocking the dipper to the floor in the process.

"I'm sorry," Lizzie said. "You first."

"No, you," he said, insisting that she drink before he. On his turn he took a long slow drink while watching her mop her wet mouth with her apron. His eyes never left hers as he drank, nor did she try to look away.

The hours evaporated quickly with him there. The smell of vinegar and sugar and cloves permeated the humid air, adding sweetness to the labor. And with the sweetness came a longing. For what, Lizzie didn't know. But she felt it.

When the girls came in for something to eat, a spot was cleared at the table for them. Lizzie and Pastor Stebbins continued to work, eating their butter and jelly sandwiches on their feet. He asked permission to offer a prayer of blessing over the meal. Lizzie was glad. She didn't do a meal time prayer when Willie wasn't home, but she certainly didn't mind him doing one.

The girls wanted to stay and help in the kitchen, but Lizzie said no. They would help best by playing outside, she assured them.

"I've been wanting to speak with you." Pastor Stebbins stood facing the cupboard when he said it, lining up the jars into perfect rows.

Lizzie was wiping up the floor but stopped momentarily to give her undivided attention.

He looked tired. His face was flushed, and the ends of his hair were curled up, especially at the temples. She wondered what he would look like if he let his hair go natural instead of slicking it down.

"Well, I guess you've done plenty of that today," Lizzie said, smiling.

"No, I mean, really talk. About important things."

Speaking of important things, maybe she should

talk to him about Jake. Maybe he could give her some
advice about boys.

"Pastor?" she began.

"Please, Lizzie, call me Jimmy."

Jimmy? She hadn't heard anyone call him by that
name before. Why would he want to be called Jimmy?

"I know. That's not what most people call me. It's
usually Pastor, or Pastor Stebbins? Some even call me
Pastor James; maybe you didn't know that. But, if you
don't mind, I'd like it if you would call me Jimmy."

"All right," Lizzie said warily. "I'll try—Jimmy."

"See! There you go. It wasn't that hard, was it?"

It wasn't that is was hard. It just felt odd—very
odd. She had come to know him as "Pastor." That title
seemed to fit him better. To be calling the pastor
"Jimmy," and especially when others didn't use that name
for him, well, it just didn't feel right. In fact, it felt so
strange that she no longer wanted to talk to him about
Jake. She should probably, and she would, she promised
herself, but not today.

"You're looking tired," she said instead.

"I'm that all right," he admitted. "It's been a while
since I helped with canning, but it's been downright
enjoyable. Every minute of it!"

"And I'm downright thankful for the help. As you
know, I can't have Rosie doing this heavy work. So,
thank you."

"Anytime! I mean it, call on me anytime." He
untied his apron, folded it, and laid it on the table. She
should probably offer him a final cup of coffee, but she
couldn't bring herself to do it. She was tired and ready to
have the kitchen to herself."

She led the way to the screen door.

He held out his hand as though for a formal handshake. "Well, maybe we can finish our talk next time."

She put her hand in his, and when she did, he clasped it with both hands and squeezed it tenderly. She looked quickly to the floor, not sure she was ready for whatever she might find in his eyes had she looked into them. His companionship for the day had been pleasant—an unexpected treat. And delightful, too, almost to the end. But now she wanted him to go.

CHAPTER TWENTY-THREE

Earlier this evening as he slopped the widow's pigs, tears of shame began to roll down Jake's face. No matter how hard he wiped, they wouldn't stop flowing. For days he'd fought with his conscience and had been, he thought, winning. But today was different. No matter how he tried to justify the things he had done, it wasn't working. He knew when he had committed the acts that they were wrong, but he had gone ahead and done them anyway. What choice did he have? Someone had to help the widow. And he had promised Mother.

After cleaning the widow's barn floor he had gone home and hid in the barn loft trying to get a handle on the guilt. But he couldn't. Mother's words kept playing over and over in his head, "Be sure your sin will find you out."

He hadn't gone in for supper. How could he eat? He didn't deserve to eat. He didn't deserve anything good. All he had done since Mother died was lie and cheat and steal.

He waited until long after dark then finally climbed down from the loft and headed back to the widow's house. What else could he do? His pestering conscience wouldn't let up. He had to confess his sins. If he didn't, his insides would rot.

With his head hanging he approached her porch step. He cleared his throat and smeared his shirtsleeve across his face one more time. He bent forward and beat the dust from his pant legs then kicked the loose dirt from his boots. He straightened his heavy shoulders and stuck his hands into his pockets.

He would get a licking, he knew that. But he had it coming. It wouldn't come from her, but once Father found out—

He knocked on the door.

"Mrs. Bannister, you still up?" he called, clearing his throat again. His voice sounded weak and stupid, like he was eight again.

He waited and leaned his ear against the door, but he heard nothing. The eerie howl of nearby coyotes made him shiver, and a fresh flow of tears slid down his cheeks. He swiped his face with both shirtsleeves.

Maybe this wasn't the right thing to do. After all, she wasn't his mother. So why did he keep looking to her in that way? He shouldn't have come.

When she finds out what I've done, she'll probably chase me off with the broomstick and tell me never to come back again. Maybe she'll march me home to Father, right on the spot, pulling me by the ear.

So be it, he thought. *I have to tell somebody.*

Somebody who would listen. Somebody who would forgive him. Lizzie certainly wasn't the one to tell. She wouldn't even hear him out. And why should she, he thought, sighing, for all he had put her through. He thought he heard footsteps inside. Again he leaned his ear to the door.

"That you, Jake?" Mrs. Bannister whispered on the other side of the door.

"Yes, ma'am," he said. She opened the door, lantern in hand.

The flickering light revealed his smeared face and weepy eyes.

"What's the matter, son?" she said, motioning him inside. "What are you doing out there this time of night?"

"I've sinned somethin' awful," he cried, a fresh flow of tears rushing down his face.

"There now, Jake, come in and sit down a minute. I'm sure it can't be that bad."

Before she had time to set down the lantern and settle herself beside him at the table he was already face forward onto his shirtsleeves, weeping outright.

He sobbed and sobbed. She didn't try to stop him. She laid a hand on his arm and waited. Eventually, when he had quieted somewhat, she reminded him of God's love and forgiveness and assured him that whatever it was that he had done, it was not too big for God to handle. It didn't matter how great the wrong; God would forgive. The crying let loose again and again as she spoke. She went for a damp cloth, took it and wiped his messy face, quoting I John 1:9.

"'If we confess our sins, He is faithful and just to forgive us our sins, and to cleanse us from all unrighteousness.' You remember that verse from Sunday school, don't you Jake?"

He nodded. "That's why I'm here. I *want* to confess."

"You realize, don't you, that you can talk directly to God about it? You don't really have to tell me."

"But it involves you."

"It does?" she said, surprised.

What involved her? She hesitated a moment trying to imagine what he might be talking about. Why, he had never caused her even the slightest worry. Ever! He had been nothing but a help and a blessing, right from the start.

"Mother said that if we sinned against another person, then confessing it to God was only half a confession. We have to make it right with the person, too."

"I agree," she said. "That's what the Bible teaches." She leaned forward and put a hand on his arm. "What's troubling you, Jake?"

He swallowed hard, then stole a quick glance at her and swallowed again.

"You remember the pigs I said I found wandering out in the field."

"I remember."

"I stole 'em from my brothers."

"You didn't!"

"And the lumber and nails I said I found under the hay in your—"

"Jake!" she whispered, disappointment showing on her face. She was silent a moment, then asked, "Your father's?"

He nodded and lowered his chin. His shoulders sagged. "Some chickens, too," he admitted. "But they'd a got butchered anyways."

Mrs. Bannister sat back.

"What about the filly, Jake? Where did she come from?"

"Oh no, she's yours for real. She was mine to give and I want you to have her."

Mrs. Bannister leaned forward again and folded her hands on the table, her thumbs massaging one another.

"Is that everything, then?" she said at last.

"Yes, ma'am." His head was bowed and his shoulders slumped as though laden with a load of timber.

Quietly she took his hands in hers and squeezed them.

"I forgive you, Jake," she said gently. Then she tipped up his chin and looked him in the eyes. He didn't look away. "I do forgive you. What've you done is wrong and you were right to confess it. I forgive you for lying to me about these things. But, Jake, it's your father and brothers you've wronged. You must seek their forgiveness."

Tears fell again and his shoulders shook. He was afraid she would say that.

"Come," she said, "Let's pray." She stood up, drew him up as well, and turned toward the sitting room door.

"I want to live with you," he blurted out.

"Jake, let's not talk like that."

"I mean it," he cried, suddenly circling his arms around her waist. "You're the only one who cares about me."

"Jake, that's nonsense and you know it," she said, feeling awkwardly ensnared. "You have a wonderful family. They love you, and need you."

"You love me more," he argued, clenching his hands together at her back.

"Come now, Jake. You're upset, that's all. Things will look better once you talk to God about it."

She gave him a motherly hug, then took hold of

his arms and put them alongside his trunk. She wasn't
sure what to think of it all. He was distraught, that was
plain to see. But why would he talk about moving in with
her? It wasn't like him.

She took up the lantern and led him by the hand
into the sitting room.

"Let's kneel down right here," she said, indicating
a carved wooden table, knee high.

She prayed first. She asked God to help Jake. She
prayed that God would calm his troubled soul and give
him the strength and the comfort he needed. Then she
prayed that God would prepare Jake's father and brothers
for his confession. Once she said "amen," she told him to
go ahead and pray his own prayer. She ached for him as
he confessed the sins he'd admitted. He concluded by
asking God to forgive him for hating Lizzie and for being
angry at his mother for dying.

"And please God, make Mrs. Bannister let me
move in with her. I could sleep out in the barn. I won't
mind. And I'll try not to eat too much, Amen."

Mrs. Bannister couldn't help but smile at that last
part of the prayer knowing he could certainly put away his
share of food.

They rose to their feet and she said, "The Lord
will help you do what you need to do. Try to do it soon."

"It might take me a couple days to work up the
courage."

"The sooner the better, Jake." She led him to the
door.

He stepped out into the night and then turned back
to her.

"Could I sleep here tonight? I'll head home first
thing in the morning."

CHAPTER TWENTY-FOUR

Ever since Jake had confessed his sins, Mrs. Bannister's stomach was in a knot. Not only because of the content of the confession but also because she had given in and let the boy spend the night. She had given him a blanket and told him he could sleep in the barn if he wanted to. He did.

The particulars of the misdeeds Jake had confessed were not nearly as disconcerting as were the signs of his deep seated anger against his family and his perceived isolation. Jake said no one in his own family understood him, and that he had no one to talk to. Not even his father.

She couldn't just sit by and watch. There was too much at stake. She loved the boy too much to allow this to go on. And since hearing Jake's confession and the words he had prayed, she felt obliged to speak with Mr. Van Ankum. Especially now that Jake was begging to move into her barn.

Instead of driving directly to church Sunday morning she took the way leading to the Van Ankum place. This wouldn't take long. She would miss the preservice visiting and possibly the opening hymn, but it was the right thing to do. She'd be back to church before the sermon began.

As she neared Van Ankum's property she wondered what sort of man she would encounter. She knew almost nothing of the man; she had not so much as seen him. The inquiries she had ventured to make regarding him had produced no clear picture of him. The few townspeople she had questioned agonized freely over his sad situation.

"Poor man," Mr. Truett at the bank had said. "I've never seen a man so crushed. It took him weeks to figure out how to put one foot in front of the other. Haven't seen him myself, you understand. He hasn't been out as much since Sarah passed."

"You could see it already at her funeral," the grocer's wife said. "He was totally undone. I dare say, I can see him in the ground himself before long, if something good doesn't happen. Mind you, I don't have it first hand, but I hear he was holed up in his room for weeks. Now that can't be a good sign. I haven't inquired about him lately, but that kind of man sets me to worryin'."

Mrs. Bannister turned the steering wheel and pulled the car to a stop near the front step of the house. She hoped he was in the mood for company. Perhaps she shouldn't have come unannounced. But it wouldn't take long. Just long enough to alert him of her concerns about Jake.

Her visit with Lizzie some weeks ago gave her little to go on in sketching out the man she was about to meet. Hopefully, he would be willing to come to the door.

"Children, stay put," she said as she stepped out of

the car. "I want to speak with Mr. Van Ankum alone. I won't be long."

Blackie wagged his tail in his usual welcoming way. A hen pecking the dirt near the step clucked and jumped aside as Mrs. Bannister's legs brushed by.

She knocked on the door. Suddenly, from inside, she heard the thud of what sounded like a body hitting the floor, accompanied by a loud moan.

What was that? She stepped back, her heart suddenly racing. Had someone fallen? Was someone in danger? She heard more moaning. She stepped forward, leaning her ear against the door.

Having been inside the house once before, she knew there was a porch-like room first, then another door between herself and the kitchen. It sounded like the ruckus was beyond the porch room, possibly in the kitchen.

She knocked again, more sharply this time, her ear still to the door. She heard an angry moan, and mumbling. Someone in there must be hurt, she thought, shoving aside all reserve. She pushed against the solid wooden door, ran to the inner door, and burst through it like a stone from a slingshot.

A man lay face-down on the floor, bone naked. He picked up his head to address his intruder, blood dripping from his nostrils. Instantly, at seeing her, his eyes squeezed shut and his forehead hit the floor, a curse bursting through his lips.

Of all times to meet the man, Rebecca scolded herself. *Was this the best I could do?*

Quickly she reached for the towel that lay near his feet and laid it across his buttocks. She grabbed the dish rag from the edge of the dishpan, dipped it in the water pail and brought it to him.

"Here, this should help."

He tore the rag from her hand and buried his nose in it.

"Are you all right?" she asked, kneeling beside him and bending over to get a look at his face. "What happened?"

"I fell on my face," he barked. "That should be plain to see."

It was plain to see. He had obviously been bathing. The copper tub was lying on its side nearby, its water spilled across the floor. He must have toppled the thing and slipped on the wet floor.

"Do you think you can get up?"

"Not with you in here," he growled.

"Are you hurt, other than the nose, I mean? No broken bones?"

"I'm fine." Though muffled somewhat by the rag, his voice had edge.

"Let me help you up."

"No!" he yelled. "I'll manage well enough on my own, if you'd be kind enough to look the other way."

"Certainly," she said, turning her back.

She hadn't known what to expect to find in Mr. Van Ankum, but what she found on the floor was not even close to the images she had conjured up of him. He was not puny and pathetic, as she expected. He wasn't old. And he certainly wasn't weak. At least not physically, she was sure of that.

The quick appraisal she'd made of him laying there on the floor revealed that Zachariah Van Ankum was much more alive and well than the townspeople gave him credit for. What she had seen of him, and she'd seen plenty, looked lean and strong. His shoulders and upper arms were thick and the muscles defined. He was bald on top save a few fine strands, but he had a good-looking face. She got only a quick glimpse of it before he buried his face in the rag, but it was definitely a handsome face.

She liked this version of Mr. Van Ankum far better than her own imaginings. He was, though presently humiliated, much more robust than she had expected. True, he was angry at her intrusion, but what man wouldn't be? She heard him pull to his feet and gather the towel around himself.

"I'm decent," he said at last.

She slowly turned around.

"Goodness sakes!" she gasped, seeing his bloody face. She grabbed him by the elbow at once and steered him toward a chair. "You need to sit down." Blood was trickling over his lips and onto his chin, even dripping down unto his hairless chest. His face, neck and forearms showed evidence of time spent in the sun, but his shoulders and trunk looked as pale as buttermilk.

"I'm fine," he said impatiently, pulling his arm from her grasp. "It's a nose bleed, is all. You never seen a nosebleed before?"

"Of course I've seen a nose bleed." She pulled a handkerchief from her pocket and pressed it against his nose. "Here, press this tight, right here."

He obeyed, casting an angry glance her way.

He's a feisty sort of fellow to be sure, she thought. But she didn't mind. There were worse things in the world.

She gathered several rags from Lizzie's rag drawer, poured cool water over them, and wrung them out in one big grouping before bringing them to the table.

"Come now," she said. "Put your head back a bit, that'll help get it stopped." She placed a thick rag across his forehead, handed him a fresh cool rag for his nose, and began dabbing up the blood on his chest. "What on earth happened to cause all this blood?"

"You came along, that's what happened. Who are you anyway?"

***

Mrs. Bannister's face beamed as she took her place at the steering wheel. Isabelle noticed, and bouncing up and down, begged to hear the good news.

"Why do you think there is good news, Sweetie? Is my smile that big?" She knew it was. But she couldn't help it. She gripped the steering wheel firmly with both hands and turned around in the yard.

Once she had told Mr. Van Ankum who she was and where she lived, she suddenly felt she had stayed long enough. He was furiously uncomfortable with her in the room and she couldn't blame him. She excused herself. It would have been cruel to stay.

Besides, if she had stayed another minute she might have burst out laughing and that would not have been right. He would have thought she was making fun of him. But that wasn't it at all. The unexpected twist her visit had taken was what tickled her so.

"I'll leave you now," she had said, patting the table lightly and rising. "You better get dressed and get on about your day. I'll do the same. That is, I'll get on my way to church."

Who but God could have orchestrated such a meeting? she thought. And something inside told her that

that's exactly what had happened.

The children pleaded. They wanted to know what she was chuckling about. But this was not something she would be discussing with her little ones. Indeed not. In fact, it was not something she would be discussing with anyone. She hoped it had not been overly humiliating for Mr. Van Ankum. She pursed her lips, harnessing another smile.

She felt ashamed of herself for enjoying the exchange so much, especially when her enjoyment came at his expense. But the surprise of it all, well, it was so...so entirely unforeseen. Something about him had totally disarmed her and the experience was exhilarating.

She glanced back at the unpainted weatherworn house unable to ward off the largest smile the children had ever seen on her face.

It was hard to identify what she was feeling, exactly. But suddenly, there was so much to smile about, so much to look forward to.

A mile down the road she hit the brake. She had totally forgotten about Jake. He was the reason she had stopped to see Van Ankum in the first place. She geared down and slowed to a stop.

Should she go back? No, she decided at last, stepping once again on the clutch and engaging the gear shift. Mr. Van Ankum had had enough for one day.

CHAPTER TWENTY-FIVE

Zachariah hoisted the last four cream cans from the wagon onto the creamery platform. Then clasping his hands together he stretched his arms up over his head and twisted his upper body from side to side.

"Ay, Mr. Van Ankum," laughed young Billy from the loading floor. "These cans gettin' to be too much for you?"

Zachariah smiled at the boy, Ben Vanderhorn's only son. "Better watch how ya' talk to yer elders, young feller. I'm just stretching is all. Don't you know stretching is good for ya?"

"It is, ay. How's that?"

"Keeps yer' muscles from cramping up on ya. Not that a boy yer age has trouble with that, I s'pose." Zachariah strode across the wide platform toward the large open doorway. "Yer pa inside?"

"Yes sir," Billy said, taking hold of a five gallon cream can. It was a full one, and just about more than his thirteen year old shoulders could muscle. "He's over at the grading table. It's good to see you again, Mr. Van Ankum."

Zachariah entered the building, his eyes detecting the lack of activity inside the creamery and noticing also the number of cream cans still unopened in the tasting corner. Not good to have those cans sitting there too long, he thought to himself.

J.C. was pouring cream into the pasteurizer, but no one else was in the room. There was no one at the tasting table and no one manning the huge butter churn.

All the way to town Zachariah had rehearsed the offer he was prepared to make Ben Vanderhorn. Maybe he wouldn't have to offer as much as he reckoned. By the look of it, the place was going downhill. Maybe he could offer less. No, he wouldn't do that to Ben. Not now.

"Where is everybody?" Zachariah called out, approaching the grading room.

"Hey Pa," J.C. called from his perch near the top of a huge metal tank.

Just then Ben came through a doorway. "Mornin', Zachariah," he said, reaching out to shake Zachariah's hand long before either was close enough to take hold. "I was hopin' to hear from you today."

Ben's face was severely bruised along one side. Purple, blue and yellow markings around the left eye and cheek bone made it look like he'd been in the wrestling ring.

"Another fall?" Zachariah inquired.

"Can't hardly stay on my feet anymore. 'Bout at the end of my rope."

"That's why I'm here, Ben. I been considering your proposal. Ifn' you're open to a new idea or two, I'd like to help you out. Maybe even relieve you of the place altogether before long."

"Now we're talkin'," the older man said, reaching

out and giving Zachariah's hand another excited handshake.

Mr. Vanderhorn led Zachariah through a door just beyond the service desk. An electric poll lamp without a shade dimly lit the small room, casting shadows across its plastered walls. A small plainly constructed table sat close to one wall. Two chairs accompanied the table, one painted, one not. Apple boxes were piled three deep, each box stuffed full of yellow and brown slips of paper. A telephone hung on the wall near the table. Empty cream bottles and several sealers cluttered one corner, some were cracked, some had their edges chipped. The Calgary Herald lay open across the table, wet coffee stains blurring a large portion of the farming section.

"Have a chair, Zachariah," the creamery owner said, pulling out the painted chair for his guest. "Isabelle!" he called, lifting his voice into the air. "Bring in another cup of coffee, will you? Make sure it's hot this time."

Zachariah heard someone stirring about in an adjacent room as he sat down. Ben crouched slowly to the floor and picked up several slips of paper. He added them to the others in the top apple box. The telephone rang, one long ring, then two shorts. Ben picked up the receiver and spoke a greeting into the mouthpiece.

A tiny girl quietly stepped into the room, setting a cup of steaming coffee in front of Zachariah.

"Cream and sugar?" she asked, her eyes not looking directly at him.

Zachariah was surprised at the size of the girl. She was nothing more than a child. Why, she couldn't be much older than Rosie, he thought to himself. What on earth was Ben thinking, having such a little thing working around the place? Surely she couldn't service the customers.

"Yes please," he said. Cream and two spoons of sugar." The girl was back presently with a small pitcher of rich cream, a bowl of sugar, and a spoon.

"Thank ya, Miss," he said. "Don't believe I've seen you here before. I'm Zachariah Van Ankum." He extended his hand to the girl. She curtsied and smiled and shook his hand but didn't offer her name. "You been workin' for Mr. Vanderhorn long?"

"Two days now. Last Saturday and this Saturday. I like it. Mama said I'd like working for Uncle Ben, and she was right."

Her smile was contagious. He couldn't help but smile back. He had not seen the girl before, he was certain, and yet she looked familiar. He wondered who she belonged to. He liked her smile. It reminded him of Sarah, so bright and ready. The girl appeared very much at home with her responsibility of serving up coffee. Rosie had never served coffee, not as far as he could remember. But that's probably something she could handle. He'd have to talk to Lizzie about it.

"So Ben's your uncle, is he? What happened to Susie?"

"She moved to Calgary. Wants to work in the city, Uncle Ben said. I better get back to work." She curtsied again and backed out the door, wisps of fine wavy hair floating about her face and shoulders.

So maybe there was some truth to the rumors after all, Zachariah thought. Word had it that Ben's daughter had run off with a smooth talking salesman from the city.

Typically, Susie, Ben's sixteen year old daughter, was the one who answered the telephone and poured up the coffee. She also did most of the paperwork for the business. She had done so for the past four years, ever since Ben's wife passed away. Susie was only a teenager, but she had a sharp head for business. The whole community agreed that she was not one to dicker with. She knew money, and she wasn't about to let you make a profit without her father's business doing the same.

Zachariah rested back in his chair not giving much mind to Ben's telephone conversation. He remembered a statement Susie had made not more that a month ago.

"Smells too much like a barn in here for me," she had said. She had thrown her nose up in the air as she said it. "There must be some fresh air somewhere out there in the world."

Word was that Susie up and packed her clothes and snuck out in the middle of the night. Too bad, Zachariah thought, looking up at Ben's bruised face. It must have been awfully hard having her go like that.

Ben was standing at the telephone empathizing into the mouthpiece, "Aha . . . I see . . . Yes, I understand."

Zachariah's thoughts went back to last Saturday.

Ben had driven out to Zachariah's in hopes of talking him into a partnership. Instead of competing with each other, he reasoned, perhaps they could consolidate their efforts and run the creamery business together, maybe put it on the map, so to speak. Business was booming at such a rate that Ben no longer had the manpower to handle the demand. He had asked J.C. and Willie to work additional hours as he had the other two men who labored along with them, and still it wasn't enough.

"Everybody's crying for more butter, city and

town folk alike," Ben had said. "And that's not even countin' the cafes and restaurants in Calgary that keep asking for more. Butter sales alone are runnin' me ragged. It's more'n I can do to keep up. And now with these bloomin' seizures, and well, family matters and such—"

Zachariah thought he saw the man fighting back tears.

"I just got to make some changes, and soon," he had said through a clouded throat. "Will you think 'bout it at least?"

Poor Ben! Zachariah looked up at his friend and business rival. Ben cleared his throat and attempted to say something into the mouthpiece but was cut short.

Zachariah picked up his cup and held it to his mouth. He heard Ben sigh, obviously frustrated at not being able to get a word in edgewise. Ben's left elbow rested on the slanted front of the telephone box, his forehead in his hand. His right hand held the receiver an inch or so from his ear.

"All right, Ruby," he said at last. "Now calm down. It'll be fine."

Another significant pause. Zachariah waited, setting his cup on the table and quietly checking the stretch in his suspenders.

"Ruby . . . all right," Ben said. "Ruby . . . now hold on and listen a minute. I'll have someone out there to pick it up right away. If not me, then one of the Van Ankum boys. How's that?"

Another long pause followed. Ben shifted from one foot to the other then back again, rubbing the back of his neck with his free hand.

"It's all right, Ruby," he said again. "Don't bother yer head about it anymore. I know it couldn't be helped."

He moved the receiver to the other ear.

"That's right. Cover it up good an' keep it as cool as you can. I'll get someone out there right away."

Zachariah slurped at his coffee. Ben hung up the receiver and fairly collapsed into the unoccupied chair.

"Poor woman. She just can't seem to keep good help. Here she is, almost 70, and still milkin' and chorin' like her life depended on it."

Maybe it does, thought Zachariah.

"I don't have the heart to tell her that we can't use her milk anyway."

"Why not?"

"Stinkweed. Her pasture's nothing but stinkweed anymore."

Ben shoved the newspaper off the side of the table with his forearm. It settled onto the pile of other such papers on the floor against the wall.

"Alright, let's talk business," he said, using his shirtsleeve to dry the coffee-splattered table top.

***

Zachariah hurried across the street. Hopefully, Mr. Bartell would still be at the bank. He pulled out his pocket watch. Good. It was not yet three o'clock. He pulled the door open and strode quickly toward the counter. Suddenly he recognized the woman standing directly in front of him in line. It was the one who had found him naked on the kitchen floor. He pivoted at once, attempting an escape. But it was too late. She had turned her head in time to see him and called out his name.

"Mr. Van Ankum, how good to see you."

Reluctantly he turned toward her, feeling a savage

redness rise up his neck and explode into his face. He had hoped never to see her again. Not as long as he lived. He had never been so humiliated in all his life. He nodded stiffly and took her outstretched hand.

How she happened upon him that morning, he had no idea. Nor did he want to know. He wanted nothing more to do with the woman.

No women but Sarah had ever seen him unclothed. But try as he might he couldn't keep the scene from replaying in his mind. His recollection of the whole miserable affair triumphed over his resolve to forget about it so that instead of getting over it, it was gaining ground, making him think in her direction more and more. The whole thing mortified him.

And to make matters worse, the children could do nothing but praise "sweet widow Bannister" to the hills. He knew of no one who had gained so much admiration in so short an acquaintance. What was it now, only five or six months since she had moved into old Bannister's place?

It seemed the girls were always talking about her: how beautiful she was, how gracious, how this, how that. How they wanted to grow up to be just like her. He, one the other hand, had hoped never to lay eyes on her again, nor have her lay eyes on him.

Now here she was, acting all comfortable and friendly—like nothing had happened. He couldn't bear to speak with her. Or look into her face. What if she made some mention of the ordeal? She better not! What was she doing at the bank anyway? Sarah would never have been at the bank alone.

He wanted to run. And turned to do so, and would have succeeded if Mrs. Foster had not come pushing through the door that very instant. Instantly, he turned back toward Mrs. Bannister, tipped his hat and mumbled an indiscernible greeting. He didn't look into her face for long, just a glimpse. The tenderness in her expression was like a warm morning sunbeam, but he quickly stepped away and went to face Mr. Bartell's desk. He didn't look back.

"Good afternoon, Zachariah," the banker said.

"Good day."

"I see you've met Mrs. Bannister," Mr. Bartell said, nodding toward the door. "Fine lady, that one. Well, what can I do for you today?"

"I'm 'bout to dive into the creamery business head first. You willing to give me a push?"

CHAPTER TWENTY-SIX

Mrs. Bannister felt troubled as she drove home. She hadn't discussed her concerns about Jake as she intended to on the day she had first met Mr. Van Ankum. And their happenstance encounter at the bank today was not exactly the time to get into it. Besides, he looked extremely uncomfortable and hurried. Perhaps speaking with *him* about Jake wasn't her best option after all. Maybe she should speak with Lizzie instead. Then, if Lizzie felt so, she could take it up with Mr. Van Ankum. He would, most likely, have an easier time taking it from his daughter.

She turned around in the road and headed west to see Lizzie. She knocked at the screen door several times but no one came to answer.

"Anybody home?" she called out. "Lizzie, you here?" But no one responded. She went out into the yard and called again, but all was quiet. The dog that had greeted her last time was no where to be seen. Disappointed, she got back into the car. Then, while backing away from the house she thought of leaving a message. She pulled a piece of paper from her purse and wrote Lizzie a note of invitation.

"Please come for tea as soon as is convenient for you. I'd so much enjoy a visit." She rolled up the note and tucked it into one of the small holes in the screen door.

***

Lizzie squinted at the sun, determining the time. There was still plenty of picking time left before they needed to head home. She and the girls had decided to stick with this patch, and it was paying off. At first the berries seemed to hide from them, but once she was able to convince the girls to get serious about picking their buckets filled steadily.

Blueberries and fresh cream! How good it would be! Father and the boys would love it. Lizzie smiled at the changes that were taking place inside her own heart. It felt good to please her family. To do things that brought them enjoyment.

She decided she would try to make some pies. Like the ones Mother used to make. Nice full ones, with fresh berry juices bubbling and boiling their way through cracks in the crust. Lizzie thought of Mrs. Bannister and wondered if she had any good picking on her place. She suddenly got an idea.

"Girls, let's pick an extra pail of berries and I'll take them to Mrs. Bannister tomorrow afternoon."

They cheered, "Yes, let's!"

***

Zachariah drove the milk truck home, thankful for Mr. Bartell's generosity with the loan. He had hardly asked a single question of Zachariah. Just wanted to hear him explain the vision he had for the creamery. And just like that, the loan was given.

How he longed to run into the house, take Sarah up in his arms and surprise her with the good news.

"Why, Zachariah Van Ankum," he could hear her say. "Did you ever doubt it? Of course you're getting your own creamery!" She'd hug his neck and fly lightly as he twirled her about the room.

"O Sarah, how I wish you were here," he whispered.

There would be a lot to talk over with the boys tonight. Plans to be made. New responsibilities for them all. As if their days weren't full enough already, especially with all this wedding talk.

Zachariah let the engine die near the barn and walked to the house. First he'd get a drink then he'd head out to the field and check on the wheat.

As he reached for the screen door he noticed a small note. It was at chest level, rolled up like a cigarette. Something from Lizzie, he supposed. He unrolled the note and read it.

"Of all the nerve!" he seethed through gritted teeth. "Will she never leave me alone?" He cleared mucous from his throat and spit it to the ground and went inside, letting the door slam shut behind him.

Water. That's what he needed. A good long drink of water. And some to rinse off his hot face. If only Sarah were here. Everything would be perfect if she were here to meet him instead of that stupid note.

What is the matter with that woman?

He squished the note tightly in his hand and flung it across the room.

***

Sunday's afternoon sun was hot. Hot, but not scorching. Sadie and Sally talked the boys into laying blankets in the shade along the grassy side of the barn so they could get the benefit of the shade and breeze while they talked details. They loved to be outside, but they didn't want to get overly tanned before their weddings.

Sadie and Sally spent increasing amounts of time at the Van Ankum's. Often when the boys were still at the creamery, working late, they'd come out and spend the warm evenings with Lizzie and the girls. Lizzie was beginning to get used to the idea of having them move in. And having them around gave her a chance to get away from the house more often.

"Go ahead, Lizzie," Willie said when Lizzie announced that she'd like to take some berries to Mrs. Bannister. "The girls are fine with us."

"Ah, we want to go, too," Anna cried. "We helped pick 'em."

"You know Rosie can't walk that far," Willie said, settling the issue.

Mrs. Bannister welcomed Lizzie with open arms and pulled her into her homey kitchen.

"Come in, Lizzie. I'm so glad you've come."

Lizzie looked around amazed at all that had been done to the place. Old man Bannister wouldn't recognize it, she was sure of that. New linoleum covered the kitchen floor. A bright cheery pattern. A new larger doorway separated the kitchen from the next room. The cupboards and stove were shiny clean. Poor old Bannister had not only been dirt poor, he had also been a very poor housekeeper. Lizzie had been invited in twice with her father when a deal was being struck over a piece of property he was selling.

Lizzie was overpowered by the aroma of cinnamon and cardamom. Immediately she thought of Mother. She drew in a deep breath, wishing her own kitchen had such charm.

Jake came into the kitchen from another room and stopped short at seeing Lizzie standing there.

"Lizzie!"

"Jake!" Lizzie said, surprised as well.

She almost blurted out her disgust at seeing him there. A dozen questions were racing through her head about why he was there and what he was up to, but she managed to remain poised and turned instead to Mrs. Bannister.

"Brought you some berries." She handed over the two-quart sized bucket. "I hope you like blueberries."

"Like them! I love them! Isn't that right, Jake?" She winked at the boy then reached around Lizzie's shoulder with a gentle hug. "Thank you, Lizzie." She took the pail to the cupboard. "Jake found some for us yesterday, but we made short work of those. This is wonderful, Lizzie. How good of you. There's enough here for two pies."

Lizzie looked back to Jake, her eyes shooting him with silent questions. He looked to the floor, then pulled out a chair and sat down at the table.

"I'm so glad you've come," Mrs. Bannister said again, taking note of the stiffness between Jake and his sister. "Please sit. I'll put on some tea."

Lizzie sat down, hoping Jake wasn't planning to stay long. She wanted to spend time alone with Mrs. Bannister. Not that there was anything especially secretive she wanted to discuss with the lady. It's just that she had enjoyed the woman's company so much on their first visit that she was looking forward to a similar chat— woman to woman.

"Yes, tea," Mrs. Bannister repeated, patting the front of her apron with both hands. Lizzie thought she looked just a bit tense when she added, "And we'll visit, all three of us."

Lizzie looked at Jake. She couldn't hold the questions inside any longer.

"What you doing over here, Jake?" she demanded.

"I live here."

"What!" Lizzie gasped.

"Isn't that right, Mrs. Bannister?"

"Well now, I don't think we can call it official just yet."

"What!" Lizzie yelped, jumping from her chair.

She looked from one to the other, trying to take it in. Suddenly, she felt sick. Sick, and dumbfounded—and sizzling mad.

"What's going on?" The question was directed as much at Mrs. Bannister as it was at Jake.

She had come calling in hopes of spending some time with Mrs. Bannister, and bearing a gift as well. She wanted nothing more than a nice little visit with her neighbor.

And now this!

It was too much.

Hadn't Jake already made her life about as miserable as he possibly could?

"Okay, Lizzie, the cat's out of the bag," the widow said. "Now let's sit down and reason together. I'd like you to listen to your brother. You need to hear him out."

I do, do I? was Lizzie's first thought. *And what gives you the right to tell me what I need?* Lizzie almost let the words come boiling off her tongue. If what Jake had to say was more of what she'd been putting up with from him since Mother died, she didn't want to hear it. What could he possibly have to say that would make up for all the sneaking around, the neglected chores and the hours gone with no idea of where he was at? She had suffered more than a few frazzled nerves and sleepless nights because of him.

And what did she mean; the cat was out of the bag? What cat? It didn't make sense. Jake didn't live here. How could he? He lived at home. True, he didn't spend as much time at home as Lizzie wanted him to. But he spent his nights at home, didn't he? Sure he did. She had to admit she had stopped paying much attention to Jake's night time activities. Even so, the whole thing was absurd. And to think that widow Bannister was in on it with him!

Lizzie opened her mouth to argue but the words never made it past her lips. Mrs. Bannister quickly put an arm around Lizzie's shoulders and encouraged her to come back to the table and sit down. The woman's soothing words touched Lizzie's soul like a soft summer rain. A welcome summer rain—the kind that nourishes the crops and cools down the sun-beaten farm animals.

***

Zachariah slid the shovel across the dirt floor scooping up a full load of manure and carried it to the wheel barrow sitting in the center of the barn. Lizzie expected some sort of reaction out of Father, but he seemed unmoved by her announcement about Jake.

"I'm not lying, Father. He means it."

"I know you're not lying," Father said, propping the shovel against the stall boards and sitting on a milk stool.

How could he be so calm about it, Lizzie wondered, fuming inside. Didn't he realize what it meant? Couldn't he see what the neighbors would think?

There was no way on earth they could manage without Jake, especially now that Father was spending more and more time at Vanderhorn's creamery and the boys working more and more hours servicing the routes. Surely Father could see that.

"Well, he just can't, that's all," she cried. "It's not fair. And besides, it's not right."

"What exactly did he say?" Father asked.

"He said, 'I live here.' Just like that. Like he was a part of the family over there or something. And he acted like it, too. Walking through the house like he'd lived there all his life. Father, you should have seen it. He acted like it was his decision to make, and we have nothing to say about it."

"Maybe there's more to it," he said softly.

Father didn't seem to be getting it.

"No doubt! A lot more over there, and a lot less over here," Lizzie kicked a hardened chunk of manure across the barn floor. It was unbelievable. The very idea! That he'd move in with the Bannister's and be their hired hand. He, Jake. The one who despised farm work. The one she had covered for every time the chores at home didn't get done. The one who has caused her nothing but misery and grief ever since Mother died.

She spit out the stem of timothy she'd been chewing on.

"And Mrs. Bannister was standing there supporting everything he said. It makes me mad!"

"What does *she* have to do with it?" Father asked, a frown forming on his brow.

"Everything!"

"What do you mean, everything? He's my son!"

"I tell you, Father, she was right there, hearing it all. Jake plans to move in with her. And she was standing there beside him with her hand on his shoulder, saying why it might be the best thing."

Zachariah pushed to his feet and took hold of the shovel. Why would she do that—encourage his son in this improper way? Suddenly he felt sticky with perspiration. He pulled out his handkerchief and mopped around his neck.

For not being long in the neighborhood she sure seemed to take a keen interest in things not her own, he thought. Jake hadn't mentioned anything to him about moving out. Why would he go talking to her, looking to a complete stranger when he had a home and family?

"Can't see why she'd have anything to say about what my boy should or shouldn't be doing," he grunted.

"I know! That's just it. It's like he's more hers than he is ours."

Zachariah dug the shovel deep into the sloppy manure mounting in the barrow and headed for the door.

"Is he over there now?"

"Think so."

***

Zachariah set out on foot. The walk would do him good. Maybe he'd have his thoughts together and his questions lined up into some kind of logical order by the time he got to her place. Maybe some revelation would come to him on the way. Something that would shed some light on why this was happening. And what this nosy neighbor was wanting from his boy.

Two things Zachariah was sure of. One, Jake was not moving in with this woman. And two, from now on, Jake wouldn't be chorin' at her place ever again.

The sun had lost its earlier heat, thankfully, but even so, he wished he had remembered to get a drink before heading across the fields.

"Blast!" he shouted, stopping short, remembering the note she'd left. This was not the time to be going over there. It would look like he was accepting her invitation. What else would she think? He couldn't go now.

He stood there weighing his options. What choice did he have? He had to speak to her. If what Lizzie said was true, he had to rescue his son from her wily ways. She had already demonstrated her lack of discretion. No other woman would have come bursting in on him while he was bathing. He hated her for it. But that was nothing compared to what she was doing with Jake—turning him against his own family. She had to be stopped.

The prospect of losing his son to someone so disrespectful and devious worked against him with every step, and by the time he reached her yard he could think of nothing but taking Jake by the ear and dragging him home to the wood shed. He might be powerless when it came to communicating with this woman, but he could let Jake know where he stood on the subject.

A little girl came running toward Zachariah as he entered the Bannister's yard. He recognized her immediately. It was the girl he saw at Ben's creamery.

"Hello, Mister," she said, smiling. "I remember

you."

Before he could say hello she was running to the house calling, "Mama, Mama, company's come!"

***

"Just want you to know," he said as soon as the woman appeared at the door. "I'm not here because of your invitation. I wouldn't be here at all if—

"Mr. Van Ankum, please, come in."

He stepped inside. He could see that her cheeks were flushed and her eyes red from crying.

"Here, take a seat," she said, pointing to a chair. She was sorry now that she had left the note. But how was she to know he would be the one to find it? And how was she to know he would think it was meant for him? How silly! She would never do something like that. "I'll put on some coffee."

"No!" he said, almost bellowing. "That's not why I came over here. I just came to . . . I have . . ."

Blasted! he thought. He couldn't remember how it was he planned to get started on the subject. He had spent the last half mile memorizing what he was going to say, but now that he was inside her kitchen, all he could do was stammer like a fool. Just like every other time he'd been near her.

He crossed his arms and squared his feet. He felt ready to take her on. It didn't matter to him that tears still wet her eyes. She better know he was serious. If she didn't back off, she'd find herself dealing with more than she bargained for.

How had it come to this anyway? Having to fight for his own son. And with a neighbor he didn't even know—and didn't care to know. And a woman at that!

He cleared the phlegm from his throat and looked around for some place to spit. He saw nothing that would hold it. He couldn't exactly walk over to the stove and deposit it. There was nothing to do but to swallow it. Determined to take the lead and bring this thing to resolve he said, "I just want to know one thing—

"You mean about Jake?" she interrupted.

"Of course about Jake. I told ya' I didn't come because you invited me."

Oh, that again, she winced.

Her eyes met his ever so briefly and it set him to rattling inside. He looked toward the window on the side wall. He felt himself breaking out in a sweat. Would he never be able to react to this woman with composure? If only she had not stopped by the house that awful Sunday morning.

"Please, Mr. Van Ankum, sit," she said, taking the hat from his hand and setting it down on the far end of the table. "This kind of discussion goes much better when you're sitting, don't you think?"

He took the chair she offered. She pulled one out for herself. He watched as her hands smoothed out a wrinkle in the table cloth on her side of the table.

He didn't rightly know how to start. Here, with her eyes on him, he couldn't think how to bring the rehearsed lines to the front.

She seemed to be waiting for him, letting him take the lead. And that was probably the proper thing. After all, he was the one who came calling unannounced. Anyway, that's what he intended to do. It was his son he came to fight for and he would be the first to make a move.

He cleared his throat again. But it seemed his voice had abandoned him. He couldn't help noticing the changes in the room. At present it held no resemblance at all to old man Bannister's kitchen.

How do I put it to her? he struggled inwardly, mopping his forehead with his handkerchief.

Just blurt it out? he scolded himself. *Jake is my son and I don't want you making 'im think he'd have it better over here.*

Somehow though, with her eyes on him, that sounded too harsh.

Watching her hands move gently over the tablecloth reminded him of the day she nursed his bloody nose and covered his bare backside. He felt an intense blush burst into his cheeks and his neck prickled with stickiness. He snorted and wiped the hankie across his nose. Why couldn't he put that behind him?

Blast! Was she reading his mind? He better get done what he came for.

"About Jake," he finally managed to blurt out.

She looked at him, waiting.

He swallowed hard, like he could hardly get the saliva down his throat.

"You need a dipper of water," she said, springing to her feet. "Forgive me. I should have known you were thirsty after that walk.

She pulled a dipperful from the water pail at the cupboard, cupped her hand underneath it and brought it to him. He guzzled every drop. She refilled the dipper without a word, and he drained that one as well.

"Perhaps I should begin," she offered as she returned to the table. She swiped her skirt under herself as she sat down, then began running her hands along the table cloth once again. She licked her lips and drew in a thoughtful breath.

"I imagine Lizzie told you what happened."

He nodded.

"I believe my enthusiasm over Jake's helpfulness may have contributed somewhat to his present discontent at home. I—well, I felt he needed some motherly encouragement. I could see his heart breaking over his need for his mother and I couldn't help but try to comfort him." She had folded her hands on the table, her thumbs massaging one another. "Perhaps I went too far."

Zachariah folded up his handkerchief and stuffed it deeply into his pocket. Just how far did her "motherly encouragement" go, he wondered, making an attempt to read her face. To the point of turning him away from his own flesh and blood, obviously.

He should say something, he reasoned, but instead he watched her fingers take hold of a loose curl, twist it, and poke it into the thick currant-colored waves pinned back from her face. When he opened his mouth, nothing came out.

She went on.

"Jake missed his mother so much in the beginning he was almost wild with pain. I could hardly stand to see him so angry and so alone. You didn't see it. I know that. How could you? Your own pain was so unbearable that it sewed your eyes shut. From the first day Jake showed up on my doorstep offering to help with the chores and fences—well, right from the start, I decided to give him whatever comfort and support I could. He was in agony. That first day he looked like a lost puppy whining for a place to belong."

She shrugged her shoulders slightly.

"I don't know. Maybe I did it all wrong. But I had to do something. I had no idea he had stolen animals and supplies from his own father's place and added them to mine. I…"

"He what?" Zachariah fairly coughed the words out, the chair legs squeaking against the floor as his body stiffened.

"I was afraid of that," she said, bowing her head then smoothing both sides of her hair and repositioning one of the hairpins. She pushed up slowly from the table. "I need some coffee."

"Coffee! Woman, how can you talk 'bout coffee? My son's been stealin' from his own pa and all you can do is talk 'bout coffee!" It was out of his mouth before he could stop it. Immediately, he buried his face in his hands.

She stopped mid-stride and turned back to him. He was crying.

***

Jake fidgeted nervously at the table, thumping loudly with all ten fingers, then stopping to bite the edges of dirty fingernails, then back to thumping. Lizzie had insisted he stay at the table until Father got home. She was taking no chances of him being nowhere-to-be-found when Father got back from Widow Bannister's place.

She busied herself with supper preparations: peeling potatoes, chopping cabbage, seasoning the roast. Carrots were also added to the large cast iron pot before the thing was slid into the oven.

"Don't go thinking you'll get your way in this," Lizzie warned, untying the damp apron and hanging it with the towel behind the stove. "Father's not likely to give in. Nor, may I add, should he."

"Come on, Liz," Jake pleaded, hoping to bring Lizzie over to his side on the matter. "You can see how she needs help over there. How's a woman with no husband supposed to do all that needs doin' on that place."

"Jake, it's not up to you."

"Well, it should be."

"Stop it!"

"Well, it should. It's what Mother wanted."

"Mother!" Lizzie cried. "That's foolishness."

"You don't know everything," Jake said, pivoting in his chair so his back was to Lizzie.

Lizzie tossed the pot holders onto the warming closest and sat down near him. Why was it that their conversations could only go so far? Would it never change? The minute she felt he was beginning to see reason, then off he'd go again on some new tangent, just to keep her riled.

If only she had a pinch of Mother's wisdom.

If only he would grow up.

"Mrs. Bannister seems a very healthy and capable woman," Lizzie said, resisting the temptation to shout. "I'm sure she knew what she was getting into when she took on the place. She knew there'd be chores that needed doing."

Jake bolted from his chair and stomped to the window.

"Of course she's capable. But she can't do it alone. She's a city woman for pity sake. You can see that."

"So, she can hire a hand."

"That's right! Me!"

"Yeah you! Like you're a man or something!" She didn't mean for it to come out like that and bit her lip, but the damage was done.

Jake kicked the window chair. Its feeble back broke when it hit against the wall.

"Serves you right you stupid chair," he said, storming up to his room.

***

Father didn't come home for supper. Lizzie had held it off as long as she could and had decided to hold Jake in the house until Father's return. Her plan was that they would all sit down together before supper and talk this thing through. But after a time she tired of Jake's pacing and thumping and throwing things and sent him outside with a list of chores.

He helped his brothers with the evening milking. And did the separating, alone. Lizzie had him pour the fresh milk into one of the new shiny five gallon cans Father had acquired when he bought Ben Vanderhorn's creamery. The cream was added to cream can #3 in the ice house.

Once he had finished the list of outdoor chores Lizzie had given him, she set him to churning butter in the kitchen and filling the flour and sugar bins. He was clearly disgusted, but he didn't dare put up a fight. He knew better than to risk it right now. If he hoped to get Lizzie's support about moving over to the widow Bannister's place, he'd better do what she said, and without any more complaining or arguing.

Lizzie had been determined that no one eat supper until Father got home. She was sure he wouldn't be long.

He was too upset to stay long. He would say his piece and be on his way.

But she was wrong. One hour turned into two, and two into three. The typical evening chores were done and extra besides, and still he wasn't home. Finally at eight o'clock she made the girls slices of bread and jelly to hold them over, convincing the boys to hold on a while longer. Surely it couldn't be long now.

The roast was drying out. Lizzie had killed the fire once supper was cooked, leaving the meat in the heavy roaster in the oven to stay warm. She wanted it out of sight.

J.C. and Willie had not been given a say in the decision to delay supper but were cooperating agreeably. They playd several rounds of checkers, discussed the future of their pig herd, and how was it another one had gone missing. They even playd dolls with the girls for a time. But at last their bellies ached and they pleaded for their supper. Lizzie had to give in. It wasn't right to make them suffer just because she had decided that there was no supper until this thing was settled.

She was dishing up their rice pudding, topping each bowl with freshly whipped cream, when Father finally came through the kitchen door. Had Blackie announced his coming Lizzie could have had his plate dished up and his coffee poured.

"Father!" Willie said, sighing with relief. "I was about to go after you."

Zachariah removed his hat and tossed it onto the spot where the window chair usually sat. It landed on the floor, but he didn't notice. Lizzie returned the cream pitcher to the icebox and hurried to the warming closet.

"Don't bother, Lizzie," Father said before she had

a chance to bring out his plate. I'm going to bed."

His voice was hoarse. It sounded like he'd been crying. He walked through the kitchen without the slightest faltering in his pace, passed through the big room, and disappeared into his bedroom, all without making eye contact with any of them.

"But Father!" Lizzie called after him. "I've kept it warm for you."

There was no reply. Things would not get talked out tonight after all. She tore her apron ties loose and ran outside.

If God does care, she screamed inwardly, pumping the water pump lever downward and up, downward and up, as hard as she could, caring not that it was forming a puddle near her feet and splashing up her legs. *If He really has a purpose for me, as Willie says, why does everything always go wrong?*

CHAPTER TWENTY-SEVEN

Zachariah pulled the curtain door closed, punched his hands into his pants pockets and paced the short distance alongside the bed. Food was the last thing on his mind. His soul was ablaze with revelation; it fueled and nourished him beyond any meal he'd ever eaten. How had he missed this? It wasn't as if he'd never heard it before. Sarah had seen to that. She had not only spoken of God's love and forgiveness, she had demonstrated it. And Willie, too. He was forever quoting the Bible. Then he would go the extra mile and do his best to translate it in a way that the rest of them could understand what it meant. It irked Zachariah at times, but for Sarah's sake, he let Willie preach away.

How come none of it had gotten through until tonight? he wondered. The words Mrs. Bannister had spoken were similar to Sarah's. She even quoted many of the same scripture passages. He remembered Sarah reading them. The very same ones! The only difference this time was that Mrs. Bannister insisted he turn the pages himself and read the verses aloud to her. How could that make such a difference?

He didn't know the New Testament from the Old, let alone the many different books within the Book; he would have been totally lost without some guidance to the right page and passage. A couple of sentences in Jeremiah were particularly meaningful. Something about God having a plan and a future for him.

He continued to pace, rubbing his chin and wishing he would have written that one down. How had he missed that when Sarah had read it to him? And the verses about God forgiving sins. He looked around the room for Sarah's Bible, but it wasn't there. No matter. He'd never be able to find the verses on his own anyway.

He went to the window and stared out at the night. He could still see the glow in Mrs. Bannister's face. She beamed like she had found the treasure of all treasures— and wanted him to find it too. Her eyes coaxed him along the path of discovery. She had helped him find the various books in the Bible that contained the verses she called out, but then she insisted he do the rest.

He turned from the window and fell to his knees beside the bed.

"Oh God," he started, his elbows on the bed and his hands folded at his chest. "Father God, thank you. I don't know what else to say." Presently he reached his hands toward heaven and wept. "Such a man as me, God. Thank you for getting through to me."

How good it felt to be released of the bitterness and anger, against God, and against Sarah. He felt like a load of lumber had been removed from his shoulders. Like he was light enough to float away. The Bible said he was a new creation. The old had passed away, and the new had come. If only Sarah could know!

He unbuttoned his shirt and pulled the tails free.

He knew what he had to do. He had to make peace with his boy. He had to let Jake know he was loved and forgiven. But first he wanted to read Sarah's letter.

He removed his shirt and laid it on the chair then knelt down in front of his dresser and pulled on the bottom drawer. He had vowed in his anger never to read the letter Sarah had written to him those many months ago.

The drawer felt stuck. Yes, of course it was. Way back in March he had purposefully lodged a screwdriver on the inside to jam it shut. He had refused to read the words Sarah had put down on paper and had determined that day that no one else would read them either.

He realized now that all that old thinking was distorted and completely off the mark. Everything had changed over the course of the past few hours; his whole perspective was new. Mrs. Bannister is an unusual woman for sure, he decided. Incredible, was probably closer to what he was thinking right now. Her ability to explain God's love and forgiveness. Her simple explanations made God so real, so believable.

Why? he wondered, as he worked the screwdriver out of the way with the end of his pocket knife. Why did it take a stranger to wake him up to the hope God offered? And to wake him up to Jake's broken heart?

The widow lady had brought him face to face with his failure as a father. She confronted him about Jake's needs, both his emotional needs and his spiritual needs. And as she did, Zachariah recognized his own need for help. Then it happened. Suddenly, he realized it was he, himself, who needed God. It was he who needed God's forgiveness. And, what's more, he was ready to receive it. Just as he was ready now to read what Sarah wanted him to know.

He tore through the seal and unfolded the stationery, tears welling up in his throat as he beheld her last written words.

To my dearest husband and friend,

How I long to hold you tight and have you hold me, too, like we used to do. How I wish I could put your supper together tonight and listen as you hum your delight in eating it. If only we could stand cheek to cheek just for a minute or two. Like we did, not so very long ago. Zachariah, you've been part of my life for so long that I can't remember a time I didn't love you. But now that I'm facing eternity, my thoughts keep turning toward heaven. I know without a doubt that there is a God. I know He's preparing a place for me, and I hope with all my heart that you will want to come and join me there. Since I surrendered my life to Christ, I have found a peace and a hope beyond anything I've ever known. I can't explain it to you and I don't understand it myself. But somehow I know I can trust God to do the right thing with me—with us.

Be strong, my dearest. God will see you through. There will be rough spots ahead, but I pray, in time, you will put your hope in God and embrace His abundant plan for your life. He wants more for you than you want for yourself. Let Him have His way. You won't be sorry. I hope you will not be upset with me for "preaching," but I cannot leave without saying it. Believe in Him, my darling, BELIEVE.

I love you beyond all words (English or Dutch).

Sarah

p.s. Do what you can to see that Lizzie gets to nursing

school, will you?

Tears dripped from the tip of Zachariah's nose to his bare chest. He dug for his handkerchief and blew his nose. In the months since Sarah's death he had given little thought to Lizzie's sacrifice. And, as Rebecca pointed out this evening, he'd done nothing to alleviate Jake's pain. In fact, until she spelled it out, he had not even noticed that Jake carried a burden of sorrow and loss. He could see it now. He had pushed Jake off to the side. He couldn't even remember when he last spent time with Jake, just the two of them. Rebecca said Jake felt abandoned—mislaid— "like an old scrap of wood, good for nothing but the heap."

The night passed quickly as Zachariah prayed and planned and, at last, decided to wake Jake up. He chose a shirt from the second dresser drawer and stepped into a clean pair of pants. He dug his dress shoes from the closet and set them on the chair. He looked at them. He'd not worn them since the funeral. Lizzie had given up polishing them. He slipped into them and tiptoed upstairs.

"Jake," he whispered, gently shaking the sleeping lad.

"Huh?" Jake moaned as he turned and saw his father.

"Shh now, get dressed and come to the shed."

Oh, oh, thought Jake. Here it comes. As a young boy he had made many a trip to the shed with Father. The shed was not a good place to be when Father was angry.

Jake thrust his tired legs into his overalls, snatched up yesterday's shirt and followed his father.

"What time is it?" he whispered. But Father was too far ahead to hear. It seemed awfully late for Father to be up. Outside, Jake glanced at the sky but had trouble guessing the time. The man in the moon seemed to wink at Jake. Was that a good sign, or bad? He wasn't sure.

Father waited, holding the shed door open. It creaked painfully as it closed behind them. Father lit a lantern then turned to speak. Jake had braced himself for trouble, his backside tight against the worktable. But Father was smiling.

"I've wronged you, Son," Father said, looking Jake squarely in the eyes. "And I'm hopin' you can forgive me."

What! Father asking for my forgiveness? Jake was stunned. He was the one who should be apologizing. It was he who had lied, and cheated, and stole.

The next hour in the wood shed the two of them confessed their sins to one to another. They each had plenty to say, and they said it all.

At last Zachariah clutched Jake's shoulders and pulled him close. Jake surrendered to his father's embrace, fresh sobs bursting their way to the surface.

"It's all right, Son" Zachariah said, holding Jake tightly. "You deserve a good cry."

Jake melted in Father's strong arms. His young shoulders shook against his father's chest. He had never let Father see him this way before. It had always been to Mother that he poured out his heart.

"I love you, Son," Zachariah whispered.

It felt good to be in Father's arms—to feel the power of Father's forgiveness erasing the mountain of guilt he'd been carrying.

When Rebecca first suggested that he had neglected the boy, Zachariah had rejected it utterly and lashed out at her.

"I have not!" he had shouted, adding a curse. "He's my own flesh and blood."

His hotheaded outburst didn't deter her. She plowed ahead.

"Then could it be that you have simply failed to show it?"

Her words tore through him like a butcher's knife slicing flesh from bone. It wasn't that he didn't love Jake, it was just that—

What, exactly? He wasn't able to tell her. Throughout the long lonely months without Sarah he had nothing to offer others: no strength, no encouragement and no time. He had no room, no recognition of anything except his own pain, his own sense of being abandoned.

He saw no one's needs but his own. His own need for love. His own need for companionship. His own desperate need for hope and a future. Until tonight he didn't realize he was holding anything back from his children. He didn't know they were shriveling up for lack of love and comfort. All he knew, and this he got hold of the evening before Mrs. Foster's visit, he knew he had to buck up and get moving ahead, investing heart and soul into building up the business, and leaving the rest to Lizzie.

But now, thank God, someone possessed the courage to wave a flag in his face and point out the error of his way.

"Even a frustrated, hurting, lonely man with a heart full of sorrow can experience the peace and love of God," she had said. And she said it as though she really believed it. She talked of her own pain, the loss of her precious husband three years earlier. Her present troubles meeting the mortgage. Her words were filled with life and hope and with such a confidence in God's goodness that she made him want to believe it, too.

She brought out the Bible and they read verse after verse of comfort. Each passage came as ointment to his bleeding soul.

When she asked if he wanted to know more, he said, "Yes." He couldn't help himself. There was something there, and he wanted it.

She explained things about God's love that he had never known and had never heard before. It was all there in the Bible. After his questions ceased and the room was still, she asked if he would like to pray a prayer of confession and belief. He did. She walked him through it, and by the time the evening was gone there was not a bitter root of anything left anywhere in Zachariah's heart. He was changed from the inside out. There was nothing left to do but seek Jake's forgiveness.

Streaks of light from the far eastern sky began to lighten the shed where Jake and his father now stood.

"Well, Jake," Father said. "What are we going to do about you and Mrs. Bannister?"

"I don't know, Father. It's up to you. I'll do whatever you say. My way of takin' care of things made a terrible mess."

Jake took the handkerchief his father offered and blew his nose.

"Father," Jake said then, suddenly thinking of a solution. "You could buy her place and Mrs. Bannister could move in with us.

"Now wait a minute, young man! Don't be getting the horse ahead of the cart. I know you've come to love her like a mother, and she cares for you an' all, but movin' in with our family, well—that's—that just wouldn't be proper. Things got to be done in an orderly and decent way. And that is not it."

Zachariah pulled Jake close again, thankful to God for the boy, immature though he be. There was such a gurgling sort of joy rising up within his soul. It was unlike anything he had ever experienced. He felt like a sheet bleached of every stain and now flapping freely in the breeze. God had cleaned his slate; he'd been given a fresh new start. He hardly knew what to do next. He heaved a contented sigh and rocked Jake back and forth, and prayed out loud.

"Thank you, God. Thank you from the bottom of my heart. Thank you for all the good years we had with Mother. Thank you that she didn't have to suffer long at the end. Thank you, God, that Jake is a sensible boy." Zachariah went on the ask God to help them work out a plan that would give Jake hope for his future.

As he prayed, suddenly he felt a surge of anticipation regarding his own future. There was so much he needed to ask Willie about. And Lizzie! What about her desires? She needed to be set free. The words in Sarah's letter came back to him, *"Do what you can to see that Lizzie gets back to nursing school."*

But how could he do that? The girls still needed a mother. They wouldn't be able to bear it if Lizzie, too, was gone from their lives. Besides, how could *he* ever get along without her?

***

In the house Lizzie hurried into her green housedress, pulled on a light sweater and quickly pinned back her hair. She must speak with Father before he left for the creamery. She wasn't about to let this thing with Jake slide by. She must know what Father intended to do about it.

The house was chilly as usual this time of morning. No matter how warm the summer days became, the nights always cooled everything down, often much more than Lizzie liked. She would build a fire and put on some coffee, but first she needed to talk with Father.

She passed through the big room and knocked on the wall beside his curtain door. No answer. She peeked inside, expecting to see him still asleep. But she was wrong. He wasn't in the bed. In fact, the bed was already made.

That was odd. Father never made his bed. That was her job. First Mother's; now hers. She pushed the curtain back on its string and looked about the room. Though she knew it was preposterous to do so she even bent down to see if he was underneath the bed.

The shirt Father had worn this past week, though dirty, lay neatly across the bedside chair. His pants lay where they fell. His lowest dresser drawer was partially open. She resisted the temptation to take a look.

It appeared as though the bed had not been slept in at all. It was just as she had made it the day before. Apparently Father had changed his clothes and left.

She knew he was upset last night, that was as plain as daylight, but she had never known him to go through a whole night without getting into bed.

He hadn't been up pacing the floors, she was sure of that. She would have heard him. The past few months she had come to discern a pattern in his nighttime pacing. He didn't do it often, but when he did, it brought a curious sort of comfort to Lizzie, probably because some new change followed soon thereafter. His pacing seemed to help him think and figure. She had come to find solace in the sound of his pacing.

Maybe he was in the barn.

She ran through the house and out to the barn. It was hard to envision Father staying up all night, even in the barn. But perhaps—

She eased through the creaky door and called for him, but there was no answer. She climbed the rough boards to the loft. Poking her head through one of the loft holes she looked around expecting to see his reclining body in one corner or another. But he wasn't there. Lifting the skirt above her knees, Lizze climbed up into the loft and checked behind the hay bails and piles of straw, but there was no sign of him.

As she walked back to the house, she heard laughing. It was coming from the shed. She went to investigate.

"Breakfast ready?" Father asked as Lizzie swung the door open, a full smile brightening his face. But before she could answer or think another thought, she was drawn into Father's strong and tender arms and rocked side to side.

Jake was there too, Lizzie noticed, looking extremely elated.

"Dear sweet Lizzie," Father whispered. "How I've neglected you. Will you ever be able to forgive me?"

Lizzie wasn't sure what was going on. She looked over at Jake, drilling him with her eyes.

"Isn't it grand, Lizzie? Father loves us."

Well of course he loves us, Lizzie thought. So what's going on here?

"Come now," Father said to Jake, releasing Lizzie.

"Let's have some of Lizzie's good coffee and tell her all about it."

CHAPTER TWENTY-EIGHT

Pastor Stebbins whistled as he steered into the Van Ankum's yard and set the brake. What better way to start this beautiful summer day, he thought, than to stop by and get a little better acquainted with Lizzie? Something he'd wanted to do for several weeks. Her increasing attendance at services, plus, the responsiveness on her face as he preached God's word, had gotten his attention. A particular question had been nibbling at his thoughts lately. A question only Lizzie could answer.

Having heard it said that "flowers speak volumes," he brought along a bouquet of freshly picked daisies. He had never cared for their potent fragrance himself but had heard that many women enjoy them and are not offended by the scent. He hoped Lizzie was one such woman.

Upon hearing the rumble of the pastor's rattle-trap jalopy, Lizzie shook the soapy water from her hands and dried them with her apron. What would be bringing him out here today? Willie always worked on Tuesdays, he knew that.

She opened the door and was surprised by the large bouquet of daisies he produced from behind his back and thrust in her direction. She jumped back as petals and stems poked her in the face. He hadn't meant to be so forceful in the presentation.

"I'm sorry, Lizzie. I— "

"Oh, for me?" she said, accepting the bundle. "They're lovely!"

"Yes, for you. They're growing wild everywhere on the church property. Thought you might like some— that is—well, I *hoped* you might like them."

"Thank you!" She twisted the bouquet to see all sides. "I *do* like them."

The aroma of sweet buns baking in the oven permeated the house, reaching even to the door, and Lizzie was pleased. She invited him in for coffee, or a glass of water, if he'd rather. He accepted. The fragrance of cardamom, cinnamon, and yeast dough already had his mouth watering.

Lizzie led her pastor into the kitchen. "Please, have a seat," she said, pointing to a chair. Assuming he seated himself she gave her attention to the flowers. She poured water into a two-quart jar and poked the stems inside, fanning out the flowering heads to create a balanced arrangement. With her back to him she plucked several brown petals from the bouquet and tucked them into her apron pocket.

Pastor Stebbins had not taken the chair that Lizzie had indicated, but instead, he stood near the cook stove with his hands deep in his pockets, a worried look on his face. Lizzie noticed him pull his hands from his pockets and clench them behind his back ever so briefly, then immediately shove them once again into his pockets. Where was his ready smile? Lizzie wondered. He now folded his arms across his chest, another attempt, it seemed, to get his arms settled into some sort of satisfactory position. But that, too, appeared unacceptable for he quickly thrust them back into his pockets and began fidgeting with what sounded like coins.

Lizzie couldn't remember seeing Pastor Stebbins look this uncomfortable. He was typically much more at ease. So steady and sure, as a rule, so in command of himself. But today he was restless. Definitely, Lizzie concluded, in a dither about something. Or possibly, she considered, possibly he had already had more coffee than was good for him.

"If you're not in a hurry," she said, hoping to set him at ease. "There'll soon be some sweet buns out of the oven."

"No hurry at all," he assured her. He was glad to wait.

He wouldn't say it aloud, but he hoped to do some prospecting today. Waiting for the sweet rolls may turn out to be just the opening he'd been watching for, the chance to turn their acquaintance into something more.

Lizzie went for a doily from the cabinet in the big room. When she returned, she noticed that his hands were again clenched behind his back. She heard him suck in a deep breath as if to say something, but instead, he swallowed loudly then turned to the stove and went about washing his hands in the dish pan on the stove. Something was troubling him. He wasn't acting at all like he had the day he had helped with the beets. What a blessing he had been that day.

Lizzie poured them each a cup of coffee. *He likes his coffee black*, she remembered. She brought the sugar bowl to the table and sprinkled a teaspoonful into her cup and stirred it slowly. She would forego the cream today.

Just because she had more cream in the house than she knew what to do with was no reason to add cream to everything.

"So, how's your church work going?" Lizzie inquired, knowing he always enjoyed speaking of the good things God was doing.

"Fine."

His answer was so immediate that Lizzie was sure he had the answer out of his mouth before she had completed the question.

Lizzie didn't go to church every Sunday the way Willie wanted her to, but in recent weeks she found herself not only looking forward to Sunday but attending more and more. She began planning ahead, and anticipating what Pastor Stebbins might preach about next. She had gotten comfortable with his eyes meeting hers as he spoke. She no longer looked down when their eyes met, unless, of course, it was to make note of something he had said, something she would need to ask Willie about later.

She admired her pastor's ability to communicate God's love through his preaching—he himself modeled that love. He showed no partiality; his love and attention poured out to all. His compassion for the widows and the elderly was unmistakable. To him, they held great worth—and great wisdom. Even those in the community who never stepped foot into the church, they, too, received his care and concern. It didn't bother him one bit to visit those who used God's name in vain, as well as those who praised God with their mouths. Instead of rejecting the God-mockers and keeping his distance, he prayed for them and blessed them. He shared his garden with them. He called on them when they were sick. He bailed and bucked their hay. It was easy to see why Willie looked up to him so. The church was to Pastor Stebbins, Lizzie had come to believe, what she had hoped nursing would have been to her. A perfect fit.

"And your parishioners, they all doing well?" she asked, making another attempt at conversation. He had his back to the stove and was fiddling very methodically with a cuff button, unbuttoning it then buttoning it again. If he kept it up, Lizzie suspected that it wouldn't be long before the thread would wear completely away and the button go rolling across the floor.

"Yes, thankfully," he answered, avoiding direct eye contact. "Everyone is healthy." Lizzie pulled out a chair for him and was glad when he sat down. He was making her tense. "And the crops are looking real good," he added. "No hail so far this year, praise God!"

His elbows lit on the table. *That's a good sign,* thought Lizzie, sighing.

She wished he would relax and initiate conversation, the way he usually did. He did it so well, as a rule. She had often been fascinated at how easy conversation was for him. He seemed always to know the right thing to say and the right time to say it. And she wasn't the only one who held this opinion. She had heard it said of him many a time by others in the community. And they loved him for it.

It was sweet of him to bring the daisies, Lizzie thought, adjusting the jar a half-turn so the best looking heads were facing his direction. She smiled at him. He smiled back; a large, exuberant smile.

She pulled her cup to her lips and blew softly across the steaming liquid. She glanced at him as she sipped. He was watching her. Their gaze locked, and instantly Lizzie understood the look in his eyes. Quickly, she looked back to her cup.

Why would he be looking at her like *that*? He had to know there was no future with her. She spun her cup slowly in the saucer, questioning herself. Maybe she had misinterpreted what she saw in his eyes. Perhaps she should ask if he was all right? But how, exactly, do you ask a minister if everything is all right with him, personally? It wouldn't be proper. She brought the cup to her mouth once again and shifted slightly in her chair, facing more toward the window.

"Lizzie," he said, the cup rattling as he set it onto the saucer. "There's something I'd like to know, if you don't mind. I don't mean to be nosy at all, it's just that, well, I've been wondering if—well—I've been wanting to ask—"

She set down her cup and looked at him. "Then ask," she said.

"Well, I've been wondering," he said, giving his hands another swipe along his lap. "That is…well…I've heard—a rumor. At least I hope it's merely a rumor. He swallowed hard, like a lump broke loose and dropped down the back of his throat. "Well, what I've heard is that there may be someone in your life. A man, I mean."

Lizzie gasped.

"I can't imagine who it might be," he quickly continued, "considering I know all the young men for miles around. So I can't accept it as true unless you say it is. So my question is this: Is there someone? I feel I'd have a better chance if –"

Lizzie stared at him. She could feel heat like a fire coming up her neck and blasting into her cheeks. Suddenly her head was in a whirl. Not the silly dizzy-headed swirl of fascination, but a flaming, intensifying indignation. She felt like a pot that had sat too long on a hot stove. The curiosity he had aroused in coming, and with flowers to boot, now turned sour in her stomach. A slender column of perspiration escaped her hairline near the right temple and she pushed to her feet.

"Excuse me," she whispered, trying desperately to bridle the inner frenzy. "I'll get some cream."

"Not for me, thank you," he said. "Black is fine."

She knew that, but she must get away, even if just for a moment. She reached the icebox, pulled out a small pitcher of cream and set it on the cupboard, her back like a wall between them.

What's it to you? she wanted to demand. *What difference does it make to you if there is a man in my life?*

No one knew of Daniel. No one! She had never mentioned him to anyone—ever. And even if there was someone, why was it any of his business?

"Yes, there *is* a man," she wished to inform him. But that wasn't exactly true, and she knew it. There *had been* a man. For one brief flash in time it had been so. But now... the reality; there was no special someone.

But what's it to him?

She rummaged about in the cupboard, pretending to get something more. She swallowed back the tears that pushed close to spillage. In an attempt to calm her trembling hands, she wadded up the skirt of her apron and forcibly dried the dampness from her hands.

"I'm sorry, Lizzie," Pastor Stebbins said, regret evident in his voice. "I've embarrassed you." He could see what was happening. He'd been wrong to assume that the coast was clear, wrong to hope for a deeper level of friendship with Lizzie. He wished he hadn't come. "I'm truly sorry. It's none of my business."

Lizzie held her stance at the cupboard, her shoulders tight.

He got up from his chair, picked up his cup and saucer, and deposited them in the dishpan. Lizzie couldn't muster up the gumption to turn and look at him.

"Lizzie?" He reached out to touch her shoulder but reconsidered at the last moment and pulled his hand back without making contact. "I'll let myself out."

She was too humiliated to stop him. She stood in silence, stiff as a stick of furniture until she heard the outer door close. Every ounce of pleasure she had felt in the pastor's unannounced visit had vaporized. She turned on a heel and collapsed into the creaky window chair.

Why did he have to go and do that?

Then there was a quick knock, and his face poked back inside.

"Sorry Lizzie, I forgot." His voice was quiet, humble. "Brother Lemont has sent word that he's coming through this way again, and he asked specifically to speak with you. Shall I set it up?"

"Uh...I guess so," she managed.

The door closed softly behind him. She listened as his rattling automobile left the yard then drew up her legs, rested her chin on her knees and sobbed into her apron.

* * *

Lizzie lay awake that night, listening to the soft rattle of Rosie's breathing and stewing over her own innate inadequacies. Downcast in both heart and soul she cried into her lumpy pillow. With great sufficiency it soaked up her tears and muffled her cries. Sobs of hopelessness shook her slender body. She felt like a buggy without wheels. Built for a purpose, but stripped of the means and material to reach that purpose. If she was ever to come to terms with the pickle she was in, she needed a miracle. She needed a change of heart and mind.

Every fiber of her being still longed to be a nurse. If only she could give it up! If only *that seed* had never sprouted in her heart! She wished she could embrace Mother's "calling," and take it on as her own. But try as she might, she couldn't. Not on her own, anyway. She needed help from above.

What was she to do? No matter how hard she had tried, she couldn't abandon the notion of tending the sick and injured. But what good was there in dreaming and wanting? She couldn't bring it about. The whole thing was hopeless. The cotton pillow slip was saturated by the time she turned over onto her back.

"He who is love, knoweth all things," Lizzie remembered Mother saying.

"Oh God, help me!" she prayed. "Take it away. Help me stop wishing and hoping. I don't want to think about nursing anymore. Please, dear God, please! You've given me a family to care for, a calling, of sorts, right here. Please let that be enough for me."

She tugged on a loose thread that dangled from the side seam of her nightie. She snapped it off and her fingers began walking their way up the string…a, b, c, d…D for Daniel. She tore the thread in two at that spot.

The words of Willie's favorite hymn began floating through her thoughts, "But we never can prove the delights of His love until all on the altar we lay; for the favor He shows, and the joy He bestows, are for them who will trust and obey."

Until *all* on the altar we lay—
What did that mean, exactly? She tried to think
how one would go about laying their *all* on the altar. Is
that what Father had done in the shed? That night he had
made peace with Jake? Whatever it was that Father had
done, it had changed his entire life. He was a new man.
Lizzie knew it. The family knew it. And from what Willie
had said at supper last night, the whole community knew
it. Lizzie pondered on her own situation but couldn't
make out what it would mean for her, personally, to lay
her *all* on the altar. She decided, at last, that it was too big
a subject for her tired mind. She rolled onto her side,
plumped her damp feather pillow with a weary fist and
went to sleep facing the wall.

Lizzie didn't go to church the following
Wednesday evening. She just couldn't. Seeing Pastor
Stebbins, *Jimmy*— well, she couldn't bear to look him in
the face and shake his hand. Not yet. Not after what had
happened between them. She'd have to face him sooner or
later, she knew that. But she wasn't ready just yet.

CHAPTER TWENTY-NINE

Thursday morning broke sunny and warm. It would turn out quite hot, Lizzie suspected. It was a good morning for a long walk; the girls would enjoy it, and she needed it. She still felt knotted up inside. So, once the morning chores were done and four rows of carrots weeded, she and the girls headed across the meadow.

What Lizzie really wanted to do was run. Run until she could run no more. She wanted to feel the wind in her face, fighting her. That wasn't going to happen today, however, for there was not even a whisper of a breeze. *So what!* She'd run without any wind in her face. But she would have to wait until later, once she had the girls settled in a good play area.

They selected branches from the ground under the large maple tree. One that felt "just right" to each of them. They took to the cow path heading east, swishing their sticks back and forth as they walked. Rosie followed Lizzie's lead and Anna took up the tail. Anna danced playfully, her bare feet stirring up little dust clouds along the lane. Red clover grew thick along the right side of the lane, its sweet fragrance stimulating their taste buds as they strolled along. Lizzie snipped off a handful of blooming heads and chewed the sweetness from their inner tips.

Life had certainly veered from the plan she and Mother had worked out on paper last fall. If someone had told her then that she would still be herding cows, slopping pigs, and separating milk, she would have shot them with both barrels.

"Can we go to the creek?" Anna called ahead to Lizzie. "Can we?"

"No Anna! We didn't bring anything to dry off with. Besides, I don't want Rosie in that cold water."

"Please, Lizzie, we'll just swish the water with our sticks, that's all."

"All right, we'll go to the creek, but no one is going swimming. Do you hear me?" As they got closer, Lizzie reconsidered and decided maybe it wouldn't hurt to let them wiggle their toes in the water for a few minutes.

At first the girls were happy putzing around, ankle deep, in the water. Lizzie joined them. It was immensely refreshing. Before long, before Lizzie even noticed it was happening, Anna was lifting her dress and going deeper.

"That's far enough," Lizzie warned when she saw it, then agreed to let them go in up to their knees. They bunched up their dresses at their waists, trying their best to keep them dry. But the rocks on the bottom were slippery, and down they went, one after the other. They were both soaked up to their necks. Since the day was so hot, and with absolutely no wind, Lizzie decided to let them play a bit longer while she stretched out on the pebbly ground to bask in the sun. She pulled her dress up to her thighs to let the sun get at her white legs.

The sun's heat felt good on her skin. She leaned back on her hands and raised her face to the sky. She stayed that way several minutes then turned over on her stomach to let the sun color the back of her legs. While braced on her forearms, she noticed a small greenish rock near her elbow and picked it up for closer examination. It was not a typical river rock. It had perfectly smooth edges. There was not one rough or jagged edge on it. She had not seen a rock this lustrous before, not down here at the creek. It felt almost like polished glass. She looked it over, inspecting the varying colors of gray and brown and green. It was beautiful.

How many years the rock had lain there, taking whatever the elements hurled upon it, she had no idea. Winter's long freeze, spring's winds and storms, summer's sun. Season after season, it lay unnoticed in this secluded spot. Lizzie pushed up onto her hands and knees, looking for others. She poked and dug at the ground with her stick, loosening several rocks from their sound setting and turning them over. Her digging produced two more, similar to the first one, yet each uniquely shaped and possessing its own splendor. She spit on them and wiped them with her thumbs. She took them to the water, dipped them in, and polished them with her skirt. Three beautiful rocks! Found in a riverbed of plain old rocks! She sat down, laid them in her lap and examined them again one by one.

How in the world had they gotten so beautiful? Here they were, stuck in a creek bed with every sort of severe weather condition beating on them day after day, year after year. Three stunningly beautiful rocks! She smiled and shook her head. How could they get so pretty when they had nothing in their favor?

"They also have me," was the message that came whispering into her soul. Lizzie sat up and listened. She knew that voice. It was the same comforting voice that had spoken to her many months ago as she cried in the hayloft. "It's those very things that pound against them that make them beautiful," the gentle voice said.

Suddenly she understood the meaning.

"But they're rocks," she replied aloud. "People aren't rocks."

"Trust me, Lizzie. I'm polishing you too."

"What do you mean?" she asked, waiting for more.

But nothing more came. It seemed the conversation was over. All was still. She rolled the rocks over and over in the palm of her hand, listening to the glassy sound they made as they hit against one another. At last she tucked the little treasures into her skirt pocket. Remembering the girls, Lizzie scrambled to her feet.

"Rosie! Anna!" she called, running into the water. She screamed louder. "Girls! Where are you?"

"We're over here," Anna called back from a bunching of tall grass.

Lizzie found them sunning themselves, their wet dresses spread like flimsy sheets between the ground and their shivering bodies.

"For goodness sake, you two! We need to get you home and into some dry clothes." Lizzie squeezed as much water out of their dresses as she could. She drew the girls close and wrapped her skirt around them for a time, warming their shivering bodies. They each retrieved the stick they came with and headed across the field toward home, Lizzie carrying the dresses and the girls following behind in their panties. They were probably better off with the sunshine warming their wet heads and quivering shoulders than they would be in wet dresses, Lizzie reasoned.

Saturday morning was as beautiful a start to a late-summer day as one would ever hope to get. Not only was it a perfect day for cleaning but also a perfect day for letting the breeze blow through the house to freshen it up. No matter how she tried, it seemed the shanty always smelled of sour milk.

Pastor Stebbins had made the arrangements he spoke of concerning Brother Lemont's visit and sent word through Willie that she could expect them for supper tonight. Pastor Stebbins would provide the dessert. Rhubarb pies, he told Willie. Lizzie's face puckered when she heard that.

Of all things to serve company! she thought. *Especially this sort of company.* But she decided not to concern herself with it, just so long as *she* didn't have to bake them. She felt a bit guilty about all the rhubarb that was going to waste in her own yard, but she didn't enjoy it enough to want to do much with it. Mother had been the only one in the family who really liked it. Instead of attempting to produce something yummy with the stuff, Lizzie usually just pulled off the mature stocks and threw them to the pigs. Perhaps she should have offered to let the pastor come and pick hers. But, she figured, it was he who had offered so he must have resources.

The housecleaning chores were much more enjoyable with the doors and windows flung open. This morning a parade of blithesome breezes worked their way through the house, playing liberally with the curtains and creating that "fresh-cleaned" fragrance she had hoped for.

By morning's end the cleaning was finished and a noon-time meal of warmed over white beans and bread was set before the girls.

Jake was away with the threshing crew; today they were at Foster's. Lizzie had packed him extra sandwiches knowing that it was very likely the woman would not have anything edible prepared for the workers. No doubt she would blame some recent ailment she'd been suffering.

After the breakfast and dinner dishes were washed and put away Lizzie began supper preparations. She had decided on roast beef, new potatoes, creamed parsnips and coleslaw. She chose the biggest roast left in the ice house, seasoned it and placed it in the oven. Then she worked on arranging the table. Mother's favorite Sunday tablecloth was pulled from the tall dresser and spread over the wooden surface. Lizzie didn't mind admitting a certain desire to impress the old man. Plus, she wanted to make Father proud.

Father had changed so much in recent weeks that there was no denying he had found God. And in finding God, he brought to the family an incredible sense of hope and wholeness. His changed life also expressed itself in regular church attendance. Most Sundays he even stayed after services to socialize a bit with the neighbors, which thrilled both Willie and Pastor Stebbins.

Something good had happened to Jake as well. Whatever had been mean and ornery inside of him had been switched off, sent to flight, washed away. He was being transformed right before her eyes. Within days of the episode at Mrs. Bannister's house he had come to Lizzie apologizing.

"Lizzie, I've been so stupid."

"Jake, don't talk like that!"

"No, Lizzie, I mean it. The day they put Mother in

that box I felt like somethin' inside me went down with her. I wanted her back. I couldn't have that, so I got mad and started hurtin' people. That's the way Father explained it. It kind'a makes sense, don't it? I didn't want to be the only one hurtin', so I did things that I knew would make you hurt too."

Jake moved from the chair he was in and came to stand next to Lizzie at the cupboard. He put an awkward arm along her shoulders. "I'm sorry, Lizzie, I've been mean and ornery, and you didn't deserve it."

It felt good to hear him say it. But she knew it wasn't all his fault. "I haven't exactly known how to be a mother to you, have I?"

"See, that's the thing. I didn't want you to be my mother. I had a mother and she was dead. I didn't want you actin' like you were taking her place. After she died, all I could think about was keepin' the promise I had made her."

"You made a promise?"

Jake nodded. "She asked me to make sure the widow lady had all the help she needed."

"Mother said that?"

"Yeah. She made me promise to pray for Mrs. Bannister every day and do whatever I could to help her."

No wonder, thought Lizzie. No wonder! Suddenly it all became clear. What she thought was rebellion from Jake was not rebellion at all. He was doing the same thing she was trying to do. He was trying with all his might to stay true to his promise. He, too, had made a promise he couldn't break. She knew the feeling. She turned to him and hugged him.

"Oh Jake, I'm sorry too. I didn't know you were trying to keep a promise." Lizzie started to cry.

Jake cried too.

"That's what I've been trying to do, too," she admitted after a few moments. They stood together holding each other and crying. At last Jake asked.

"What did you promise?"

Giving Jake a final squeeze and pulling away, Lizzie smoothed back her hair and lifted her apron to wipe her face.

"I promised to take care of Father and raise you children in her place."

"But Lizzie," Jake said, "how could you promise that when you knew you were going to nursing school?"

She shrugged, fresh tears pouring down her face. She buried her face in her apron.

"I had to. There was no one else."

"I'm sorry, Lizzie. I didn't know."

Jake understood now, for the first time, Lizzie's anguish. She had laid everything down to be true to Mother. He understood it, but he couldn't stand it. It ought not to be that way. Never before had he seen in Lizzie what he saw in that brief exchange. Her sacrifice; her pain.

Before leaving Lizzie to stand alone in the kitchen he took hold of her upper arms and planted a quick kiss on her cheek. Then he was gone.

He couldn't bear to stand by and watch. Something had to be done.

***

Well ahead of suppertime Lizzie called the girls inside and had them clean up and dress for company. She had them brush out their hair, a full one-hundred strokes each. Lizzie fixed Anna's hair into two long yellow braids but left Rosie's loose, with bows holding it back behind her ears.

Anna skipped and sang around the table, trying every chair. "Where's the preacher going to sit? In this one?" Then she'd hop to another. "Or this one?"

"Anna, come away from the table," Lizzie scolded, "before you knock something down."

She hoped Father and the boys would get home and in from doing chores before Pastor Stebbins and his guest arrived. It would be nice to have everything come off in a nice, orderly fashion. Now if she could just pretend the pastor had never asked that awful question. If she could just treat him like the pleasant young man he was the day they had canned beets together, then all would be well.

Father's milk truck clattered into the yard right on time, much to Lizzie's relief. The girls heard it as well, and climbing on the window chair, they cheered its arrival.

"Oh-oh," Rosie said, her laughter suddenly gone.

"What?" Lizzie asked, stirring hard to keep the white sauce from boiling over.

"The truck!" Rosie said quietly.

"Oh-oh," Anna echoed, sliding from the chair and heading outside.

"For pity sake, girls! What?"

But they didn't answer. Lizzie stirred furiously and finally dragged the pot to the cooler end of the stove so she could go take a look.

***

"Honestly, I don't know how I managed to steer clear of the fellow," J.C. said. His hand was still shaking as he poured another ladle of gravy over his entire plateful. "First thing I knew, there he was, coming right at me. Then, just when I thought I was clear of him, there he was again. There was nothing to do but crank it hard and hit the ditch."

The truck's left side was badly crinkled, and several cream cans had gotten crunched so badly that their lids would never fit again, but as for the three of them, there was not so much as a scratch.

"You did the right thing," Father said. "Better to hit the ditch than him and his horse."

J.C. seemed unable to let the incident go; he was visibly shaken by it. He talked almost feverishly about the man. He supposed it was a man. Some desperate or foolhardy soul, whoever it was.

"Acted like he was trying to kill himself or something," J.C. said, looking intently at both Pastor Stebbins and Brother Lemont, as though they should be particularly interested in the man's mental and emotional well-being. "You shoulda' seen him!" J.C. scooped up another fork of mashed potatoes and filled his mouth.

Lizzie was as astonished as the others over the ordeal, but she had to admit, she was thankful for the diversion it brought to the evening meal. Pastor Stebbins and his guest, Brother Lemont, had arrived just as the boys were coming in from the barn and they all gathered around the dented truck to look it over before converging upon the kitchen like a ravenous band of marauders. Once inside, Pastor Stebbins handed Lizzie two lovely looking pies.

"Hope these will do," he had said with a ready

smile. There was no awkwardness in his manner; he seemed completely at ease with himself, and with her, like Tuesday's unpleasant conversation had never taken place at all. The friendly way in which he spoke put her instantly at ease. All the worry she had been hauling around over their next face to face encounter slipped away like butter off a hot knife.

"They most certainly will do," she said, smiling back at him. But she couldn't bring herself to look him directly in the eye.

"Well, son," Zachariah said, "I'm glad you had your head about you. I hope the poor fellow got home safe and sound."

"And thank goodness none of you got hurt," Lizzie said, putting a spoon of creamed parsnips on Anna's plate and passing them on.

Anna turned to Rosie and wrinkled up her nose. Parsnips made her gag.

"I think it's the Lord we ought to be thanking," Willie said.

"Amen!" was echoed by several around the table. Willie had been practically speechless since they arrived home.

"Well, enough said 'bout that," Zachariah said at last. "It's behind us, praise be." He picked up the platter of meat, passed it to Brother Lemont and said, "Willie tells me great tales of your beloved north country. I'd like to hear more."

"I was hoping you'd ask," the preacher said. Brother Lemont's gangly left arm reached to receive the plate of meat. He forked off a small piece and passed it on to Pastor Stebbins who welcomed another slice of roast. "Let's see. Where to start! It's all so exciting and challenging, and, I admit, terrifying at times. Sometimes I feel that my vision for the northern regions should perhaps be passed on only to those who are ready to commit themselves to being part of the solution. Whether that be through their prayers or through their presence, either way we need people who are committed to seeing God bring hope and help to the masses migrating north."

"Seems to me," Zachariah interrupted, "you have to get the facts to people first before you can expect them to commit to the thing, wouldn't you think? I confess; I'm fairly ignorant about what's going on outside my community, as are many others, I'm sure. So try us out. There might be someone sitting around this table tonight that will be part of the solution you're lookin' for. What do you say, children?" Zachariah looked around at his family for confirmation. All but J.C. were nodding their heads in full agreement. Zachariah looked back at Brother Lemont. "See what I mean."

"Well then," Brother Lemont said, wiping his mouth with the linen serviette near his plate. "For starters, let me say, opportunity abounds like never before. Land is plenteous. There's a wealth of water, fish and game throughout the Stony Plain region, the area of which I'm most familiar. The homesteading possibilities are endless, if a fellow has nothing against hard work. Or if one preferred to live in town, businesses are booming. Been that way ever since Stony Plain was featured in the Edmonton Evening Journal almost twenty years ago. Seems to me it might be a right good spot for any young man dreaming of starting his own business."

Zachariah sailed a glance across the table at Willie and saw what he expected, a young man brimming with desire to strike out on his own. He'd seen it coming for a couple months now. Zachariah wondered if Brother Lemont could see it too.

The visiting pastor took a drink from his cup and continued. "Sawmills are running full tilt with more starting up every month. You don't even have to go that far north to get a sense of it all. Take Rimbey for example, you wouldn't believe the lumber coming out of that area. Of course, there's the downside: broken dreams, poverty, illness and disease. Not for all, but for some."

"I'll tell you one thing, Mr. Lemont," Zachariah interjected. "If anyone could make a go of it in a spot like you're describing, Will could. He's got what it takes."

The words pleased Will.

"Better ask Sadie before you go jumping on that one, Will," J. C. advised. The others laughed, but J.C. was serious. "I mean it. It might not be that funny to her."

"Don't worry," Willie said, a contented smile taking over his face. "I already have."

A slight frown crossed J.C.'s brow and he turned his attention back to his meat and potatoes.

Brother Lemont said, "The three things I'm praying hardest for are these: men with a heart to teach the Bible, nurses with a calling so passionate that the hardships and hazards won't get the better of them, and for the faith to accomplish all God gives me to do."

The man's excitement about the northern regions was infectious. There could be no denying he loved it. He spoke for a good half hour before Rosie and Anna became restless. He talked about his dream of seeing a trail of churches being built in many of the budding communities. His zeal for launching these churches reminded Lizzie of the way she used carry on about nursing. But of all the things Brother Lemont said during the evening, his parting words captivated Lizzie the most.

"There's someone I want you to meet, Lizzie. Someone who may be able to persuade you to come up north to learn your nursing."

The idea of her going north was absurd and she knew it. But the man did not seem to pay attention to her explanations. In fact, he seemed not to comprehend her situation at all, nor her obligations. It seemed he didn't fully grasp *why* she remained at home.

"They'll be in church tomorrow," he said. "Don't miss it."

Lizzie tried to get him to say more about the person he wanted her to meet. Who could it be? A doctor perhaps? Maybe a nurse like Nadine! She could learn plenty from someone like Nadine Taylor. With someone like that to teach her she might not even need to go to school. If only Nadine could have taken her under wing, she'd be prepared already to go up north.

But that was unreasonable and she knew it. It would never have worked. She couldn't have left the girls and the chores long enough each day to spend time in town with Nadine.

Brother Lemont did not act the least bit discouraged when she explained that she had not had the slightest opportunity to learn nursing since his last visit. He seemed only to revel in the fact that her desire had not changed, that she still, as much as ever, hoped to someday gain nursing skills, even though she knew not how. His enthusiasm didn't waiver in the least when she explained that she was needed at home to care for her younger siblings. She would not be free to go anywhere, for quite some time.

"God will provide," was all he said.

Lizzie was determined that he not foster any kind of false hope and reiterated that as far as she could tell, she would not be able to give herself to nursing for at least ten years. But telling him so didn't dampen his spirits.

"You tell him, Pastor Stebbins," she said at last. Someone must make him understand her situation. But the pastor simply shrugged and smiled, as if to say, "He may be right about this thing."

"Just keep pursuing the desire of your heart, Lizzie," Brother Lemont said as he and Pastor Stebbins said their good-byes. "Pray about it. I'll be praying too. Remember, nothing is impossible with God."

She promised she'd pray. Willie said he'd pray too.

"Me too," Father added, winking at Lizzie.

Lizzie said she would pray, and she did. As she cleaned up the supper dishes and readied the girls for bed, it never left her thoughts. It had been a long time since she felt such a surge of hope. Brother Lemont had cranked on the starter and now the motor of possibility was rattling along under its own steam, anticipation rising in Lizzie's chest with alarming thrust.

After tucking the girls into bed Lizzie sat beside them and talked to them about saying bedtime prayers. Like they had done with Mother.

"Can I go first?" Anna asked, bouncing to a sitting position in her spot next to the wall.

"All right, you go first tonight."

"Dear God," Anna prayed, clasping her hands and holding them close to her chest. "Please make Lizzie into a nurse. And please bring us a new mommy. Amen."

Anna opened one eye and looked up at Lizzie.

"Was that a good prayer?"

"Yes, Anna, it was a good prayer." Lizzie tucked the child's hair behind her ears and kissed her forehead. "Now you, Rosie."

Rosie bowed her head and folded her hands on her lap as the children had been taught to do at church services.

"Dear Jesus, I love you. Thank you for taking Mummy to heaven. Thank you for Father, and Lizzie, and Anna, and Jake, and Willie, and J.C., and thank you for giving me enough air to breathe. Amen."

"Amen," Lizzie echoed and rose from the bed.

"Aren't *you* going to pray?" Anna asked, a frown forming on her face. "Mother used to pray, too."

Lizzie sat down again, took one of their hands in each of hers, and bowed her head. Of course, she should pray as well. And though Lizzie knew she wasn't nearly as good at it as Mother had been, she was now their example.

"Dear God, thank you for these precious girls. Please protect them while they sleep. Bless Father and help him not to be too lonely. Thank you for helping him to turn to you. As for me, Lord, I put my future in your hands. You know what's in my heart. You know what's best. Amen."

Lizzie slipped her summer nightgown over her head and dropped onto her bed. *What do you think about how things are going, Mother?* she asked heavenward. *Are you pleased?* The double wedding was set for the last Saturday in September. Hopefully, the haying would be about finished by then. The wedding day would be in upon them before they were ready, Lizzie felt sure of that.

It helped knowing that Rosie and Anna would be back in school by then. Jake would return to school once the haying was done.

Hopefully, it wouldn't rain that day. The brides both longed for the ceremony to be held on the grassy patch next to the garden. Mother would be glad about that. Had Sally and Sadie's parents not decided to sell their place and move to Calgary this past summer, the wedding would have taken place in their flawless flower garden.

Pastor Stebbins would perform the ceremony. Mother would definitely like that. She had always appreciated the young pastor's courage in using weddings, funerals and the like to get the message of God's love out to the whole community.

Lizzie sighed, pulling the cotton sheet up to her chest. It had been another hot day, and though she knew the cool night-time air would soon make her shiver, she was not ready for any blankets yet. Lizzie let out another happy sigh. The bride's dresses were not her concern. That was a relief. Nor were the decorations. These things and many more details were all being cared for by Sadie and Sally, and their mother. And to hear the boys talk, everything was well in hand.

Lizzie's list of responsibilities was really rather short. The garden must be freshly weeded, each row that by that time had not yet been harvested. The boy's suits must be cleaned and pressed, and their shoes polished. In regards to food preparation, Lizzie had only to prepare a large bowl of fresh coleslaw and a roaster full of J.C.'s favorite baked beans, the kind that were sweetened with molasses. The cabbage heads she had her eye on for the coleslaw were almost fully formed. And yes, there was

one other thing. By the wedding night she must have the
boys' upstairs bedroom divided into two rooms. J.C. and
Willie would have gladly put up the partition themselves,
but between their long hours at the creamery, serving on
the threshing crew, and their trips into the city for
wedding preparations, well, if it depended on them, it
might not get done.

"Don't worry!" Jake had offered one evening
while wedding plans were being hashed out at the supper
table. 'Lizzie and I can do it. We know how to throw up a
wall of plywood, don't we, Sis?"

It felt so good having their sensible, hard-working
Jake back. Such wonderful changes had come about since
he and Father had worked out their differences, out there
in the shed. Lizzie sighed again thinking how Mother
must surely be doing some sighing of her own over the
recent changes in Jake's behavior. It was good of Father
to let him continue on at Mrs. Bannister's place. A bit
lavish, Lizzie thought, but good. She felt it was especially
generous of Father to let him bunk down most every night
in the widow's shed. But now that Jake was pulling his
fair share at home, life on the farm was taking on an
increased measure of satisfaction. She dare not murmur
for even one moment about what Father was doing with
Jake.

Lizzie smiled thinking of how silly her older
brothers were getting. And at their age! Father said they
acted more like teenagers than she did, and she agreed.
J.C. laughed more than he talked, and Willie, well, he
hummed and whistled so much that she could hardly keep
from clapping her hand over his mouth at times.

"It must be something to be in love," Lizzie
whispered, rolling over onto her side and looking out at

the moon. *To be so exhilarated by hope and expectation.* Her mind went back to last winter. She remembered how she had marked off the days, and weeks, and months as she prepared for nursing school. That was a kind of love, too, she reckoned. A love for doing something that really mattered. Something that filled your heart so full that it yearned for nothing more.

Suddenly, as she lay there watching the moon, the image of Daniel's face darted as sharp as lightning across her thoughts. It came with such clarity and was so full-color that she sat up in bed. Her stomach quivered strangely.

His face hadn't flitted across her mind's eye in ages. She had almost forgotten how he looked. But just now, for that brief moment, it was back as clear and sure as on that long ago day in the city. His intensely dark eyes and wavy brown hair. His straight back and square shoulders. Those warm calloused hands clutching hers in not one, but several hearty handshakes.

Memories of that day came flooding back. Sharing her sandwich on the bench, and his giant slice of gingerbread cake. Walking together down the path to the water. Him thumbing the rim of his hat, then suddenly, without warning, running off to meet the coming train. How she wished she could have kept her promise to him.

Lizzie adjusted the sheet and turned over onto her stomach. She had spent more than enough time dwelling on what would never be. The hope of meeting him again, the thought of falling in love—

All of that falling in love business was out of the question now. There was only one place for her. Right here on the farm.

Nothing short of a miracle could change that.

CHAPTER THIRTY

Lizzie rose to clear the breakfast table. "Come on, girls. Finish up your porridge. It'll soon be time to go."

It was a lovely Sunday morning; a perfect day to walk to church, Lizzie decided. She hated to see summer moving so quickly toward autumn. There would not likely be many more Sunday mornings as pleasant as this one, at least not this year.

She set the breakfast dishes to soak in a pan of water, shooing off several pesky flies with the dishrag. The dishes could wait and be washed up later in the day.

Father scooted his chair back a bit, and with some command, cleared his throat. Everyone looked his way. The twinkle in his eyes was what caught Lizzie's attention.

"We'll do things a wee bit different this mornin'," he said. He thought the children would not mind the announcement he was about to make. In fact, he expected them to be downright happy about it. Especially Rosie and Anna.

"I offered to pick up Mrs. Bannister and her children for church today. Anyone want to ride along?"

As anticipated, both Rosie and Anna squealed

with delight. Yes, yes, they wanted to go. Of course they did. This would be their first ride in the brand new automobile Father had purchased and had delivered to the farm yesterday. Father smiled. Lizzie noticed his face was glistening.

"Not me, Father," Willie said, wiping his mouth with his serviette and pushing away from the table. "I'll take the wagon. You know how much Sadie loves bouncing along on that wagon bench. Anyways, those modern vehicles can hold only so many bodies, you know. Wouldn't want you and the dear Mrs. Bannister to have to squeeze too tight." He laughed and flung a wink in Lizzie's direction. "You coming with me, Lizzie?"

Lizzie could see what Willie was doing. He, too, must have read the eagerness in Father's face.

"No," she said. "I feel like walking today. And if you girls will help me clear the table, I'll have plenty of time to make it before the church bell rings."

The girls jumped from their chairs and began gathering up the bowls, spoons and cups.

***

A split second after Zachariah knocked on Rebecca's door both Frankie and Isabelle shot through the doorway, racing each other to the car.

"Children!" Mrs. Bannister called, "Aren't you forgetting something?"

They stopped in their tracks and turned toward Mr. Van Ankum. Frankie took on the posture of a small soldier and bowed slightly. Isabelle gave a quick curtsy. "Good morning, Mr. Van Ankum," they greeted in unison. Then off they ran.

Mrs. Bannister tossed the long tail of her decorative scarf over her shoulder and pulled the door firmly shut behind her.

This morning Zachariah had no trouble agreeing with the complimentary statements he had heard the townspeople speak of this woman. She was undeniably attractive. Strikingly beautiful, Zachariah had heard Ben Vanderhorn say. Even his own young daughters called her a queen.

Indeed, Zachariah thought, looking at her now, she certainly looked the part today. The plum colored dress with its cream colored trim at the neck and wrists—it elevated her somehow. Or was it she who elevated the dress? Whatever the case, she was a sight to behold. Hardly someone to be slaving away in the muck and manure of the barnyard, Zachariah thought, recalling Jake's concern over her the night they had made amends. And the poise with which she moved. That bit of lift in the chin. She was enchanting. Yes, he could see royalty in her all right.

Zechariah squared his shoulders and heightened to full stature as he offered his arm. With a smile and nod she accepted the offer and the two of them walked slowly to the car.

He was glad he had decided to buy the new automobile. He had been considering the purchase for quite some time and over the past few weeks had investigated prices, models, horsepower and the like, but until he could be absolutely sure that the creamery was standing on two sturdy legs, financially, he just couldn't bring himself to spend the money. But upon Friday's thorough review of the books (which took the entire day), he finally gained peace about it and gave the salesman the nod.

Frankie and Isabelle ran full blast and joined Rosie and Anna in the back seat of the shiny black and brown Tudor Sedan Model T. The four of them bobbed up and down on the springy upholstered bench seat as the adults approached the car.

Zachariah wasn't in the same hurry the children were in. He took his time. In fact, he held Rebecca's pace in check. He had been wanting a moment alone with her. Ever since he had gotten permission to stop by and pick her up, he had wondered how he would carve out a few moments to speak with her privately. This walk to the car might be his only chance all day, or all week, for that matter. He had hoped for an opening yesterday on his way out to pick up Ruby Van Buren's milk cans, but Frankie said she was not available to come to the door right then. Frankie did not invite him in. Zachariah asked Frankie to ask his mother if it would be all right if he picked them up for church the next morning. Frankie ran inside saying he would be right back with the answer. Within a minute the boy was back.

"Mama says, 'We'd be delighted'."

Zachariah had felt a surge of vivacity come upon him at hearing the answer and shook Frankie's hand intensely. "Thank you, Son. I'll see you in the morning." Of course, hardly knowing the older gentleman and being yet a child, Frankie did not notice the combination of relief and elation in the man's smile.

Now here it was, Zachariah's moment alone with her. He had put considerable thought into his approach, knowing it was upon him to take the initiative. Nothing was likely to happen otherwise. He stalled as they neared the automobile. Then turning his back to the shiny thing

and to the children inside, he took her hands in his.
Surprised, she looked at him. His face was
glowing. His eyes were brimming with—something.
What exactly, she wasn't quite sure. He was studying her
face, her eyes in particular.

Just as that moment Frankie rolled down the
window. "Mother, I forgot my Bible. Do I have time to
run in and get it?"

"Yes, Son," she replied without taking her eyes
from Zachariah's face. "But hurry!"

"We'll help you," Anna cheered, and three of the
children ran to the house. Rosie remained in the
automobile.

The commotion had not deterred Zachariah in the
least. He continued to study Rebecca's face, as though he
was after something. But what? It seemed to her that he
was endeavoring to say something, but apparently, he had
decided to let his eyes do the talking for him, relying
solely on them to transcribe the message that lay within
his heart. At last he did attempt to speak. But nothing
audible came out. He ended up licking his lower lip but
that was all.

She felt his hands tighten around hers and again
his eyes examined hers, furrowing as best they could a
pathway to her soul. She could feel it. He was searching
for something, and telling something, all at the same time.
But what it was exactly, she couldn't tell.

"What is tromping around in your head?" she
wanted to ask, but didn't. Their eyes held fast, neither pair
letting go. What was in his heart? Could it be the same
thing that was trawling the groundwork of her own? She
couldn't, and shouldn't, tell him of her feelings for him,
she knew that. Not yet. She had humiliated him enough

already in their short acquaintance. No, if any other dimension was to be added to their relationship, it would have to come from him. She would not risk injuring the newly formed bond that had been established that night at her kitchen table—that of sister and brother in Christ. Anything beyond that would have to start at his end. So, all she could do at present was gaze into his eyes and hope that her own were not giving too much away.

She continued to wait, thinking he must surely be about to speak. But apparently he wasn't. Instead, he took hold of her shoulders and looked at her sternly. For the briefest moment she felt like she might get a good scolding. But then, to Rebecca's surprise, he gently pulled her toward himself and embraced her. She sucked in a soft gasp. Her purse slipped from her shoulder and dropped to the ground. She wrapped her arms around him and her cheek felt the warmth of his neck. Being that her eyes were closed, Rebecca didn't notice Rosie's face pinned up against the window, taking in every move and smiling merrily. Zachariah didn't say a word. Neither did Rebecca. But it was the beginning, their new beginning, she could feel it.

CHAPTER THIRTY-ONE

The singing was already underway as Lizzie walked into the church yard. She didn't realize how poorly her Sunday shoes would hold up to the two mile walk, nor did she know that they would slow her down as much as they did. She should have worn her running shoes or her rubber boots, anything but her Sunday shoes. Her feet hurt. She sat down on the church steps, slipped the flimsy things off and clapped them free of the dust they had gathered. Then she patted the dust from her feet. The congregation was singing the hymn "What a Friend We Have in Jesus."

Lizzie rested back against the sun-baked door and sighed, listening to the rich harmony of the voices inside. She raised her face toward the morning sun, closed her eyes and hummed along.

The harmonica moved into a higher key and the people sang out the final stanza fervently. "'Are we weak and heavy laden, cumbered with a load of care?"

A smile spread across Lizzie's face as she sat soaking in the warm rays. She could say for certain that she no longer felt heavy laden, at least most of the time. The struggle was over. She no longer hated being "mother" to the family. She no longer felt angry. God loved her, she knew that. And He loved the family. And not only did He love them, she, too, loved them. Mother had not asked too much of her after all.

"Excuse me," a man's voice spoke, disbanding Lizzie's contemplations. Something inside quickened at the voice and she opened her eyes. His hat was tipped shielding his face. She jumped to her feet, brushing out the gathers of her skirt and apologizing for blocking the doorway. She looked up at the man. When she saw his face her heart rendered such a cry that her lips could not hold it inside.

It was him.

It was Daniel!

Embarrassed at the noise she had made, she covered her mouth with one hand and reached for the wooden railing with the other.

Her mouth hung open and her eyes looked so much like saucers that he laughed out loud and tipped his hat. He stepped closer. Before she could think about what she was doing she jumped toward him, clasping him tightly around the neck. He wrapped his arms around her as well and his soft breath touched her hair.

"Lizzie!"

She clung to him, praying he was real. *It really is daylight, ay, and not the middle of the night?*

Suddenly a gush of self-awareness smacked across her senses. What would people think? What was she doing hugging a stranger? She pulled away; and he gently set her down. She wanted to stare, uninterrupted, into those deep dark eyes of his. But instead, she stepped back, lowered her eyes and spoke as if to the boards under her feet.

"Daniel! How did you?— What are you?—"

What was she asking? *She* didn't even know. A million questions pitched around in her head, tying her tongue to the floor of her mouth. There was so much she wanted to know—so much she wished to explain.

"We'll talk later, Lizzie. I need to get back inside."

"You do?"

Then it came to her. "You mean, you're the—"

"Hurry, get your shoes on." He held the door for her. She pressed into her shoes and eased through the doorway, quickly taking her usual spot between the girls. She didn't see where Daniel sat. Near the back, she supposed. Pastor Stebbins called out another hymn number and there was a general rustling of pages as Sister Flynn played a few introductory notes on the harmonica.

Somewhere near the back a child let out a yelp. Typically Lizzie tried not to look in the direction of noisy children and had scolded the girls on numerous occasions for doing so, but today she threw a glance toward the back of the room, as did several others. She was thankful for the cranky child. It afforded her the perfect opportunity to locate Daniel. So now she knew. He sat on the back bench, next to the aisle, beside Mrs. Foster. Lizzie looked back at the hymnbook, fumbled for the correct page and instantly felt a rush of heat rise up her neck and into her face. She could feel Rosie's eyes on her, as in reprimand, but Lizzie refused to look at her.

In his typical, capable manner Pastor Stebbins directed the congregation through each verse of "Rock of Ages" then welcomed the visitors from up north. He asked Brother Lemont to share with the people and to introduce his young friend.

Lizzie heard almost none of what Brother Lemont said once he asked Daniel to come to the front. Her eyes were too busy soaking in Daniel's physical features, especially his face, and her mind was too busy trying to justify flinging her arms around his neck.

Daniel Winslow greeted the congregation with warm enthusiasm. He briefly explained his family ties with Brother Lemont and expressed his appreciation to Pastor Stebbins and the congregation for allowing him, a layman like them, to share his burden for the people up in his beloved North Country.

"I come from a territory of challenge and opportunity," he announced proudly.

"I've come appealing for workers," he said, getting right to the heart of his mission. "For people with grit. For people who are not afraid of hard work and won't give up when hardship comes. I'm looking for individuals, and couples, and families who believe in the power and provision of God and who have an appetite for adventure. I'm asking God to reveal His love for the folks up north to people who are willing to face challenge upon challenge, and persevere through them all, come what may. I'm looking for those who have eyes to see God's open door. I've come seeking people who will lay down their lives for the sake of others."

Daniel's shoulders were square and broad, the way Lizzie remembered them. His suit was charcoal-colored and his tie a blend of burgundy and deep blue. He moved comfortably in front of the group, like he had stood in the spot of spokesman before. Lizzie saw no sign of nervousness in him, no self-consciousness. No fear or fumbling. She liked that. Her shoulders relaxed and her countenance lightened just listening to the sound of his voice. It must be something to speak to a crowd and remain calm when all eyes are upon you, she thought.

"Homesteading has stretched far north," Daniel continued. "Miles from here. Mills are starting up like wildfire. And there's land for the taking. Sure, it takes hard work, but there's plenty of reward for your labor. Are there any young men here today with a dream of owning your own land? Do you believe in God's provision and protection? Then I plead with you to think about coming north. Pastor Stebbins has told me there are some here with a passion to share the gospel of Jesus Christ with those who have never heard. Well, don't think you have to go across the sea to do it. There's plenty of spiritual drought up north. 'The fields are white unto harvest,' as Jesus said. But the laborers are very very few.

"And what about you who have medical expertise," he said. His eyes looked over the congregation and came to rest on Lizzie. "We are crying for you up there."

Lizzie listened with intense interest. Medical expertise! If only she had gotten to school, she would gladly help meet the needs he spoke of. If she were not responsible for the children, she would volunteer right now. She'd stand up right now and offer her services. And why not? So what that she would be living miles away from home and family. This was Daniel who was speaking. He would take care of her in his beloved North Country. He'd give her the nursing opportunity she yearned for.

Stop it Lizzie, she chided herself. She took out her handkerchief and mopped her sweaty palms. *You're not going anywhere and you know it. Weren't you just outside reveling in God's love and confessing that you were in the*

right place, in the place God had designed for you?
She looked to the floor. Tears suddenly toppled over her lashes and slid down her cheeks. Why? Why had she promised Mother? Why hadn't she insisted on following her dream? Father would have figured something out. Then she'd have been ready for this. She'd have been equipped to respond to Daniel's plea. She'd have had over six months of nursing under her belt by now.

Quickly she brushed the tears away and looked at Daniel. If only she had gotten to know him. Even just to have been allowed to meet him that day as they had planned. But she was robbed of that, too. It seemed there was nothing for Lizzie Van Ankum but a life of misery and loneliness, just as Mrs. Foster had predicted months ago.

Her thoughts continued to war against her heart as Daniel spoke. She seemed unable to keep herself in check. Why did it hurt so to see this new opportunity go by when she had so assuredly felt at peace with the circumstances of her life just moments earlier?

Daniel's words had several of the young men in the congregation sitting up and paying attention, including Willie. Daniel said he felt God was looking for people who were willing to serve and sacrifice for the sake of their neighbors. He spoke about God's love and compassion for those up north. For those who were suffering from illness and injury, and from loneliness and despair and the hurt of broken dreams.

Daniel ended his appeal and Pastor Stebbins offered a final prayer. Those who wanted to speak with Daniel further were invited to gather at the front. Willie took Sadie by the hand and the two of them practically flew to the front. Others quickly joined them there.

Lizzie slipped quietly from the bench and started for the door. There was no sense in going forward. She wasn't available. She wasn't trained. She wasn't anything she needed to be.

She couldn't look Pastor Stebbins in the eye but shook his hand and muttered something about what a nice service it was and hurried toward the door. She moved to a quiet spot along the back wall and watched as several more gathered around Daniel.

How she longed to join them. Better yet, to be alone with Daniel. But what good would that do? She had nothing to offer. Her head was buzzing with questions for him, many of them having nothing to do with his plea to go north.

How was it that he was here? In her community? In her church? How had he found his way? It seemed nothing short of divine intervention. But the timing was lousy. Here he was, at last, but would she even get to talk to him at all with everyone else swarming around him?

For a time she lingered there against the wall. She wasn't about to risk losing sight of him—not this time. That had happened before, and she wasn't about to let it happen again. One minute he was there, and the next he was running down the pathway toward the train. Up and gone, before she even had a chance to object. If only she could spend some time with him now—alone.

"Lizzie," Mrs. Foster called, waving her handkerchief and waddling toward Lizzie. The woman took a moment to catch her breath and wipe her forehead with the embroidered hankie. "Now see here," she said, nodding her head in Daniel's direction. "This is exactly what I spoke of. This very thing! Don't think I can't read the longing in your heart to get acquainted with such a fine young fellow. And why shouldn't you? What young woman your age wouldn't run after him? Yes, even if it meant leaving everything and everyone behind. But see, that is one choice, you, my poor sweet Lizzie, will never get to make. I still say it's a pitiful shame, the fix you're in.

"I'll tell you this though," the woman went on, wiping at the perspiration that speckled her pudgy jowl. "If your father improves in his manners, I may be tempted to marry him myself and put an end to your misery."

A sickening wave of despair hit Lizzie and she excused herself immediately, saying she needed to tend to the girls.

It seemed to take forever for folks to start clearing out of the church. A grain of wheat could have been sown, watered, and reached full maturity by the time Daniel was free to come outside, but at last the ravenous inquisitors were satisfied, each taking with them something fresh to chew on, something new with which to enter their prayer closet. Finally only these remained: Brother Lemont, Daniel, Pastor Stebbins, Willie and Sadie, the children, and Lizzie. And yes, Father and Rebecca Bannister were there, but they were across the yard, standing beside Father's new automobile, talking.

"Oh, Lizzie," Rebecca called, beckoning Lizzie over to the car.

Lizzie approached Mrs. Bannister. Father was climbing in behind the steering wheel and the children: Rosie and Anna, Frankie and Isabelle were all sitting together on the back seat.

"O Lizzie," Rebecca said excitedly. "Isn't it

thrilling? I've invited Brother Lemont and Mr. Winslow for dinner. Please come. Your father has agreed to join us." Rebecca took Lizzie's hands in her own. "Isn't it fantastic? All this talk about God calling folks from here to minister to the people up north! I'm just about beside myself. Did you get a chance to talk to the young man?"

"I—I really didn't. I just—he got pretty swamped."

"I'll say! I've never seen such eagerness in our people, such interest and desire to reach out and be used of God."

Rebecca gave Lizzie a quick hug, then reaching for the car door said, "I'd better go. Your father is waiting. Ask Willie and Sadie to come too, will you? Let them know there's plenty for everyone."

CHAPTER THIRTY-TWO

There was such an impassioned exchange of questions and answers around Mrs. Bannister's scrumptious Sunday meal that Lizzie couldn't get a word in edgewise. Not that she would have known what to say if she had found an opening.

Looking at Daniel now, sitting there across the table, and seeing him looking back made her hands tremble. She shook so that she had to use both hands when she passed him the bowls of steaming mashed potatoes and thick beef stew. When she dished Anna some carrots, she bumped the child's tumbler and knocked it over. Thankfully, Mrs. Bannister had not yet poured the children's milk.

Try as she might, Lizzie couldn't keep her eyes off Daniel. The sparkle in his eyes was much brighter than she had remembered, and his voice deeper and happier. She was glad that Mrs. Bannister had placed him directly across the table from her. His smile was warm and broad, and his enthusiasm magnetic. It was hard to look elsewhere.

"Come on, Lizzie," Willie said, teasing. "Pass

some food our way. Daniel's not the only hungry soul at this table."

All Lizzie could think about was getting a chance to speak with Daniel. Just the two of them. Even if it was just for a few moments. She needed to explain herself. She needed him to know why she hadn't met him as she had promised in the spring. She needed to explain why she had leaped into his arms earlier this morning. Truth be told, she wouldn't be able to explain why she did that. It just happened. But the least she could do was apologize for it.

"How about some bread pudding for dessert?" Mrs. Bannister asked the group, but Lizzie noticed that the woman's eyes looked only for Zachariah's response. "Topped with whipped cream, if you like."

Lizzie witnessed the not-so-fleeting glance that passed between her father and Mrs. Bannister as the lady set his dessert dish in front of him. Intrigued, Lizzie watched to see what might transpire, but momentarily, she got caught up in something Daniel was saying to Willie.

"Not yet. Why? Do you think *you* could start one?"

Will looked at his father. "What do you think, Father?"

"Well," Zachariah said, sinking his spoon into his bowl of bread pudding. "Are the farmers up there keen enough to keep their cows out of the stinkweed?"

The men howled with laughter. Rosie and Anna cackled at the top of their lungs, like they knew what it all meant, and Lizzie was sorry she had missed the joke.

Rebecca suggested the men move to the sitting room to finish their coffee and dessert in comfort. The four younger children ran outside to play. Frankie invited

Jake along, but he said he was too old to play kiddy games and stayed inside with the men.

Under Mrs. Bannister's gentle direction Lizzie and Sadie made short work of the mountain of dirty dishes that had accumulated beside the dish pan then they joined the men in the sitting room. Before they could be seated, however, Daniel stood to his feet.

"The thought of another train ride makes me want to stretch my legs," he said. He then looked directly at Lizzie and asked, "Would you care to join me, Lizzie?"

She nodded, lowering her eyes. Of course she would care to join him! She had wanted nothing other for the past several hours. She felt the silent query of what seemed a thousand eyes upon them as they left the room together. She hoped she wasn't turning beet red but knew she probably was.

He held open the door and she led the way. It was a lovely September day: warm, bright, happy. All too soon the warmth would be over. Northeasterly winds would come along, bringing with them the snow and bitter cold. It wouldn't take long for them to pilfer all the pleasure out of being outside.

How good it felt to walk alongside Daniel. To hear him taking in deep breaths and letting them out slowly. To watch him, out of the corner of her eye, surveying the land with a look of pleasure on his face. Halfway across the yard his arm brushed against hers and she felt the tingle of it all the way to her stomach. Her breathing quickened and she glanced his way again. It really was Daniel. He was here. Beside her. After all this time.

They walked toward a field of harvested wheat and stood for a few moments at the fence, looking out into the distance, at nothing in particular. Lizzie turned to walk on. Daniel stopped her with a gentle hand on her arm.

"Lizzie," he said softly. "I thought I would never see you again. I didn't know what to do when you didn't meet me as we had agreed. I didn't know how to find you."

So it's true, we had agreed, I hadn't just imagined it. Lizzie turned toward him.

"I'm so sorry!" she said, looking up at him. "I should never have promised to meet you, not with Mother as sick as she was."

"No, it was my fault," he said. "I should have asked more questions. It was unfair of me; you had told me of your mother's condition. I was being selfish and thoughtless." Then taking her by the shoulders and turning her to himself he said, "You don't know how I've ached not knowing if I would ever find you again. For months I scoured my memory, searching for some clue, for something you might have said that would lead me your way. But nothing! It was futile. Then, when I saw you this morning on the step of the church, I thought—well, at first I couldn't believe it. I thought I was seeing things. All of a sudden there you were, close enough to touch."

Lizzie's heart raced as he spoke, and she wanted to hold him again, like she had this morning on the church step. She wanted to reach around his neck and pull him close. But she didn't. Just because she was bursting to do it didn't mean it was the right thing to do.

He still had his hands on her shoulders. His eyes were searching her face.

"When I saw you there I—"

His voice cracked and Lizzie saw tears come to

his eyes. He blinked them back then his eyes held hers steadily. She had no desire to look away. She peered deeply into the dark eyes she had hoped never to forget. Eyes she thought she would never see again. Eyes that seemed at present to sparkle with such an odd mixture of anticipation and discovery and regret.

He took in a full breath as if to say something but checked it. He released her shoulders and turned around to face the fence. He ran his fingers slowly through his hair and propped his elbows against the top rail.

He was pondering something, she could see it. He seemed to be deliberating with himself. His countenance looked almost sad. And at the same time determined. He reached for the wooden rail and gripped it in both hands. It was plain to see there was a struggle going on inside. She didn't know him well enough to know what it might be and didn't feel she could ask. Maybe she should divert him from whatever it was that troubled him.

"You game for a walk out to those poplars?" she asked, pointing south to a huddle of trees in Mrs. Bannister's cow pasture. "If you have the time, that is."

He nodded agreement but said nothing. They walked along together in silence, each alone with their own thoughts. Lizzie's thoughts were working along the line of trying to guess why he was being so quiet. She hadn't seen any reserve or hesitation in him at all while he was in the larger group. She couldn't tell if he was upset, or if he was just mulling something over. Whatever was going through his mind, he gave no clue.

Lizzie picked up a dried twig and swished it across the tall drying grasses. She glanced his way from time to time as they walked along but wasn't sure what to say. Halfway to the bunch of poplars she quickly slipped off her shoes and started running.

"Catch me, if you can," she called, leaving her shoes behind. She ran as hard as she could. As hard, that is, as she could in her Sunday dress.

Just as they reached the shade of the trees he caught her. Laughing and panting he took hold of her. He turned her around and drew her close. They stood laughing and gasping, their hearts beating wildly against one another. When he let go, they both collapsed onto the ground.

They rested against separate tree trunks, laughing and catching their breath. Lizzie noticed the number of colored leaves that had already fallen from the trees, reminders that autumn would soon be forcing its way through the door.

"I can't remember how long it's been since I've done that," Daniel said, his eyes alive with pleasure.

"Me either," Lizzie admitted, huffing. She had not run like that once, not just for fun, this whole spring and summer. There had been no time for racing, or for games, or for kicking off her shoes and frolicking around in the fields. But enough of commiserating, she wanted to get to know Daniel.

"How long's it been since you raced a girl?" she asked.

"Can't remember when. Since grade school, I guess."

"Come on! Not even your sisters?"

"Have no sisters," he said, smiling at her.

"Then what about cousins? Or neighborhood girls?"

"Have no cousins, at least none that I know of. And no, there were no neighborhood girls close enough to spend time racing with."

"Okay then, brothers. You have brothers to race, don't you? I can't believe you haven't raced since grade school."

Daniel's smile went quickly away and his shoulders sagged noticeably. He picked up a crimson colored leaf and twirled it slowly by the stem.

Her question seemed to cut him. She wished she hadn't asked. But no, she wanted to know. She wanted to know as much as she could about him. And not only him, but about his family. About his whole life.

"Lost both my brothers," he stated quietly. "Then Dad. My mother died when I was five, I've been told."

Lizzie covered her mouth, very sorry she had asked and shocked at his great loss. How horrible! His whole family! How? She wanted to ask, but couldn't. To do so would be cruel. She sat silently, so sorry she had pried so hard. At last she reached out and placed a hand on his shoulder.

"I'm so sorry!"

Lizzie saw tears on the rim of his eyelids but he turned his face to the north so she couldn't see. She heard him swallow.

"Do you still plan to be a nurse?" he asked without looking at her. His voice sounded flat.

The question caught her off guard. She had wanted to get to know *him* better, and here it was happening again. He had turned the focus back on *her*.

"Uh...well, I still dream of it, for sure. But it's not something I can bank on anymore. At least not 'til the girls are raised."

"So if it wasn't for Rosie and Anna you'd be pursuing it?" He still wasn't looking at Lizzie.

"Definitely! With everything in me! It's just that now is not the time. I've come to accept that. I promised Mother I'd raise the children in her place, and, well—that's the way it is."

"So there's no way you'd leave here. Is that what you're saying?" He turned and looked at her then. His eyes seemed cool and detached. Not hard or mean, just very distant.

She had no idea what her future held. All she knew was that she had to live one day at a time. She adjusted herself on the ground, tucking her legs beneath herself, side-saddle like, and folded her hands in her lap.

"All I can say," she said, shrugging. "All I know to do—I'm trusting God with my future, is what I'm trying to say. I don't know what else to do. Staying home, raising Jake and the girls—well, it's not what I would have chosen. But I know my life, my whole future for that matter, is in God's hands, and I choose to trust that He knows what is best, for all of us, not just me." She knew she was probably disappointing him with her words, but what choice did she have? She had no power to change the way things were. And furthermore, life wasn't just about *her*. There were others to consider. She didn't say this aloud but she knew it to be true.

"Remember the day we bumped into each other in Calgary?" he asked, changing the subject.

Of course she remembered. It was the single most replayd event in her memory. She would always remember that day.

"Sure I do."

"Word had come to us that some generous contributors to the Calgary General Hospital's School of Nursing were willing to provide living expenses for one year to any student nurse, or beginning doctor, should they be willing to serve in certain remote areas of the province. But before they would release any money, the community applying for medical assistance had to demonstrate their need for such a person. It had to be documented need, you know, facts on paper. Well, our district had plenty of need.

"After Dad died," Daniel said, pulling out his handkerchief and swiping his nose, "Uncle Lemont helped me work up a strategy. I set out to document as many needs as I could find. I went from homestead to homestead, bunkhouse to bunkhouse, shanty to shanty. I gathered notes on every medical condition that existed. And the deaths—smallpox, typhoid, all kinds of ailments. Some folks lost their lives because of some sort of injury or another, while others were fortunate enough to loose only limbs. I canvassed forty miles in every direction from the home place.

"That day in Calgary, the day we met, I had spoken with the hospital board. They agreed to consider sending someone up north on a trial basis. They just needed to find someone willing to go that far north. They assured me that by summer they would find some willing soul.

"Then when we ate together," he continued, "you and me, there on the bench under the weeping willow, and I heard you talking of your dream—"

He paused. Then he took her hands in his. "Well, you were so fired up about it. You wanted to talk of nothing else, that's how it seemed to me. You ignited hope in me and made me believe that God truly would provide someone for us. Maybe even you, in time."

Lizzie sat spellbound as he talked. So that's how it

was that day. She had wondered how it had come about that he was in Calgary on that particular day. He was on a mission, a help-seeking quest.

"Talking with you that day and hearing your passion for nursing made me hope like I hadn't allowed myself to hope since my father died. And the more I thought about you, the more I hoped you would be the one. I prayed that God would help you see it, too. When you didn't show up, I didn't know what to do. I felt lost. I hadn't gotten enough information—"

Lizzie opened her mouth to apologize, but he stilled her lips with his fingertips and went on.

"I had no way to track you down. It was my own fault and I kicked myself for months over it. I had no one to blame but myself. I asked the hospital staff about you, but they said they had no such student nurse. They could not help at all. Then to top it off, the matron of nursing told me later that despite her most earnest efforts, no nurse could be found who was willing to move north. She found one who was willing to go to Edmonton, or some other good sized town, but no one was willing to live out in the feral countryside.

"Needless to say, I went home dejected. As the months passed I lost hope of ever seeing you again, of ever getting anyone to come and help us up there."

Suddenly Daniel stood, extended a hand, and pulled Lizzie to her feet.

"Lizzie Van Ankum," he said nestling her hands inside both of his. "Will you be my wife? Will you come north with me?"

What? His words stunned her. She stared at him, feeling too dumbfounded to speak.

Marry him? How could she? Hadn't she just told

him she couldn't leave, not until the children were raised? He, too, did not seem to understand. Had he asked what she thought he asked? If so, what did it mean? That he would be willing to wait ten years to get married? She continued to stare at him, praying for the ability to discern his intent.

"I love you, Lizzie," he said. "I've loved you since the day we met." He touched her chin just barely and tipped it upward. All she noticed were those dark cocoa eyes. Those eyes that looked too old for their years. Now she knew why.

"Please say yes," he said, drawing her into his arms.

Lizzie's heart wrenched with the perplexity of it all. Here he was, the man she had ached to know more intimately. The one she had come to love, even in his absence. Here he was, asking her to do the very thing he knew she could not do. It was bewildering.

Tears spilled down her face and she pushed away from him. He reached out and cupped her face in his hands, gently rubbing the tears away with his thumbs.

"What's the matter? I had hoped you felt the same."

She nodded, and then shrugged. She did feel the same. Her heart was howling yes, yes, capital yes. But in actuality, her circumstance made it all impossible.

"I can't. I can't leave the girls—"

She bowed her head against his chest and sobbed.

He held her a few moments then said, "But your father said the girls really like Rebecca and he thinks they'll be as happy as songbirds when he tells them the news."

"The news?" Lizzie barely squeaked. "What

news?"

"About your dad and Rebecca."

Father and Rebecca? What about them? What was he saying? He was making it sound like Widow Bannister and Father were—

Lizzie drew back and searched his face. "What are you talking about?"

It was obvious to Daniel that Lizzie had not yet heard the plan. Perhaps she had never even considered the possibility of it.

"Lizzie, I'm sorry. I thought you knew. Your father mentioned it while we visited in the sitting room. I assumed it was common knowledge."

Lizzie collapsed against his chest, and Daniel bit his lip. He wished he had kept his mouth shut. He didn't mean to upset her. He smoothed her long blonde hair as she shook and sobbed. If only he had kept quiet.

Could it be? he thought, as she trembled for some moments in his arms. Yes. Yes, it was. She was laughing? He held her out at arms length. Yes, she was laughing. And crying. All at the same time.

CHAPTER THIRTY-THREE

The day of the double-wedding arrived at last, and even though the happy occasion had had to be delayed for two weeks, the wedding party couldn't have asked for a nicer day. The warm weather had extended in October, much to everyone's satisfaction and delight; the twins would be wed outside after all. Neither J.C. nor Willie cared one way or the other, just so long as there were no more postponements.

"A man can hold his breath only so long," J.C had said to Lizzie the night they received the news that both Sally and Sadie were diagnosed with pneumonia. "We should be hitched by now," he had moaned.

Lizzie adjusted J.C.'s bow tie, spun him around, and yanked his coat tail down hard. It didn't fit as well as it had when he bought it two years ago.

"If Sally's not careful, she may have a moose on her hands before long," Lizzie teased.

"C'mon, Lizzie, 'nough of this fussin'," he complained. "Let's get on with it."

"Just hold onto your horses," she said sternly. "Nothing important is going to happen 'til the brides get here anyway."

Willie took another look in the hand-sized mirror Lizzie had propped atop the warming closet, spit onto his fingertips and smoothed the sides of his light-colored freshly-cut hair.

"Then why are you making us get into these already?" J.C. said, his tone on the verge of bellyaching. "I can hardly breathe in this thing, ya' know."

"Well, dear brother, that was your choice. You could have bought a new suit like others have done." She smiled across the room at Willie.

"Right," groaned J.C. "And spend my hard earned dollars on clothes instead of hogs. Not likely."

Lizzie laughed. That was J.C. alright. His animals came first. She hoped Sally was prepared for this big galoot.

"Let me see your shoes," Lizzie said, pulling up his pant leg. "Good. What about yours, Will?" Willie stuck a foot in her direction, rotating it side to side for inspection.

"Who polished them?" she asked, knowing she had not gotten to it herself. "Rosie?"

"Of course not," J.C. grumbled, his face turning into a bright sunbeam as he announced proudly. "Our brides did the job."

Outside, the yard was beginning to fill with horses and wagons and automobiles. Jake worked out a particular pattern and insisted that the wedding guests park according to his plan. Horses were led toward the barnyard and tethered along the fence.

Lizzie went to the window and assessed the progress. A company of automobiles was just then turning into the lane, the parents of the brides, no doubt, among them.

"All right, boys, out to the shed. Hurry up, before they see you." The boys left quickly, and the kitchen was suddenly as silent as she could ever remember. Father and Rebecca had offered to keep the girls with them, along with Frankie and Isabelle, leaving Lizzie free to concentrate on getting the boys ready, and also herself.

Lizzie went to the small mirror to check her own hair. She had tried something fancy; a high French roll with several loose ringlets dangling down her back. Amazingly, after her morning food preparations and readying the boys, the ringlets still had some curl left in them.

If only Daniel could see her now, she thought. Fancy hair, a lovely dress. The dress was the bluish gray one that Mother had made and worn at Aunt Emma's wedding. A few basic modifications were all it had needed, and Lizzie managed them without difficulty. She ran upstairs to take a look in the full-length mirror. She twisted side to side in front of the mirror, feeling satisfied, and then lit lightly on her knees beside her bed.

O God, thank you for everything that's happening today. And for all that is about to happen.

How could so much have happened in such short order? Daniel hadn't been gone two days before Father called a two-family meeting and exposed his feelings for Rebecca Bannister and his intentions to marry her. In fact, right there around the old oak table, stretched out to its fullest, he proposed to her. Every member of both families was present, including Sally and Sadie, the two who were, at that time, just days away from joining the family.

Lizzie smiled now remembering the hoots and

hollers that flooded the room. Mrs. Bannister blushed. Lizzie had never seen that much red in the lovely lady's face. It was refreshing, and brought on a new surge of frivolity from the young men around the table. Eventually Zachariah hushed the cheers and restored order. Then he turned to Lizzie and asked her what she thought about it all.

"It's beautiful, Father. Everything's beautiful."

She didn't mean to but she began crying then, right there in front of them all. She covered her face with her hands and wept. She didn't know it, but all of them were giving each other the "what's this?" look. Willie reached over Rosie and Anna's heads and gently squeezed her shoulder.

"I'm all right, really I am," she sniffled, pulling up the corner of her apron and wiping her eyes. "It's just that everything is happening so fast, and it's all so marvelous that—"

"You're sure right about that, Lizzie," Mrs. Bannister said softly, reaching across and patting Lizzie's hand. "Tell us again though. I don't think everyone in the family heard about what Daniel Winslow offered you while he was here."

It was true; only three of them knew of Daniel's dual proposal: Father, and Rebecca, and Willie. Lizzie had not yet told the others what decisions lay before her concerning her future, in fact, what decisions she had already made.

"Yes, Lizzie," Rosie begged. "Tell us! Are you getting married too?" The girls giggled and jiggled on the wooden bench they shared, their eyes sparkling with wonder and excitement.

"No, she's not!" J.C. and Sally exclaimed in

unison. The question was absurd.

All Lizzie could do was shrug and smile. "That's what he asked me. Would I marry him? And would I be willing to learn my nursing up north, somewhere near Edmonton?"

"No! I can't believe it!" Sally said, definitely tutting. "You've barely met him. You surely can't be considering marriage?"

"Not only can she," Will spoke up on Lizzie's behalf. "She is! Aren't you, Sis?"

"I've talked with Father about it, and Mrs. Banni—to Rebecca" Lizzie said, looking at them both, then back to J.C. and Sally. "Father has given me permission, if that's what I choose to do." Everyone looked at Zachariah.

"It's her decision to make," he said. "I'm sure it'll ease your minds to know that I've spoken to Daniel. Or should I say, he's spoken to me." Father rose to his feet. "I trust that his motives are pure; I have no reason to doubt his sincerity. Plus, Brother LeMont will be a guide to them. I want you to know I've given them my blessing; I can't help but believe that God's had a hand in it all." Not a scrap of worry showed on Father's face as he spoke. "And I for one am all for it."

Sally shook her head, unable to believe what she was hearing. She hadn't met Daniel, but she was sure there was no way on earth such a "spur of the moment" marriage could work out. "I hope you won't be sorry, Lizzie. Marriage is an awfully big step to be taking at your age. And you don't even know him."

J.C. put his arm around Sally, showing his support of her opinion.

"I don't see how I could ever be sorry," Lizzie

said. "The man I love loves me. And besides, he holds the key to my nurses training. He's getting it all set up."

Not everyone around the table was as sure of a good ending as Lizzie seemed to be.

A commotion downstairs brought Lizzie back to the here and now. It must be Sadie and Sally. Hurrying to her feet, she straightened her dress and headed down the stairs to the kitchen. She knew it wouldn't be the boys who were making the raucous for they were told specifically to hide in the shed until she, herself, summoned them to their places at the front of the grouping of wooden chairs and benches that had been set up for the guests.

Lizzie nearly melted when she entered the kitchen and saw the twins in their wedding dresses. She gasped and clutched her throat in awe. And to think, her own wedding day may not be as far off as she had recently imagined. How wonderful! How almost delirious she suddenly felt!

"How do we look?" Sadie asked, twisting this way and that so that the large underlying hoop swayed gracefully as she moved about the room.

Lizzie took hold of Sadie's hands and squeezed them, kissing Sadie on both cheeks. "You are beautiful beyond words! I hope the boy's knees won't give way when they see the two of you coming down the aisle."

Lizzie turned to Sally and admired her dress as well. She could hardly wait for Aunt Emma to see all this satin and lace.

As Lizzie left the house and made her way to the shed, suddenly she had an overwhelming sense of accomplishment, like she had just passed a test. It was an odd feeling, and an odd time to get it, but it was there nonetheless. She thought of Joseph in the Old Testament. He was stuck in jail and abandoned there until just the right time. And at the proper time God opened the way for him to get out and get on with what God had for him to do.

Perhaps all of life is a test, she thought. And now, well, now Lizzie felt she was being given a gift from God. She was being given the desire of her heart, after all. She could see now that it all had to do with God's timing, not hers. His way, not hers. It seemed so clear just now. *God's way turns out to be so beautiful*, thought Lizzie. If only she could learn to trust Him more.

She tapped on the shed door. "Alright boys, you're up."

CHAPTER THIRTY-FOUR

Almost at the point of collapse Lizzie ascended the metal steps of the train, leather knapsacks weighing down both shoulders. She had hugged and kissed and cried with every member of the newly blended family until she was sick to death of good-byes. How good it would feel to sit down, alone, and rest for a few miles. These past several days had taken their toll with all the shuffling of beds and household furniture, the scrubbing of floors and walls, and the packing and repacking of clothing and bedding and personal belongings. Not merely her own things but also those of the children, and Rebecca's children.

Four days before Lizzie was to take the train north, Father and Rebecca had changed their minds and decided to get married immediately rather than waiting until November as had been previously planned.

"I can't bear to think about bad weather keeping you from getting home for the wedding," Rebecca had said to Lizzie. So, with no big to-do the two families gathered together and Pastor Stebbins preformed a quiet happy ceremony in the big room of the farmhouse.

The rest of that day and the following two days Lizzie had her hands full moving, shifting and shuffling the belongings of the amalgamated family while Zachariah and Rebecca enjoyed a couple of days in the city. And now Lizzie was exhausted through and through. Heading north had begun to look better and better with every passing hour, and now...if she could just get some sleep along the way.

She chose a seat near the door on the right side of the train and collapsed into it. The family would be able to see her on this side; she wanted to be able to watch them all and wave to them as the train chugged away from the station.

When she looked out the window a strange sense of panic raced through her, but it didn't last. It was followed by an enormous wave of adventure and excitement. Was this really happening? Was she really aboard a Canadian Pacific Railroad passenger car, headed for Edmonton? She patted the coat pocket that held the ticket. She could hardly wait to review the stops she'd be making. She was also anxious to give special study to the enclosed instructions regarding the turntable in Lacombe, but she would have plenty of time for that. She stowed her bags under the seat and looked again to the family standing on the loading platform.

The whistle blew loud and long. Lizzie pressed her face against the window pane, making a funny face for the children. Anna especially loved it and waved wildly, jumping up and down. The whistle blew again and both Rosie and Anna covered their ears. Something about the sight she was beholding made tears come to Lizzie's eyes. She wanted to run to her sisters and protect them from the fierce noise. But that was not her place anymore.

God had provided a new mother for them; a mother so
beautiful and capable that Lizzie sighed at the magnitude
of God's goodness.

The train started to move and Lizzie waved again.
She kept waving until the family was no longer in sight,
and then she started to cry. She felt too weak and weary to
cry and yet she did. Muffled sobs poured forth from
somewhere deep inside, she knew not where. Tears
tumbled down her cheeks, soaking her new white gloves.
How very tired she felt!

"'S'cuse me, Ma'am," a bearded man said,
shaking Lizzie's shoulder roughly. "Ain't ya s'pposed to
be gettin' off one of these times? Or are ya plannin' to
live your whole life on this 'ere train?"

Lizzie straightened and pulled away from the
man's touch. He was as dirty a man as she had ever seen,
and smelly, too. But despite his ragged appearance she
saw only kindness in his eyes and managed a soft "thank
you" before peering out the window. It was hard to make
out where they were at; she saw no familiar land marks.
But why would she? She'd never been this far north
before.

She turned around to ask the man how close they
were to Lacombe and how soon they would arrive, but he
was nowhere to be seen. In fact, there was no one to be
seen at all. She looked to the front then turned again to the
back of the train, but she was the only one being carried
along. Where had everyone gone? When she had boarded
the train, the seats were almost full. That same peculiar
sense of panic she'd felt earlier in the day returned and
with it an overwhelming urge to find other passengers.

Surely others besides herself were on the train, she
thought, tightness seizing her breath. What about the man

who had just awakened her? Where was everyone? Lizzie
deserted her bags and made her way to the front,
searching each seat. Finding no one she spun around
quickly and ran to the other end of the train.

She wished she knew where she was at. Hopefully
she hadn't missed Lacombe. That was her connection
point to the train going west.

"From Lacombe you'll go west to Bentley,"
Daniel had said. "Then north to Rimbey, then Bluffton,
and at last to Hoadley. I'll meet you there. Now
remember, you change trains in Lacombe. I've got it all
marked out, here on the map."

At Hoadley Daniel would introduce her to the
folks (Daniel's friends and neighbors) that she would be
practicing her nursing skills on once she had spent a few
months in Edmonton under Dr. Haley's instruction. From
Hoadley Daniel would accompany her by train to
Edmonton and introduce her personally to Dr. Haley.

"Hello!" Lizzie called out. "Is anybody here?" She
felt foolish shouting out to an empty train, but fear
compelled her. The train seemed now to be racing. She
went back to her seat and looked out the window. There
must be something out there that would give her a bearing
on where she was. But she could see nothing. No sign of a
town up ahead, only acres and acres of land, some
cleared, most not. The longer she peered out the window
the less she saw. As she strained to get a better look, she
realized there was nothing out there but dark desolation,
no town, no track, not even sky.

"Miss, isn't this your stop?"

Lizzie jolted. The conductor was tapping on her
shoulder. "Miss, we're almost into Lacombe. Better
gather your things. The train you'll be wantin' to take is

called the Peanut Train. Ask anybody, they'll direct you."

The man moved calmly down the aisle, waking others who had fallen asleep in their places. Lizzie felt almost faint with relief.

Thank you, Lord! Thank you! She had not missed her stop after all. It had been a bad dream. And though it was only a dream, she still shivered from the fear of it. She pulled her two bags from the floor and set them on her lap, one in front of the other. The train whistle blew— a loud lonely racket. Yes, she was almost there. She could see the buildings of Lacombe. It wouldn't be long now. Soon she'd be in Daniel's arms. Soon she'd be a nurse. An honest-to-goodness nurse!

LIGHTHOUSE PUBLISHING 2012

Made in the USA
Charleston, SC
30 November 2012